ALONE ON THE ROAD

The Mystery Begins

a novel

S.R. ELY

*"Every new beginning comes from
some other beginning's end."*
Seneca the Elder

ACKNOWLEDGEMENTS

Through the years I have been so blessed to have good friends, who have tirelessly used their red
pencils on my book drafts. It is a pleasure to have such wonderful women (and an occasional
man) on my team. Many thanks to Elaine Clark, dear friend from my long ago high school years.
Many thanks to Diane Weaver, a great teacher of one of my daughters in her high school years.
And joining the team, Melody Bywater, generously volunteering to be my "one last look"
person. "Alone on the Road" couldn't have happened without you!
I am so appreciative of the all the work you have done.

Sonja R. Ely

CHAPTER ONE

The day had started to get hot before Cora Mason arrived at work that morning. That was to be expected this late in June, on the northwest edge of Nebraska. She was dressed for it though, in a short sleeved blouse and light linen skirt.

When she drove into the parking lot, she pulled into one of the shaded spots. Her solar batteries were fully charged so the car didn't need to be in the sun. She smiled as she noticed a few of the older cars, still plugged into electric charging stations. Her car might not be new, being a 2042 model, but it certainly wasn't as old as those. As far as she could see there were none of the older, almost antique, gas fueled cars in their parking lot on that day. As she got out and walked into the only medical facility in town, she heard the beep of her car's locking system. It was a good day and she felt light and happy.

With a sigh, she entered the building and headed to her office. She was the senior clerk for three doctors on the main floor of the building. The doctors rotated days in the clinic, two of them coming in from Grand Island three times a week. There were days when the work could be deadly dull. At such times she had to remind herself that it paid well.

Cora was glad her building was air conditioned as she hefted boxes of old medical records to the downstairs storage area. She had to pass through the main part of the basement, which housed a communal break room and lockers for the staff of the several doctors in the building. This part of the Medical Center wasn't kept as cool as the two floors above, although it got pretty warm up there late in the day, because of all the windows.

Three employees from the upper floor were sitting at a table having coffee. None of them offered to give her a hand as she walked by, juggling her three boxes of retired files. "Good thing. I'm young and strong," she mused to herself.

There was a sub-basement that was only used for long term storage. She hated going down into that dungeon like area. It was eerie to be that far underground. It was probably because almost nobody went down there except her and a couple of other clerks. She had visions of someone using it to hide out. Of course, it didn't help that it felt cold down there, even though it was middle of summer outside.

Cora didn't know the staff who worked on the second floor very well; she'd seen them coming and going. The second floor housed the doctors' staff for day surgery folks. The back of the building was the emergency department. It was pretty busy and had it's own staff of clerks. Doctors and nurses usually didn't mingle with the general office staff, unless there was a problem with their billing or payroll. Cora shrugged, it was just the way things were.

As she walked on she reminded herself that the job was good. It paid well and she now earned three weeks of vacation a year. With one week she could fly home to Austin to visit her mother and sister, which she always did once a year. She smiled as she thought of how she was going to use her other two weeks. Last year she had spent five great days in London and five more in Paris, the year before she went to Hawaii for ten glorious days. This year she had booked a Caribbean cruise from Fort Lauderdale. The cruise was to be six days, which left her a few days to explore the Keys after she came back.

Life in general for her was good. She loved the little starter home she had purchased in town and really liked her neighborhood, but getting away from Nebraska for a little while always appealed to her. Her friend Linda, whom she'd become friends with when she was in business school, was planning to meet her in Florida for the cruise. Linda lived a few hundred miles away in Kansas, but had visited Cora several times over the last three years. She was single too. Having something to look forward to always made the day-to-day grind worth it.

The double doors to the lower storage area were heavy and it took all her strength to get one side open. Somehow she managed, but the minute the door closed behind her, she sat her load down. She caught her breath a bit before going down the next set of stairs. For some reason the hair on the back of her neck was standing on end. She had a momentary feeling that something bad was about to happen, but she chided herself, "Silly!" The stairwell was dark, illuminated only by the lights in the employee lounge shining dimly through the glass on the doors. She flipped on several light switches before starting down. It wasn't a great place to go and she counted her blessings that almost everything now was digital and they didn't have to come to the creepy room that served as their archives very often.

Cora decided to carry the boxes down one at at time. "Probably safer to do it this way," she grumbled as she used the handrail with one hand and carried a heavy cardboard file box with the other. At the bottom of the stairs was another equally heavy set of double doors. The door she chose was as hard to open as the one upstairs had been.

Looking around the large room, she saw a spot in the rows of shelves for her files and put the box on a fairly high shelf with its date and name showing. She doubted if anyone would ever look at any of the files the clinic had stored, but, just in case, she wanted it to be an easy search. In minutes, she had all three boxes in their final resting places.

Cora glanced around for a moment, enjoying the coolness of the room for a change. She'd always been in a hurry to leave this desolate spot. But as hot as it was upstairs, it felt kind of refreshing. The rows of shelves took up about half of the room. Walking to the center of the space, she could see what the room had most likely been built for. It was probably intended as a shelter, which was understandable. This part of Nebraska could get tornados often, especially in late June. This room was big enough for the forty or so people who worked in the building. As luck would have it, in the eight years that she had worked as a clerk at the medical center, there had only been one time anyone had to use the room. It had been on a Saturday and it had only been the emergency crew in the place.

There were three tables with chairs and several long benches along the walls with thick cushions. She saw a small fridge at the back, next to that was a cupboard with a two burner hot plate and a microwave on top. A kitchen sink was in a cabinet of its own. Several cases of bottled water sat next to that. Cora wondered how often those were changed out. "Does bottled water go bad?" she asked aloud. "Never thought about that."

Cora shrugged and turned to go back upstairs to her desk. Suddenly, she felt dizzy. Her ears rang with an unusual whirring sound and she felt herself almost being lifted off her feet for a second. It was all she could do to stagger to the nearest bench before she felt herself going down. She tried to lay down, but only got her shoulders on the padded seat before darkness closed in over her. Without feeling it, she slid all the way onto the cold concrete floor.

Time seemed to stand still, there were no thoughts, no dreams, nothing. It was a sharp, cold, stabbing pain in her hip that was the first hint that something had happened. As Cora opened her eyes, the room above her seemed to be swirling around her. It took a few minutes to be able to focus and realize she was laying on the floor.

With a deep sigh she rolled over on her stomach and sat back on her knees. A pen lay on the floor. It seemed to be the source of the pain that had awoken her. She got up and sat on the bench beside her for a moment, trying to remember how she'd wound up on the cement. The dizziness came back to her, but not much else. "I wonder if I'm coming down with something?" she asked herself.

Slowly she shook off her disorientation and started for the door. Then something caught her eye, "Oh, my gosh!" She looked at her watch. "It's nearly six! I've been down here since ten this morning?" She didn't know whether to be angry or scared. "No one came looking for me in all that time? The others in the office knew I was coming down here. Those guys at the table knew I was down here!" It hurt her feelings to think no one missed her. She began to recognize the anger building in her.

Stomping towards the door she tried to calm herself down. Everyone in her office would have gone home by this time, only the emergency department would be on duty. They wouldn't have been aware she was in the sub-basement.

She opened the door to the stairs and started up the steps. About half-way up she realized that the light on the steps was odd. She gasped, "Oh Lord, what has happened?"

She continued to look up as she slowly made her way to the doors into the regular basement. Opening those doors, she found another surprise. Cora was looking up at the sky, one that was slightly purplish. The basement was empty, nothing, no chairs and tables, no vending machines and no lockers. The ceiling was just that strange colored sky. "Was there a tornado?" she asked the emptiness aloud.

Normally she would have taken the elevator to the first floor, but that was gone too. Luckily there was the emergency exit that had stairs that lead to the ground level just behind the building. She climbed the stairs and found herself standing on the sidewalk that led to the street one way and to the parking area the other. Looking around, she saw no clinic or any cars in the lot. Even her beloved car wasn't there. Again the hair on the back of her neck seemed to stand on edge when she realized that all the shrubs and landscaping trees were gone too.

It was so confusing. Cora walked to where the front of her building used to be. All the direction arrows on the pavement indicating which way to go were there, but no signs, nothing to

8

say a large building ever stood there, nothing but an empty basement. Walking out to the street she looked left and right. From where she stood she could see the junction with Highway 30, a heavily traveled thoroughfare that ran through the main part of town.

In minutes she was standing in the middle of should have been a busy road at this time of day. But today was different, Cora looked back and forth several times. There were no cars, even worse when she looked towards what had been her town, she saw no houses, businesses or buildings of any kind. All there was to see was the rolling prairie, not even trees to break the horizon.

She stood there for several minutes, breathing hard, trying to gather her wits and try to imagine what had happened. Nothing made sense. Was she dead? Was this a mental breakdown? How could something like this happen? She had no idea what to do.

All she could do was whimper and continue to look back and forth for answers. One thing she did know though, was she was on the highway that she'd taken home every day for the last eight years. It might as well have been Mars, it seemed to alien now. The most obvious thing was that she was totally alone on that road.

Cora looked up at the sky and noticed it was getting darker. The sun wasn't down but clouds were forming. Off in the distance, for a moment she thought she saw something simmering just above the horizon. It was huge and like nothing she'd ever seen before, but before she'd had a chance to really get a good look at the object, a bolt of lighting lit up the sky. At this time of year that could mean a thunderstorm or worse. She passed off what she had seen as a mirage or hallucination. At almost a dead run, she headed for the only offer of protection she knew of at the moment, the shelter in the sub-basement.

Her legs felt like rubber as she hurried back towards the clinic site. Distant rumbling of the approaching storm urged her on. It took her much longer to get back to the scary place that now offered the only safety available, than it had taken to reach the main highway. Cora was out of breath when she finally closed the door behind her.

It dawned on her that the lights were still on. "Wonder how that's possible?" Looking around she heard the hum of a generator and realized there was a door she hadn't noticed before.

She cautiously walked over and opened it. Feeling around the wall inside the door, she

9

reached a switch and found herself in a utility area, complete with a small generator that evidently came on when the power went out. She grimaced, "That won't probably last long." There was no sign of extra fuel for it.

In one corner of the room was a small closet like bathroom with a toilet and sink, which she was happy to find. There wasn't any soap for washing, but the cold water still ran.

Continuing the search around the storage area, she saw several blankets, a box of candles, some very outdated cans of food and two survival handbooks that looked old. The best find was a package of batteries and two flashlights. Those looked newer than anything else. The only other things were a few small boxes that had some military "ready-to-eat meals" and some industrial brooms and mops plus cleaning supplies that had all but dried up.

Cora took one of the blankets, the books and the flashlights with the batteries to the other room. She sat down on a bench after wrapping the blanket around her. It had been nice and warm outside, but down here it was chilly to begin with. It took two or three of the batteries before one was found that was still good. It felt better knowing she could find her way around if the generator ran out of fuel.

"Time to see if that water's still good," she said as she got up and went to the kitchen area. She opened the small refrigerator to see if there was accidentally anything in it, but there wasn't. "There are those military meals," she reminded herself. It only took a minute to retrieve one of the boxes and bring it to the table. She tore open the box and looked at the choices. There were four smaller cartons in the box. "Wonder how safe these are? They could have been down here for years."

It took a few seconds to open the first carton. There was an interesting assortment of small cans and bags. One bag was labeled beef slices, Cora carefully opened it and discarded it immediately, "Not taking a chance on something that looks as old and dried out as that." She continued opening the other small containers. A small round one held some crackers. Cora tasted the corner of one and found it a little stale, but passable. There was also a small tub labeled peanut butter that was solid and beyond using. The packet labeled 'peaches' was freeze dried and the contents tasted pretty good.

One of the two remaining packets held a couple of brittle, but good tasting chocolate chip cookies. The last packet contained instant coffee, creamer, sugar. Cora wished she had a way of making that. She left the other things on the table and went to see if there was anything like a pot or pan to heat water in.

Her search was rewarded with not only a small sauce pan, but also a couple of pie tins, and a small pitcher, plus a box of styrofoam cups that were in the cupboards under the sink. Somehow there was still running water in the kitchen sink and in the bathroom. "Wonder how that's still working?" She didn't dwell on that too long, instead just felt grateful for the blessing of a cup of hot coffee to go with her meager meal of crackers, dried fruit and cookies. It only took a few minutes to have her cup of hot brew back at the table. She didn't normally put cream and sugar in her coffee; today it would at least taste more like food. She noticed that there had been a package of gum, two pieces of caramel candy as well as a small package of tissues, a plastic spoon and a box of a dozen or so matches in the packet. "This may come in handy," she told herself as she put the items back in the bag.

It was nearly eight by the time she began to wonder how she was going to sleep. The bench was too narrow to be very comfortable. Then she had an idea. There wasn't much need for the files now that the clinic was gone so she got down four of the boxes and put them next to the bench then by taking the cushions off half the benches and putting them on the boxes it made an almost twin sized place to sleep. A blanket run over and tucked under both sides of the cushioned area made a passably secure place for her. With one blanket rolled up as a pillow and two more as covers she felt pretty sure that she'd be warm enough.

Just before she went to lay down for the night, she secured the doors with one of the heavy mop handles. There hadn't been any sign of anyone else around, but she was there so others might be too, at least she hoped there would be others.

With a deep sigh, Cora got one of the candles and put it on the little cracker container lid and sat it on the cement floor by the utility room door. She lit the candle and watched its little dancing flame for a moment before walking over to the light switch by that door. With the wave of a finger on the switch the generator stopped. "Maybe it will last a little longer."

Quietly she walked through the dimly lit room to her makeshift bed. It was pretty solid, but as tired as she was, she welcomed the warmth of the coarse wool blankets and had no trouble falling asleep. She hadn't realized just how exhausted she was. Her last thoughts were to hope that when she awoke she would find that she'd been dreaming and everything that had happened was just some bizarre nightmare.

Outside the thunderstorm raged, rain drenched the newly exposed earth. Here and there a small animal darted from a hole, where it had slept through the day deep underground. A few went in search of a drier den. Some looked around at an unrecognized landscape, then darted back into their wet, but familiar space. Others hardly noticed and kept on going. Daylight would come and the real challenge for all of them, man and beast, would begin.

CHAPTER TWO

Cora woke up with a start. It took her a few minutes to become orientated to where she was as she lay there in the dark. Once sitting up, she sighed. The memories of the day before came flooding back. It hadn't been just a dream. It took a minute of feeling around to find the flashlight, but with it she was able to get to the door. There was sunlight coming through the upper doors windows. It was a relief when it was apparent that things were all right in the shelter.

After a trip to the bathroom she came out and sat at a table. It was cold in the room so she got up to fetch one of her blankets. Wrapping the scratchy wool cover around her she went over to the little hot plate and put some water on to heat. Cora knew there would be more instant coffee in the other cartons of ready to eat meals so she grabbed one and rummaged through it until she found the coffee and sugar. As soon as the drink was made, she sat at the table and sipped her coffee while she looked at the food in the carton. The main choices were chicken ala king, which she tossed in the garbage without even opening, some fruitcake which she did keep, some more stale crackers and a package of cocoa mix. It made a very meager meal but at least it was something in her stomach. The cocoa was hard to mix but it tasted better than the coffee.

With the blanket still wrapped around her, she looked out the window in the door, then opened it slightly. Warmer air rushed by her. It seemed like it was going to be a hot day so she propped open both of the doors in the shelter and at the top of the stairs. Upstairs it had obviously rained during the night, the floor was still wet and there were small puddles of water here and there. But the sky was clear, though still a little on the lavender side.

Cora put her blanket back on the bed, then dressed and walked to the ground level again. She was hoping to see something now that it was broad daylight. It was disappointing to her that nothing had changed. She still saw no signs of the world she knew just twenty-four hours before. There was also nothing like the large silver thing she'd seen in the distance either. She was sure she just imagined it.

The clothes she'd worn to work were not very conducive to walking. Her skirt was pretty tight and her shoes had four inch heels. In spite of that, she decided she needed to try to walk into what had been town. Her house had been on the other side of the main part of the downtown area, some fifteen or so blocks from the clinic, which was just outside the city limits.

By the time Cora had reached the first streets that had been the town's newest subdivisions, she was feeling sick to her stomach, thinking of all the families who had lived there.

As she passed one of the homes she felt her heart leap. They had a storm cellar, probably built in case of a tornado. Cora rushed over, hoping that the family had gotten to it in time before whatever happened occurred. When she got close she could see the door was gone. She slowed down, peering down into the dark hole. She saw steps going down so slowly she walked down, hesitating after each step to let her eyes grow accustomed to the low light. It smelled dusty. It was simple and mostly empty except for a couple of bins of things.

Benches lined the walls so she sat down on one and looked at the items in the bins. "Must have had three kids," she said softly, picking up three pairs of tennis shoes in small sizes and tee shirts. Underneath the children's things she found a pair of hiking boots that looked like a mans and a jean jacket. The other tub held some blankets and a flashlight that was the kind you wound up to charge the batteries. Cora sat for a few minutes making the flashlight usable. Once she had light she could see that there were other things stored under the benches. There was a box of toys and games, another conformation of the family having young children. Then there was a little overnight case. It held real treasure for Cora. It had a package of disposable tooth brushes, hand sanitizer, travel sized soaps, a stack of wash clothes, some individually packaged hand wipes, candles, matches, bandaids, and a six pack box of peanut butter and crackers. She took one of the packs and ate the crackers without hardly chewing.

"Well, there doesn't seem to be anybody to object so I'm going to take the case and the jacket. The shoes are way too big," she slipped the jacket on and started up the stairs. There was a straw hat hanging next to the door that she hadn't noticed before so she took that too.

It had been early, just passed eight when Cora had left her shelter but it was already getting too warm to wear the coat. She tied it around her waist and was grateful for the hat that shaded her face. "Darn, my sunglasses were in my purse in my desk!" Then she thought about her purse, "Oh no, I've lost my purse!" She stopped and looked around, then began to laugh.

14

"I'm standing here in the middle of a whole town that no longer exists and I'm worried about losing my purse?" Shaking her head, she started walking off again.

Occasionally she saw a place where a house had had a basement and would stop and look. All of them were completely empty. After awhile, she stopped looking. Until she got to where she guessed her house must have stood. She didn't have a basement so it was hard to figure exactly how her house had sat. There was nothing there to find so she started back to the shelter.

Cora wandered through some of the neighborhoods she wasn't familiar with, hoping to find more bunkers that were still there. She was pleased to find one just after a few blocks. Its front door was set back under the bank a bit and was still there. "That must be the secret; it had to be under dirt to be spared," she told herself "like the shelter I have is." The door had a padlock hanging on it but, thankfully, it wasn't locked.

Throwing the door open wide, Cora walked in and turned on her flashlight. Just inside the door was a small dolly for moving things. She noticed it was the kind you could use upright or move the handle so it was more of a cart. "That could come in handy!" She decided to take it when she left. This bunker was bigger than the last. It looked like the owners had used it as kind of a root cellar. There was a small set of shelves with jars of homemade jams, all labeled, several jars of green beans and some jars of canned fruit from the previous fall. On the floor were two plastic tubs, one with a few potatoes and one with onions. Both looked like all that was left from last year's harvest. No doubt there had been a garden at one time on the now barren land.

Just like the other place there were a few usable things, some canned goods, ramen noodle cups and blankets stored near the near the rear of the room. Two apple crates were being used for end tables on either side of a couple of folding chairs. She put the onions in with the potatoes in one tub and used the other to load the blankets into. She used the crates to pack up the canned foods. Once she was satisfied that she had all she use she took the dolly outside and converted it into the cart. At least she wouldn't have to carry things back to her shelter.

She was just walking across the small sideless cement bridge over a dry creek near downtown when she heard a sound. It was soft, but definitely something alive. She walked to the edge and listened. There it was a sound like a small animal. It seemed to be under the bridge.

Cora walked to the edge of the bank on the far side and picked her way down into the ditch. There was a large culvert pipe under a layer of dirt beneath the bridge. Cora leaned over and, using the flashlight, looked into the tunnel.

"Oh honey," she said softly when she saw the creator of the sound. A cat had given birth to kittens. "If you wait here I'll go get one of the bins I got earlier and I can take you back with me to my place.

Cora lined the bin with a blanket and went to the tunnel. She had to crouch down to get into the tunnel; the cat seemed to sense she was there to help because she didn't move. Cora was rewarded with a purr from of the mother cat after petting her lightly. The babies seemed to be only a day or two old, their little umbilical cords stubs were still attached where the mother had chewed off the rest. The cat had cleaned them and they were dry, but their eyes weren't open yet at all.

Cora gently picked them up one at a time and put them into the bin. There were three kittens, when the last one was in the basket the mother jumped in with them and lay down, curling around her precious family. "Okay girl, we'll go now." Cora said softly as she carried her only companions to the cart.

The day was getting pretty hot by the time they reached the clinic site. The kittens were the first to go downstairs to the coolness of the shelter. Cora used one of the pie tins to put water down for the mother cat, who came immediately to drink.

It took a while to get everything downstairs, but when it was done Cora felt a little better, although she wondered how she was going to feed the cat. It was still fairly cool in the shelter so Cora left the door open to let the warm air in to try to take advantage of the day. She didn't want to run the generator anymore than she had to, using it only at night.

It was well after noon. The energy gained from her meager breakfast was long used up. Cora opened a jar of the fruit, which was peaches and smelled it. It looked good and had no sign of spoilage so she carefully ate four halves of fruit. It felt good to have that much food in her stomach. She was so tired that she was unable to resist going to her makeshift bed and laying down. It only took seconds for her to fall asleep.

When she awoke, she sat up with a start. The kittens were mewing as loudly as they could. Cora got up and looked into the basket. The mother cat was gone. Panic set in, "Oh Lord, I hope your mother didn't leave you alone with me. I was worried how I was going to feed her let alone you little guys," she whispered to herself as she watched the tiny creatures call for help. She tried to pet and comfort them as she looked around for anything she might be able to give them. Just then the mother cat came through the door.

Cora was amazed, "Where have you been?" she asked of the cat as she jumped into the basket and was rewarded with three hungry mouths each seeking the warmth and comfort of their mother as well as her precious milk.

With a sigh of relief, Cora got up and walked to the door. She started to go upstairs to the basement to see if she'd left that door open wide enough for the cat to get out. When she got to the upper landing in front of those doors ,she was surprised to see the innards of what must have been a mouse or rodent of some kind. The cat had evidently gone hunting. Looking up, she was amazed to see that it was a good eight feet to the top of the cement wall. "Holy cow, cat! You really had to work to get up that!"

Cora went to the shelter with an idea. She brought up several boxes, one at a time and stacked them so they kind of made a stairs of sorts that only left about four feet for the cat to jump the next time she needed to go feed herself. She propped the upper and lower doors open just enough for the thin mother cat to come and go. At least while the kittens were nursing, it seemed a good solution, if the mother would come back, she could feed herself.

Dinner that night was a feast. Cora had a few more peaches, a pack of the peanut butter crackers and a microwaved potato, using the salt and pepper from one of the ready to eat packages for flavor.

From the light coming in from the doorway she could tell the sun had set. It was a sort of a dilemma whether or not to leave the door open for the mother cat. There were other things that probably had been underground like snakes, even foxes or coyotes. It felt scary to think of leaving the doors open. Cora emptied one of the boxes of its files and went outside for a few minutes. She came back with half a box of dirt. "Here's a litter box and you have water. You'll have to wait until morning to go outside again," she said to the cat who just looked at her without seeming to care what she was saying.

Cora picked the cat up and put her in the box. "That's yours, use it, please." Cora walked over and closed the door, flipping on the light as she did. It pleased her to hear the cat scratching in the loose dirt she had brought in. Cora went to the bathroom and gave herself a sponge bath. It felt good to be semi-clean. She hadn't noticed before there was a pair of coveralls hanging on the back of the bathroom door. When it had been just her in the shelter she hadn't bothered to close the door. Holding them up to her she guessed she'd have to roll the legs up but they would fit her, at least she could get out of her other clothes long enough to rinse them out. It felt strange to stand naked and do laundry but it was necessary. She hung her things up where she could around the storage room and then slipped on the coveralls. They were coarse and dusty smelling but one in her circumstances couldn't be choosy.

She mentally went through her ritual of closing up for the night, barring the door, lighting one of the candles, turning off the lights before laying down. This time, however, she had four new roommates to say goodnight to. As she looked down at the sleeping little family she saw for the first time they were all slightly different in size and coloring. The mother cat was a gray stripe, one of the babies was more solid gray, another was gray with a couple of white patches and the third was mostly white. On a whim she decided to name them. "Mother cat you will be Eve, because you may be the mother of all cats from now on." Petting the first kitten gently, "Since you are gray I'll just call you Gray." The next one she touched had the white areas, "Okay, you'll be Spots, and this last one, the largest of the three, will be BB, which will either stand for Big Boy or Big Babe, depending if you're a boy or girl." She smiled down at the little family, warm and safe together.

She couldn't help tears as she thought of all those families she couldn't find during her trip to town. It was just overwhelming! Exhaustion overtook her again to the point that she almost couldn't get the lights off and the candle lit before feeling like she would not make it to the bed.

Again it was the kittens mewing that woke her. She sat up and looked around, the mother cat was at the door. "Okay, Eve," Cora said as she got up and staggered towards the door. She undid her make shift security system and opened the door. Eve was up and over the top of the stairs of boxes without hesitation. Cora propped the door open for her return and went to check on the litter. The three babies were sound asleep, their little round tummies filled with the food their mother had provided. Again tears welled up in her eyes as she tiptoed into the storage room to see if her clothes were dry.

After a little time in the bathroom she decided to just put on her underclothes and continue to wear the more rugged coveralls for another foraging trip into the remains of the town. She wanted to investigate the other side of the downtown area and, for that matter, the main part of town itself. She had left her little cart at the base of the stairs to the side of the building.

With not much fanfare she set off once again, determined to find anything that might help her survive. At least this time, she knew what she was looking for.

CHAPTER THREE

When Cora was standing in the middle of what had been Main Street that ran through the town, she just stood for a few minutes listening. Silence had taken on such a new, frightening meaning. Silence was the true meaning of being alone. No sounds of motors running somewhere, no sound of people talking in the distance, no sounds of cars whizzing by, none of the things that mean life as normal. There was nothing, no insect sounds, no wind in the trees, just the sound of her own breathing above the slight breeze she could feel around her ankles.

Shaking off the eeriness of it, Cora walked to the where the stores should have been. Meandering down the barren street, she came to one business that had a basement, now empty, but with a small door at the side. There was no way to get to the door though, the stairs that must have been there were gone. Moving on, she saw no other basements on that side of the street.

Cora crossed the street and walked the other side. There were two shops that had basements but both were as empty as the first had been. It dawned on her that there was, or had been a gas station and a little strip mall at the other edge of town. It was several blocks. Figuring it might be worth it, she decided to make the effort. Her feet were hurting but it didn't matter, she had to forage for whatever she could find if she and her little family were going to survive.

There was no reward for making the extra effort. There was a basement that ran the entire length of the mall that had existed at one time but it was completely empty except for two rats that were scurrying around. Cora laughed aloud, "You seem as confused as I am," she called to them. At the sound of her voice, they darted into a drain pipe and out of sight. "At least the cats won't starve." She turned and walked back towards the main part of town.

It felt odd to be walking down the middle of Highway 30 in the heart of what would have been a busy workday in normal times. Trucks with all kinds of things to fill the stores would have been lined up at each of their back doors. How Cora missed the ordinary things that she could now only imagine as she passed the empty lots.

Just as she was making the turn to go back to the shelter, she froze. Straining to hear, there seemed to be a slight droning sound. The wind had picked up so she wasn't sure it wasn't just dust in the air being blown against her. Cora stood transfixed as she waited to see if the sound went away. Her heart sped up when the noise didn't go away, in fact it got louder. She looked to the east as a speck appeared on the horizon disappearing now and then as it went over the rolling landscape. Finally, when it was only a mile or so away she could tell it was a vehicle.

It was a dilemma for her, should she stay and hope the driver was friendly or should she hide in case he was some sort of hostile person? In the end she didn't have time to do anything but stand there. The person driving had sped up when they saw her.

An old pickup covered in dust roared up and stopped a few feet away from her. An older looking man got out and stood staring at her for a moment.

Cora thought about running when the passenger door opened and another man about the same age as the first stepped out. Then a third passenger, a young teenage boy, jumped out and ran around the door and right up to her, stopping just a couple of feet from her. "Hey lady? Where's all the people?"

Cora sighed, "Honey, I wish I knew." She opened her arms and he rushed into them, hugging her tightly. The other two men walked over to join in the hug.

It felt good to not be alone after all. When the embrace was over they all stood back and looked around. "Think we're all that there is?" one of the older men asked. He looked at Cora and extended his hand, "I'm Jay Breeden and this is my grandson, Jake." He pointed to the other guy with a wink, "This old guy is Mike Spaulding."

Cora nodded as she shook Jay's hand, "Good to see you. I'm Cora Mason."

Mike laughed and looked at Cora, "He can call me old because I'm sixty-seven and he's only sixty-five." He shrugged his shoulders, "You got any more idea of what has happened than we do? How come you're still here like we are?"

Cora shook her head, "I can't say what happened, but what I do think I know is that what ever was underground at the time was spared. I was in a tornado shelter that we were using for a storage area where I was working. What about you?"

Jay was the first to answer, "We were visiting Mike in Missouri. We were going camping, but first he took us into this little narrow gorge where he'd found a series of caves to explore. We were in one of them when all of a sudden we all got real dizzy and passed out. When we came to, we didn't notice anything. We'd planned to camp out close to there, but since none of us were sure why we fainted like that, we thought we should get back to town to see a doctor maybe. Our

21

truck, Mike's here, was still sitting under this rock ledge where we'd parked it. The little stream was still running and there were deer grazing close by in that narrow little canyon. Birds were singing and everything seemed normal. It wasn't until we drove out of that area back into the more open area at the top of the ridge that we saw everything was gone."

"We found a little town," Mike continued their story, "we could tell where the store and homes had been. We saw a place that was a gas station and discovered there was still gas in their underground storage tanks so we figured out how to get a siphon hose down into them and filled up the truck and the two gas cans we had with us. We did that a couple of times when we came to towns. Never found any supplies though. Guess we weren't looking in the right places."

"I've been looking for storage areas," Cora said. "There's one store in the down town area that has a door on the side but the stairs are gone."

"Let's go see what we can find," Mike said, motioning everyone back into the truck. Jay and Jake hopped up into the back, taking Cora's cart along. Cora got in the front seat. Mike drove slowing following Cora's direction.

When they got to the right place they stopped and all got out. Mike got a rope from the tool box in the back of the truck. He fashioned a foothold for Jake and lowered him down. The door wasn't locked as the boy quietly opened it. "I can't see anything!" he called up.

Jay fetched a flashlight from the truck and tossed it down to him. "There are a lot of boxes in here." He went inside and brought out one into the light. Opening it he laughed, "This must have been leftover from Valentine's Day!" He held up several heart shaped boxes of chocolates

Cora shook her head, "I suspect that they were keeping them cold to sell them next year. This must have been Green's General Store."

Jake kept bringing boxes out of the cellar until he had about fifteen in total. "That's all of them," he called up. "Shall I open them all?"

"Sure, let's see what we can use," Jay answered.

"Okay," Jake began the process. The first two boxes had winter clothes, mostly mens. The next three boxes had Christmas decorations. There was one carton that had fancy soaps and bath products. Another had cans of coffee in bags for regular coffee pots and powdered creamers.

As Jake continued to pry the cartons open, he found there were two boxes with bags of dog food and cases of cat food as well as a few pet toys.

Cora considered that a miracle as she let out a little joyful cry, "Oh, my gosh!"

Mike looked at her in surprise. "We can't eat that stuff!" he said.

"No, we can't but one of the earlier finds I made was a cat who had just had kittens. I have her back at the shelter. Now I can feed her and the babies, at least for awhile."

Mike nodded, "For a while."

Jake was just opening the last of the boxes when Cora looked back down at his finds. The last two cartons were canned goods. It was decided they would take the clothing, animal food, and anything edible back to Cora's shelter. It took a little ingenuity on their part to rig the rope around each box so the men could pull them up out of the basement. By mid-afternoon they were all comfortably out of the heat in Cora's shelter.

Eve was a little nervous as the newcomers looked down at her and the kittens, but when Jake began to stroke her softly and admire her, she calmed down and lay with her precious babies quietly.

There were three or four boxes of clothing to go through so Mike started pulling the items out to see if anything would fit any of them. He found three jackets, looking to be kid sized and too small for Jake. "Those could be used as pillows, they're nice and fluffy," Cora said, thinking practically. Mike nodded and laid those aside.

The next pieces he pulled out of the box were knitted sweater vests. They were too small for Mike or Jay, but Cora reached out for one and handed one to Jake. "I think these will fit us."The things that followed were all men's pants and at the bottom of the box, house slippers in varying sizes. Cora went into the bathroom and tried on the smaller pants and two fit well enough to claim. It meant rolling the legs up quite a bit but it was better than the coveralls or her tight skirt. She put on the vest and a pair of twill pants and went to join the men. She tried on all the slippers and found one pair that would work for her. She put them on immediately. It felt great to get out of her heels.

By the time they had gone through all of the clothing, everyone had at least one change of clothes and underwear, even though for Cora it meant wearing a pair of boxer shorts. It was a relief to at least have something that came close to normal.

Taking stock of the can goods they found; they had a jackpot of a case of spaghetti with meat sauce and a case of brick oven baked beans with bacon. "Can we eat now?" Jake asked, "We haven't eaten since we had lunch in the truck after we woke up in Missouri."

"Sounds good to me," Jay answered. He looked at Cora, "What have we got to open cans with?"

Cora picked up one of the cans of beans, "Pull top cans." She got the spoons that she had saved from the ready to eat meals. "We can eat these cold." She handed a can and spoon to each of the men. "It's not a steak, but it will be filling. And we have dessert." She laughed as she fetched one of the boxes of chocolates and put it on the table they were all sitting around.

No one argued with the plan. The lids of the cans came off quickly and everyone made short work of their first solid food that day.

Even Eve didn't have to go hunting. When she'd finished her meal, Cora made sure she opened a can of cat food for her little charge. Using one of the file folders she'd carried into the storage area, Cora placed the food on the floor for Eve. There was no hesitation on the cat's part, she hopped out of the basket and eagerly accepted what was offered. Then after a trip to the dirt box she was right back in the bin with her babies.

Mike and Jay made a trip to the car and brought in the camping gear they'd had with them. "We got three sleeping bags for us," he nodded to where Cora had been sleeping, "I can see you don't need one." He had a box of things, "I'll make a pot of coffee. Seems we got plenty of that." He walked over to get a bottle of water.

"Somehow we have running water," Cora said pointing the the sink. "Let's use that and save the bottled for when we go exploring the town again."

Mike nodded, "The water pipes for the town are underground, and pressure is probably still strong enough to let the water run. But I'm sure that will eventually end when the pipes are empty. So use it while we can I guess." He filled his old, well used, enamel coffee pot and turned on the hot plate.

24

Immediately, the little generator began to run in the other room. "Hey, that's good. We got gas." He went into the other room to look at the generator. Then he came into the main room. "Well, someone was smart enough to know to vent that to the outside. Shouldn't have a generator inside though, can get carbon monoxide poisoning real easy with those things. I'd feel safer to move it outside, at least into that open space beyond the door." He looked at Jay, who nodded in agreement.

"You haven't been sleeping in here with that running have you?" Jay asked of Cora.

She shook her head, "No, to save the gas I turned it off when I closed the door. Guess without thinking about how dangerous it might be, I was saved by being conservative."

They sat a few minutes after the coffee was ready. They each took a cup of the strong brew to sip on. Jay looked around the room. "You know I think this was an old bomb shelter. From the way it's built and the storage area it has; it's a lot like the one my great uncle had. Built it back in the 1950s, when everyone thought an atomic bomb could be dropped at any minute. His son, my uncle, owned the house later and his kids, my cousins and I used to go down there to play games."

Jake went to lay down on Cora's bed while the grownups talked over coffee. "So what do we do from here?" Jay said to no one in particular.

"I haven't seen any planes in the sky or birds or signs of life of much around here. The cat caught a mouse and I saw a couple of rats. I did see something strange. A big shining thing, seemed to be stationary, looked like it was several miles up. Didn't get a good look at it though because it started to rain. Until you guys came along, I felt like I was going to be the last person on Earth." Cora sighed.

"We were glad to see you too. Finding you though has led me to believe we're not going to be the only ones. If we were saved by being underground think of all the others who could potentially have been saved. People working in tunnels, or just being in them, coal miners too," Mike thought for more examples.

Jay nodded, "Tourists visiting places like Luray Caverns, or even people in other canyons like the one we were in that seemed untouched." He smiled at his grandson and said quietly, "It

25

probably means that people in submarines might have been spared too. My son is an officer on a sub."

It was the first hope that any of them dared express. Mike thought a moment then had an idea, "I know one place we could start looking. There's that place in Colorado that's supposed to have an underground military base. I think they call it Crystal Mountain or something. I don't think we should stay here." He looked around. "We don't have enough supplies to last more than a few days. And think about when winter comes, gets mighty cold out here on the prairie with no wood for a fire."

Cora shrugged and gave a little laugh, "Well, we do have all these useless old medical files. We could burn them and no one would care." She sighed, "You're right, I think that we should go into town again and find any thing there might be left, maybe rest up for a day and then head west to see if we can locate that base."

"I think if we don't find it in a day or two we should head south. We can get into California or Arizona where it will be warmer for the winter. I think it would be smart to wind up somewhere by the ocean where we can fish more than up here," Jay added.

Cora and Mike nodded in agreement. Just then Jake woke up, "Did someone say something about going fishing?"

Jay laughed, "You heard that didn't you!" He shook his head, "Not today, but soon. We're going back into town and see if we can find anything else." He got up and unrolled his sleeping bag. "Time to turn in." Everyone followed his lead.

The next morning after everyone had another can of beans and a turn in the bathroom they were all back in the pickup and headed back into what had been the town. To save gas they parked in a central area and walked off in different directions to cover as much ground as they could.

They could see each other from blocks away and when Jake started jumping up and down ,the others hurried to see what he'd found. Cora was first to join the boy. "Wow," she said. They were standing at the edge of a swimming pool full of water. "This must be the municipal pool." She looked at Jake, then smiled and took off her slippers. It was another hot morning and it was just too tempting. Clothes and all, she jumped in. Jake didn't hesitate, he followed her example.

When Jay and Mike arrived at the scene, the other two were racing each other to the end of the pool. Jay looked at Mike and shrugged, "It won't be heated but who cares!" He just stepped in at the midline of the pool where it said 'five feet.' It was just up to his chin; he dog paddled to the shallow end of the pool. By that time Mike was in the pool floating on his back. It was a refreshing pleasure for all of them. In about fifteen minutes, the unheated water began to chill them so the little group got out and lay on the wide concrete deck around the pool to dry out.

It didn't take long for the heat of the day to begin to feel oppressive. Their clothes were dry in just a little while too. There was still a damp spot here and there, but they decided they needed to continue their quest.

"We smell a little of chorine, but that was the closest I've come to a bath in several days," Cora laughed. "It felt wonderful. A bath and washing our clothes at the same time, can't beat that." The men agreed and started off again.

Their afternoon of searching didn't improve their supply situation too much. They found two shelters. One was empty and the other had been used mostly for garden storage, but it netted them four hand gardening tools and two shovels. There had also been gloves, bottles of seeds, all carefully labeled, and three pair of garden clogs. Cora was glad to find one pair of them were close enough to her size, so she traded her slippers immediately.

By the time they returned to the shelter, everyone was hungry again. Cora boiled a couple of the remaining potatoes she had and added a chopped onion. Then she added two cans of the spaghetti with meat sauce. Once it was ready, she served the food in the styrofoam cups. It made a strange, but good meal. For dessert, she opened one of the jars of canned fruit she'd found. This time it was cherries.

Jay made another pot of coffee and they took their hot drinks outside and they sat on a curb and watched the night come on. "You observe how well you can see the stars without all the city lights?" Jay said as he gently ran his hand over Jake's head.

27

Jake didn't say anything, just smiled and leaned against his grandfather. "Do you think there will be any kids left anywhere?"

"I'm sure there will be son, I'm sure there will be," Jay said softly, but gave a questioning look at Cora and Mike. It was a hard thing to know for sure.

"It's so odd to be so quiet isn't it. I can hear each of you breathing. There's no sound of bugs flying around, no mosquitos even. I kind of miss the sound of cars going by and people talking, sitting out on their porches on a warm night like this." Mike said. "I didn't live very close to anyone there in Sedalia, but I did have neighbors I really liked. Old retired farmers like me."

Cora looked away trying not to cry. So many that she knew were just gone. There was no sign of anyone. What happened to her mother, sister, cousins, even her co-workers? Was she the only woman left? What could all this mean? She decided to try and change the subject. "Where are you from Jay, you said you were visiting Mike?"

"I'm from Spokane. Jake here is from San Diego. His father is a sailor on a sub, as I mentioned earlier. His mom, God rest her soul, died when he was pretty young. He usually spends summer with me, which has been a blessing to me for sure." He hugged the boy around the shoulders.

Cora pressed on, "How did the two of you meet?" she asked, motioning between the two older men.

Jay laughed, "Seems like another lifetime now. but we were both in Kuwait when it was attacked. I was a petroleum engineer with an American company there. Mike was working as the manager of an import goods shop. I happened to be there that day to buy some knick-knacks to brighten up my rather tiny, dreary apartment and we wound up hiding together in the basement of his store for several days, during which time we got to know each other pretty well. By the time we were liberated, I was staying at his rather palatial house and we have remained friends for all these years. Since we both retired, we've been visiting back and forth at least a few times a year."

Mike looked down at the ground, "Yeah, neither of us have any family close anymore. My wife and I split years ago, after the last kid got out of high school. She remarried and lives in

Ohio. My son lives in Wisconsin and my daughter is in England working for a medical clinic as an x-ray tech. They lived with their mother for a bit after we divorced, then moved on with their lives. I seldom saw them. I always thought they'd come back to where they had spent their high school years and see me, but they never did. They send Christmas cards and birthday cards but that's about all our correspondence. I've offered to go see them and their families but they were always too busy to have me come." He sighed, lost in memories.

Jay looked at Jake, "I'm lucky. My son has a house in San Diego and every time he's in port he calls me. Emails me almost every week, and sends me his wonderful son every summer."

Jake sighed, "I love coming to Washington every year, Grandpa. We go fishing, swimming and hiking. It's been a lot of fun," he sighed, "at least it always was. I don't know what it will be like now that we're probably not going back to your home and I probably don't have a home in San Diego."

Jay hugged his grandson, "Our home has always been wherever we are together, son. I love you and we're going to be just fine. I believe God brought us through this and will carry us on. Got to have a little faith. And we're not alone. We got Mike and Cora, we're kind of a new family."

A slight breeze began to chase the heat of the day away to the point that Cora felt a chill. "I think I'm going in for the night. I don't run the generator at night so I close the doors so it won't get too cold."

The men nodded and followed her into the shelter. Eve, the cat had been outside on the steps with them. She seemed to understand what was happening and returned to the basket with her kittens.

There was enough coffee left for a cup more each. They opened another box of chocolates and enjoyed a few treats. Then Cora remembered something, "I have something for you, Jake." She got up and went to a box she had come back from town with. "On my first day of foraging I saw some toys and games in a root cellar. I didn't bring all of them back because they weren't something I could use at the time. But I did bring one box. There might be something in this box that you could have some fun with."

Jake looked excited as the took the box to the floor and began to sort through it. A couple of things were too young for him, but he did find a small remote control vehicle and a package of batteries. He had that working and buzzing around under the feet of the grownups quickly. He stopped playing with that to continue his search of the box. He found two jigsaw puzzles and an adult coloring book of exotic birds with some colored pens. He took that to the other table and began to color.

"That looks like a good find," Jay said with a sad smile. "He's such a great kid. He hasn't asked about his father," he added quietly as he looked at Mike who nodded.

"Got to be wondering and thinking about it though," Mike answered equally as softly.

Jay nodded, then glanced at Cora, "Wonder what that thing you saw in the sky was?"

With a shrug, Cora looked away, tears were running down her face. She couldn't help it. Getting up without saying anything she went to the bathroom and washed her face. It was a journey into an unknown world now, but soon they would have to leave the safety of this shelter and try to find what was left of humanity, no matter what the danger. If not for themselves, for Jake.

CHAPTER FOUR

Following Highway 30, they set off the next day just before noon, packing up everything, including the cats. They constructed a sturdy, cardboard crate for Eve and her babies. The cushions from the benches made passable seating in the back of the pickup for Jake and Cora.

The trip across most of the width Nebraska was painfully easy, since there was nothing to see and not a thing to impede their way. Mike's pickup was old so they weren't able to travel at top speed, but nevertheless they made pretty good time. They only stopped where it looked like a community or town had been to find evidence of a gas station. Because they hoped to get into Colorado before sunset, they pressed on after finding their fuel, not taking time to explore any area for extra supplies.

As they began to climb towards the mountains, they stopped at what must have been a planned tourist stop. All that was in view were the naked rolling land of Nebraska behind them and the looming mountains of the Rockies ahead of them.

They had gone more than two hundred miles when Mike abruptly stopped the car and backed up. Up a side road he had seen something that he wanted to investigate. Cora tried to look ahead, but couldn't see what Mike had seen. It was a rough, unpaved path more than a road. The dust was stifling even though Mike was driving slowly.

When they'd gone about a half a mile, Cora saw something she never expected to see. There were three or four antelope running ahead of the truck down into what looked like a small gully. Mike followed them as closely as he could, but they were running at full speed and the road had gotten very rough. When the pickup finally crested the top of the hill where antelope were last seen, the travelers found themselves looking down into a deep, narrow canyon with a willow lined creek at the bottom. Here and there were wider grassy areas and some good sized trees. It looked like the valley ran north for at least three miles or more.

Carefully Mike made the way down the rocky trail to the bottom of the canyon. He stopped the truck and everyone got out. Birds could be heard and seen skittering along the creek bank, almost unaware that the world beyond this valley had all but disappeared.

"Well, this is good news. Maybe there will be many places like this that weren't touched by whatever happened. This is what we experienced outside the cave that saved us," Jay said happily.

Mike looked up, "It's been a long, hot drive today. What say we make camp here? This seems like good fresh water and there's a grassy spot to make camp. We can put the cat in the cab of the truck for the night. She can move around and see out. At least that will allow her to stretch her legs a bit."

Cora smiled at him, "That's really thoughtful. I think it's a great idea."

Jay didn't say anything, just started to unpack the supplies from the pickup. Jake headed for the creek and looked around. "Grandpa, there's fish in this creek. Can I try to catch one?"

Jay just smiled and nodded, noting the boy was already holding his fishing pole. "I don't think it matters that you don't have a Nebraska license, at least today."

Jake immediately went hunting for a grasshopper or worm he could use for bait while the men figured out the space for the camp. Mike and Jay got several fair sized rocks from the creek side and made a place for a fire. Cora went along the edge of the embankment to find dry twigs and sticks for the fire. It took quite a while, although she had a nice armload by the time she returned to the camp site. "Gotta remember there's snakes that were underground around here," she reminded the men. "We should be careful."

"Already saw one," Jay said pointing to a dead reptile, "I think that's a prairie rattler." He held up a hatchet, "Only way to be safe around those critters." He put the ax back into a holder on his belt.

Mike waved a pistol, "This would have been safer, from a further distance too."

Jay nodded, "If you have time and distance when you spot one." He looked around, "Well, I think we're ready." He looked at Cora, "We've spread the cushions out in the bed of the pickup for you to sleep on. Eve and the kittens are in the truck cabin, she wasn't too happy but we put her water and food down as well as her little box of dirt. That quieted her."

Cora was impressed, "Thank you, again. You've been most considerate of my little family. I know it's probably a silly thing in the light of everything that's been lost, but she means a lot to me."

"I can appreciate that," Jay looked away. "I've had a dog for the last ten years since I lost my wife. He was my constant companion, but he was getting arthritis and since we were flying to see Mike I left him in a kennel in Spokane."

Cora could see the pain in the older man's face, probably that kennel like everything else was gone. It hurt too much to think of all the things that were lost. She told herself it was better just to concentrate on the here and now. Life was fragile, and if there was to be a tomorrow, it needed to be guarded.

Cora unpacked four cans of their supply of beans. After the fire was going she popped the lids a bit and put the cans at the edge of the fire to heat. At least they would have a hot meal. They could use the cans for some of the canned fruit after they finished eating their hot food. Jay got water from the creek for their coffee. He sat the coffee pot on some of the hot coals from the fire that he pulled aside. It took quite a few minutes to get to the point that steam could be see rising from the spout.

Jake came back from the creek. "No luck today. Saw some fish but nothing was biting. I may try again tomorrow." He sat down by the fire. "After dinner can I go swim? There's a good sized pool just a few yards down the stream."

Cora looked at Jake, "Is it big enough for me to take a bath in?"

Jake wrinkled up his nose, "I guess so."

"Good," she laughed, "I promise to be quick so you can get your swim in. In fact I'll do it while you're eating your dinner." Cora got up and gathered a towel and one of her treasured little fancy bath soaps.

It only took a few minutes to reach the spot that Jake had found. He had been right, it was a perfect, if small, swimming hole about ten feet across and maybe twelve feet long. It looked like there were several deep spots amid the boulders at the bottom. The little stream seemed to move slowly at this point. Cora chose a spot down the creek near the shallow end of the pool. She stripped off and eased her body into the water and just sat a moment while she got over the shock of going from the ninety degree day to the cold water. She dove under the water and came up shivering. Quickly soaping down and then rinsing off underwater was all she could take. She made her way out of the water and dried off as fast as she could, shivering as her numb fingers struggled to redress herself.

Her hair was still dripping when she made it back to the fire. "Wow, that was, to say the least, refreshing. That water is really cold. Jake if you go swimming you can probably only stay in about five minutes. You might get hypothermia if you're in longer than that." Cora fetched her can of beans from the fire. The men had already finished theirs.

Jake looked at Jay, "Okay, five minutes at least?"

Jay nodded, "You can go, but I'm going with you." He looked at Cora, "Was it deep?"

"In spots," she answered, "and there are a couple of places where it's very deep between boulders. He needs to be careful not to get stuck under one of those."

Jay got up and motioned to Jake, "Let's go before it begins to cool down. It's still warm enough to bring your body temperature up before we go to bed."

Jake joyfully jumped up and ran ahead of his grandfather. "Come on Grandpa," the boy urged.

The pair was back in the no more than twenty minutes. Jake was shivering and hurried to be by the fire. "Told you it was cold," Cora said with a smile. Jake nodded.

Jay came back to the fireside and sat down heavily. "I stuck my feet in the water and about froze. No way was I getting in. I guess you're going to have to put up with the way I smell for a while longer."

Mike laughed, "I wondered what smelled like something had died."

Jay looked around, swatting a mosquito away, "Well, here's those bugs we were missing the other night." He moved a little into the direction the smoke was moving. "They dislike the smell of smoke more than they love the taste of human blood. At least that's what I've been told."

"I think that's one of those urban myths my friend," Mike said poking a stick into the fire. "Keep the fire going gang, cold or not I'm going to risk washing myself off. Been so hot and dusty today it will feel good." Mike got up and started off to the creek, "Got any more of that soap Cora?"

She reached into her pocket and fetched the small bar, "Happy to share."

34

Jay called after Mike, "Want me to come be lifeguard?" That was met with a shrug and a rude gesture, "Don't say I didn't warn you!" Jay laughed loudly, the sound echoing through the canyon.

It was only about six or seven when the last rays of sunlight reached down into the canyon. Immediately it began to cool down, everyone huddled around the fire. Those who had braved a dip in the water still shivered a bit, even though their hair had dried and they were wrapped in blankets.

On the bank above them a lone coyote cried for his pack, but there was no answer. There was plenty for him to eat. They had seen prairie dog mounds all over the place on their way to this valley. Here in this tiny oasis they had discovered birds and rabbits as well as the antelope. The coyote wouldn't starve, but loneliness might be the thing that would plague him. Cora thought about that as she had started to feel that deep emptiness that being alone brings. She'd seen that in some of the elderly patients that had come into the clinic. Many widows whose spouses had died years before and those with no children had that vacant, lost look. Looking up toward the canyon rim she felt sorry for the coyote. She sighed and watched the fire dance in its little enclosed space.

Their fire was just embers by the time she realized how tired she was. It was dark and Jake had already found his sleeping bag. She didn't say anything, just nodded to Jay and Mike. It only took her several minutes to crawl into the back of the pickup and stretch out on the mats. It was a hard bed, but she pulled the blankets up around her and fell asleep without any problem.

In the middle of the night, she was awaken by something moving close to her, she smiled when she realized it was Jake. He'd brought his sleeping bag and lay down next to her. He didn't really seem awake. She laughed to herself, the ground couldn't be much harder than this bed. She covered herself back up and snugged up close to the boy, immediately they both felt warmer and it was easy to get back to sleep.

Just as the first hint of sunlight touched the top of the ridge, Jake sat up and rubbed his eyes. He was surprised to find himself in the back of the pickup. He didn't remember moving himself there.

35

Cora had been awake for a few minutes but didn't move, so as not to wake Jake. She smiled, "Good morning. Got tried of sleeping on the ground, huh?"

Jake looked embarrassed and looked at his sleeping grandfather, still tucked up tight in his sleeping bag. "I'm sorry, I didn't mean to..." he looked at Cora.

"Hey, it was nice of you to think I might be cold. I appreciated you keeping me warm," Cora said before he could finish his sentence.

"Sure," Jake stammered as he hurriedly slid out of the pickup bed. "Anytime."

Cora wanted to laugh, but thought better of it as she headed for the bushes on the far side of the camp to an area she had staked out as "her" private spot. After that, she headed for the creek to wash her hands and face. The water felt twice as cold as it had the night before, however ,after that she was wide awake.

By the time she got back to the camp, the men were up and working on getting the fire going again. Jake had gone off to fish in hopes of something besides beans for breakfast. Cora went straight to the truck to take care of Eve and the kittens.

"Hi baby," she said to Eve as she added water to her dish and put down some more cat food. She stroked the kittens and saw that their eyes were beginning to open. "Oh, how sweet you are," she cooed to them. Eve got up on the seat next to the kittens demanding a little petting herself. Cora happily obliged. After a few minutes of getting the attention she needed, Eve climbed back into the bin with her babies and let them have breakfast. Cora cleaned the litter box and then went to see what she could fix them for their first meal.

The fire was going well and the coffee pot full of water was steaming. Jay threw a coffee packet in and everyone waited for that wonderful smell that would announce it was done. Cora was about to offer a choice of their two canned good options when Jake returned from the creek with three fair sized trout. Within minutes the fish were prepared on skewers of willow and roasting over the open fire. Normally Cora didn't like fish but now her mouth was watering as she hoped to have a portion of Jake's catch. They had added other sticks holding the last of the potatoes and onions. At least breakfast seemed like it was going to be a pretty good start for the day.

Cora got about a quarter of one of the fish, half an onion and half a potato. Scant as it was, it tasted like a banquet. There were still salt and pepper packets from the ready-to-eat meal packages that they shared to make it better. They enjoyed the coffee and then emptied out the pot to boil water to fill the water bottles that they had saved. It was a rare treasure to find a water source like the little babbling stream.

Time came to pack up and head on. "We should be in Colorado most anytime. I've never been to Denver, except the being at the airport to change planes, but I think where we want to go is south of there," Mike said as he took out a well worn map. "I think it's close to Colorado Springs, and I know that is south of Denver."

"I've seen pictures of that entrance to the underground base in movies, but I never knew if it was real or not," Jay said doubtfully, "I hope it is, and I hope there are people there."

Cora nodded as she put Eve and the kittens back into their makeshift crate. Jake was already up on the pickup bed. He offered a hand to Cora as she struggled to get onto the back gate. Then he helped her close and secure it.

When Mike saw that everything was where it should be, he put out the fire, stirring the ashes to make sure it was out. He got in, started the reliable old vehicle and turned around and headed out of the little reminder of Eden. There was no sign of the antelope once they reached the top of the ridge. Again the traveler's found themselves in a barren looking land.

Even though the day was promising to be a hot one, there was a subtle difference in the air. They were climbing, it was hardly noticeable, but they were leaving the prairie lands for the higher altitudes.

There was a fork in the road ahead, one obviously heading more south. Mike turned that way and they continued on. Cora saw that junction as they passed it. "This must be Highway 76 that goes into Colorado. We're not on Highway 30 anymore, that would have taken us into Wyoming," Cora said to Jake over the noise of the truck.

Jake nodded, but didn't say anything. He just kept looking out at the naked land. Here and there, a small animal would run out of a burrow to another one, but other than that, there was nothing to see. After a while, he just lay down and took a nap with his head next to Cora's legs.

She reached down and stroked his hair gently. His hair was coarse compared to the soft fur she had been petting earlier of Eve's; she was growing very fond of this boy. It made her wonder what it would have been like if she had children. She looked down at Jake. Her sister had gotten married right after high school, had three kids. The opportunity or the right man had just never happened for Cora. Now she was twenty-eight, the chances of that happening seemed very slim. Somehow that make her feel sad and a bit disappointed even though she had what she considered a very good life. A bump in the road shook her out of her melancholy and she shrugged and looked back out over the countryside.

CHAPTER FIVE

They pushed on through, stopping only to stretch their legs and relieve themselves or find fuel. The hope was that they would either find people or another little oasis like the one they had camped in the night before. As much as they hoped for that, the miles passed without them seeing anything encouraging.

The day wore on; it was nearing mid-day when they reached the outskirts of what must have been Denver. The broad streets with intricate looking street patterns was the only hint that a major city had been there at one time. It was strange and quiet. Mike stopped the car in what must have been an underground parking structure. It was the only shade offered for miles.

Cora walked out on the four lane highway at ground level. Putting her hand up to shade her eyes, she strained to see any signs of life, but just as it had been all day; nothing moved except an occasional dust devil.

It was very hot on the road, so Cora didn't stay long. "Didn't see anything," she told the others when she rejoined them. "There does look like some thunderheads building up over the mountains, we might get some rain."

"Wouldn't be bad, if we don't get a flash flood," Mike said shaking his head. "I've seen some of them nearly wash out the road in Arizona when I was down there once. We need to keep an eye out. The storm itself can be miles away but all of a sudden a wall of water comes down an arroyo." He started towards the truck, "We best keep going."

No one said anything else as they all got back in the pickup and made themselves as comfortable as possible. Cora fed Eve and gave her more water just as Mike started the engine. She hurried back to her place behind the cab.

Mike had somehow found his way through the maze of criss-crossing intersections and finally they were on what looked like the main highway heading south. Without signs, buildings, trees or anything that that lended clues, it had taken much longer than normal to get through the town site. To make things harder, the sun was swinging lower all the time and dark ominous clouds were now approaching.

They were about forty minutes out of Denver when Mike slammed on the brakes.He hopped out of the pickup and stood looking up. Jay got out of the car, trying to see what Mike had seen. Jake and Cora stood up in the back of the truck. Cora was open mouthed when a fancy little drone helicopter hovered right in front of her and then sped away. "Oh, my gosh," she shouted as she pointed, "did you see that?"

Jake was jumping out of the truck and running to his grandfather in an instant, "That means there are other people doesn't it?"

It was the first hopeful sign of human life they'd seen since they had met each other. Before they could get back into the pickup, their second surprise arrived. A humvee pulled up in front of them and quickly stopped. Two soldiers got out and ran up to Mike and Jay.

"Is your pickup still working? If it is, you need to follow us quickly," the first man said.

Cora saw Mike and Jay get back into the truck as fast they could and the soldiers get in to their rig and turn around. She and Jake sat back down as Mike sped down the highway, straining his old pickup to its limit to keep up with the humvee.

They only went about another thirty-five minutes before they pulled up in front of what Cora had only seen in the movies, that iconic entry into a mystical underground base. Just before they entered, the soldiers guarding the gate stopped them and motioned them over to the side.

The two men in the lead humvee walked back to the truck, "You'll have to leave your truck here, but we need you to get inside. Take what you need for your personal use. We have supplies inside." One of them walked to the back to help Cora and Jake to the ground.

Cora looked at the box crate, "I have a cat with kittens?"

"No problem, Miss, we have cats inside too. You can bring them."

Cora immediately got the bin and put the Eve and the kittens in it. She covered it with a towel and started to carry the basket, but one of the young soldiers took it and hurried to the waiting humvee. Cora got in and he handed Eve and the babies to her.

When everyone was seated in the military vehicle, they started off into the mountain. Cora had never had a sense of claustrophobia before. Now she understood what people talked about as she looked up at the hewn granite above her. Looking back at the daylight disappearing made her feel anxious and a little nauseous even though the area they moved through was well lit. She was glad when the truck stopped and she was able to get out and stand up.

It was eerie, to say the least, to see men and women going about their business like nothing had happened. There were several vehicles parked next to the one they had arrived in. Cora could see the parking area they were in was not as well lit as the area just beyond it that seemed to be more of a court yard. The soldiers escorted them across that area to a barracks type building. "You'll be assigned rooms here," one of them said as he took them to a young woman sitting at a desk. He stepped crisply aside, as he did he whispered to Cora, "I'll get the cat some food and a litter box, I'll bring it by in a little while." He nodded to the woman at the desk and then the two young men left.

The woman at the desk stood up and extended her hand to them, one by one. "Welcome, I'm Sergeant Lois Wilkerson" she said, "you'll be our guests. I can tell you we were are glad to see you. We are housing people here, rather than outside, until we're sure it's safe to be outside." The Sergeant looked about the same age as Cora, but a bit taller and certainly more muscular.

Cora felt like hugging her, but resisted, "We are certainly glad to see you too."

"Let me give you rooms to rest up in. Are you one family or a couple?" She looked at Cora with a questioning look.

Cora laughed, "No, I was alone and then these three showed up. I'm Cora, this is Mike and his friend, Jay and Jay's grandson, Jake."

"Okay, Gentlemen, would you be able to share a room?"

They nodded their agreement and so she motioned for all of them to follow her. Cora carried her basket and fell in step with the group.

Her room turned out to be just big enough for a twin bed and a tiny table with two folding chairs, but it did have a attached private bathroom with a shower. Cora was thrilled. It didn't have a closet, instead had just a coat rack. She put the basket down and let Eve out to explore. There was a small, inch deep plastic tray under the two glasses in the bathroom next to the sink that she took to use for water for Eve. Once that was done, all Cora could think of was that shower. Everyone else had moved on down the hall, so she locked the door, threw off her clothes and headed for her first real bath with hot water in what felt like a very long time.

Lois had said they would be briefed before they went to dinner at six, so they had a few hours to rest. Cora had just gotten out of the shower when she heard a knock at her door. She hurried into her clothes and wrapped a towel around her wet hair, "Just a minute," she called out.

When she opened the door the soldier was standing there, Lois by his side. He had a small plastic pan with a bag of dry cat food and a bag of litter in it. "I found some other things including catnip toys," he said with a smile. "Some of the others here have cats, so our little BX has little treats." He walked in and sat the items on a chair, nodded and left.

Lois walked in and put an arm load of clothing on the bed. She smiled, "I guessed that you were about my size so I went along and picked up at least a change of clothes for you. You can go back and get what you want later. We don't have much choice. We used to just order what we wanted and it would be here in a day or so from Denver," she sighed. "Guess that's not going to happen anymore."

The two women stood looking at each other for a moment, the weight of what happened hitting both of them at that moment. They reached out and hugged one another. Without saying a word, Lois moved back and left the room.

Eve meowed and reminded Cora she had taken on new responsibilities. In minutes the cat was happily crunching away on the dry food. Cora remembered she had some cat food left in the pickup. She wondered if she could go get that. Chills went through her body again as she thought how far they had traveled into the mountain. That closed in feeling came over once more and it was hard to shake off.

The clothes turned out to be fine. Lois had brought two tee shirts, a military style jacket and two pair of light weight slacks. Best of all there was a package of undies and a bra. The bra was a little big, but it would do. Cora felt totally renewed having showered and in clean clothes.

Another knock on the door reminded Cora she wasn't all by herself anymore. "Come in," she called as she put on her slippers.

Jake came in quickly, "Hi Cora," he said breathlessly, "Grandpa and Mike are headed for the briefing and he told me to come get you. Grandpa said to hurry you along."

Cora chuckled at the boy's excitement. "Okay, I'm ready." She grabbed her jacket and made sure the cats stayed in the room as they left for the meeting. Jay and Mike were waiting just outside the barracks door.

"The Colonel asked us to come to his office," Jay said as they headed for a row of box like offices that lined one corner of the part of the cavern they were in.

The office was fairly large considering where they were. There was a small conference table with just enough chairs for them to sit. Three other officers came in and stood behind the seated folks.

With a nod, the meeting began, "I'm Colonel Herbert and I'd like to welcome you to this facility. I know that you've experienced the loss we have. We will share what we know about what has happened, at least what we think has happened. For some reason our systems were out just as the event was taking place, so we're relying on those who may have seen something of what happened. We'd like to know who you are, how you all survived this whatever it was and then got here." He looked at Cora, "Let's start with you, Miss."

Cora took a deep breath. "Well, I'm Cora Mason, I was at work in Nebraska. I went to our file storage area which was in a tornado shelter underground when it happened. I felt dizzy, then fainted. When I woke up several hours later. I was able to forage for a couple days until these guys showed up." She leaned back in her chair as Mike sat forward.

"I'm Mike Spaulding and my friend here, Jay Breeden, and his grandson Jake, were visiting me in Missouri. We'd been going to go camping and had stopped to explore a cave I'd found earlier in this narrow canyon. My old truck was parked under a rock outcropping. We were in the cave when this all took place evidentially, because we, too, felt dizzy and passed out. When we woke up, we drove out of that canyon only to find everything, trees and everything were gone." He thought a moment, "We have kind of concluded that if you were underground or down in a very narrow canyon you might have been spared. We ran across another pretty deep gorge on our way here that was just as it was, right down to fish in the creek."

Colonel Herbert looked around at the two other officers in the room, "I guess what we've thought is confirmed." They nodded in agreement. "Somehow you were unaffected if you were either underground or in one of those rare untouched areas."

43

He leaned forward a bit, "I will share with you folks what we know as of now. There was solar flare activity predicted for this time period. NASA and everyone else had been monitoring it, but no one expected the size of the one that happened on that day, it was huge. Just as it was about to hit the Earth, all our monitoring systems went dead. After it happened, and it was quick, there were no reports coming in from anywhere, at least for a few hours, which must have been when you people experienced the passing out. We, in the bunker, didn't experience that because we are so far underground it would seem. However, the guards at the entrance did. We found them unconscious and brought them to the infirmary. They did recover with no ill effects, just like you did."

"As I understand it, you've got state of the art communication equipment here, have you been able to reach anyone else?" Jay asked.

The Colonel nodded, "Major Harvey, would you address that?"

Major Harvey walked to the head of the table and pulled down a map from a roll above a white marker board. "We projected where the solar flare hit first." She pointed to a spot, "Our best guess is it first hit the Earth somewhere around Portugal and Spain into France. We had always thought that a flare that big would wipe the Earth out, leave us a burnt out planet like Mars. Since we're still here, we were wrong. But our conclusion is, what we didn't count on was the speed that it was traveling. We estimate that it was three to four hundred times faster than expected and passed over the Earth so fast that it didn't have time to burn everything up, in fact there isn't any sign of anything being destroyed by fire." She shrugged, "Maybe we only got a glancing blow, whatever happened, it did not do what was expected, and because it came so fast and was so much bigger than anticipated, there was no time for warnings or anything else. As far as where everything went, we haven't a clue."

Colonel Herbert sighed, "Yes, this was not anything like what we had ever imagined. To get back to your question Jay, we have made contact with others. As Major Harvey said, we know where we think it hit first, and oddly enough the only populated place that seems somewhat intact is part of the south end of North Island, and north end of South Island, New Zealand. Half of each of the islands have experienced what we have, but that one little tiny place on Earth seems to be okay. Although they did report something strange being reported by the

44

crew of an airplane that was just landing as this whole thing happened. Just as their wheels were about to touch down, they saw a huge shimmering silver disk, as they described it, in the sky. But it disappeared before the plane rolled to a stop on the runway. "

Cora shivered, "I saw something like that too."

The Colonel looked at her and nodded. "We have no idea what you saw or what they saw. Nothing appeared on our radar or on anything that we had running here. It's an unknown."

Major Harvey just looked at the map, "We really don't know where everything went. There's no debris, no bodies, no clues except the cement on the ground, the water levels in the ocean, reservoirs and rivers dropping a few feet, and a few survivors."

Cora looked up, "Besides us and part of New Zealand, what other people have you found?"

"In Denver there was a crew working in the tunnels under the airport. Several workers had been cleaning and painting when it happened. So we were able to round them up pretty quickly. There is a total of about forty others that were working in offices and various places under the main part of the airport or in underground maintenance sites around several larger cities, too. You'll meet some of them at dinner. We suspect that there might be a lot of people in all the big cities around the city who were in the subways at the time. We just haven't been able to communicate with them yet."

Colonel Herbert took over the conversation, "We also have been in touch with several submarines, mostly ours and a couple of other friendly countries, who were submerged at the time. They are reporting the same conditions in any port they go into. The ones who were top-side went missing like everything else. There probably are a lot of others out there who were in various places that haven't had the resources to contact us."

Major Harvey turned around and walked back to where she had been standing. "We think it's safest for you all to stay with us until we've got a better idea of what happened. We've been sending out signals for anyone who hears them to try to let us know where they are and what is in their area. Our satellite system of course is gone, one of the first casualties of all this."

"Yes, we're not sure and have no way of knowing if that flare was a one time thing or if there are more coming soon. Or if this was an attack of some kind by an unknown enemy. So far it feels more likely it had to do with the sun flares," the Colonel said with a shrug. "I think it is time for dinner so Major Harvey will show you the way. Normally this would all be a highly restricted area, but you have unprecedented access in an unprecedented time." He smiled and got up.

The Major nodded to her superior and then opened the door for Cora and the men, "This way please."

Cora's head was still reeling, there was just too much to think about. She hardly noticed as they walked into the cafeteria like dining hall.

There seemed to be plenty of tables close to the serving area, but the Major lead them to two tables at the back of the hall. "Normally we go through the line but for you, someone will come and take your order tonight. Tomorrow you'll be able to come to breakfast here and go through the line. This will be where all meals will be served. The schedule is posted on the door, you'll all be in group C. We stagger the meal times because this isn't big enough for everyone at the same time. There are a few hundred people on duty here most of the time." She nodded and left them alone.

Jake looked around, "I wonder what they have that's good Grandpa."

Jay sighed, "I hope it's better than when I was in the Army. I spent a year in Turkey as a radio man. I was stationed at the main headquarters so didn't get shot at, but it still was a scary time." He looked away, lost for a moment in his memories.

A young man with two stripes with a "c" above it came to the table. "Evening folks, tonight we have either hamburgers or fried chicken. We have french fries or mashed potatoes, peas or corn, fresh biscuits, apples slices, jello, and for dessert we have ice cream or cherry cobbler. We have serve yourself coffee or tea, milk and soft drinks," he pointed to a service area. "That's where you can get your silverware and drinks." He managed a smile, "What can I bring you."

Jay looked at his companions, "Tell you what young man, we are perfectly able to go through the serving line like everyone else. You don't have to bring things to us unless you just have to."

With a smile the man held out his hand to Jay, "I'm Juan, if you want anything just ask." He stepped aside and motioned for them to join the people cueing up at the buffet line.

Jake was up and ready to make his choices. He didn't hesitate, pulling Cora along with him. They both took a tray and waited for their turn. Somehow it had sounded better than it looked, however they were hungry enough to be happy to get anything. Cora chose a piece of chicken, some mashed potatoes, peas and the apple slices. She was first back to the table so she went and got a large cup of coffee with cream and sugar. The others were at the table by the time she sat down.

Jake was half way through his hamburger when Mike leaned over started talking quietly to Jay and Cora. "What do you think of all this? I mean did you ever think we'd see the inside of this place?"

Jay shook his head, "I wasn't even sure this place really existed. I thought someone in Hollywood made it up."

"I think it's cool," Jake said as he got up to see about getting dessert.

Cora sighed, "Could a solar flare do all that? I mean where did everything and everybody go?"

Mike leaned back in his chair. "Yeah, that is the million dollar question. Where? How can a world of things almost entirely disappear in the batting of an eye?" He looked at his companions, "Then there's the other question, Why? Why are the four of us here? Why is this place still here and why of all places is New Zealand still there, even partially?"

Cora shook her head, "Is there anyone left that can tell us that?" She sighed, "That's just too much to wrap my head around. I have some hungry little critters waiting for me in my room that I need to get back to. So I will say good night. Hopefully I'll see you in the morning."

The two men nodded and said good-night as she walked off. Cora stopped by the door to look at the meal schedule posted there, group C's breakfast would be at eight. She wondered if she'd be up by then. She started to open the door when a hand reached around her and opened it for her. "Thanks," she said turning to see who it was. She recognized him as one of the other officers who had been at their briefing. He hadn't said anything, just stood listening.

"You're very welcome," he smiled down at her. He wasn't terribly tall, just a nice height, and athletic looking. He waited until she was outside the dining hall then exited himself. "May I walk you back to your quarters, Cora? May I call you that?"

"Of course, and you are?"

He tipped his head, "I'm Lieutenant Eldon Elroy, but please call me Eldon, my friends do."

Looking a little closer at him in the dim light, she could see he was probably not too much older than her, and while not quite really handsome, he wasn't bad looking. She chuckled to herself, "I'm being silly. Here in the middle of a world in crisis, I've found someone interesting." She glanced at his hands and saw no rings. She smiled again.

CHAPTER SIX

During the next week, several new people arrived at the base. Three people, a man and his wife and teenage boy, had just entered a tunnel on I-70 just west of Denver. They reported that three cars ahead of them, just 300 hundred feet or so, but outside the exit, were simply gone when they felt dizzy and passed out. Luckily the father had slammed on the brakes before he lost consciousness and the car had came to a stop against the side wall. When they awoke, they found themselves alone in the tunnel except for two other vehicles a few yards behind them that had crashed head-on into each other and drivers in both cars were killed, along with one passenger. They'd turned around and headed back towards Denver when the drone found them.

Eight more people came. They had been fighting a fire in the mountains near Cottonwood Pass. It had been getting close to them so they had taken shelter in an old mine shaft they found. They were pretty well exhausted when they were picked up by a patrol. They'd walked for three days getting out of the mountains. They had reported that when they came to, even the fire was gone.

Cora listened to the stories of everyone and became more confused, just as everyone else was. There were theories galore, but no one knew for sure. No one other than Cora, and the folks on the plane in New Zealand, had reported seeing the silver thing in the sky though.

Cora didn't see much of anyone except at meals. They'd been asked to stay inside until there was some assurance it was safe.

Eve and the kittens were Cora's companions, which was fine because they were all so sweet. The little ones were now roaming around, BB had began to climb up the side of her bed if the blanket hung down. It turned out that BB and Gray were male and only little Spots female. All of them were now using the litter box which was a relief. Cora was allowed to go get the cat food out of the pickup and so there was food for the family, at least for awhile. Lois had claimed Spots, when she was old enough to leave her mother, if no one else wanted her. Cora was actively seeking owners for the other two kittens, but so far no takers. Cora had become very fond of Eve and if at all possible would keep her.

The hours and days seemed to melt together. It was odd but everyone seemed to grow quieter as the time passed. Even Jake seemed to be more reserved. He had made friends with the other teenager, Eddie, that had newly arrived. They played pool together in the base rec room and had their video games to play, but something had changed. Cora saw it more everyday. She thought it might be that the new reality was really was setting in, or maybe it was the tons of rock over their heads. She no longer looked up, not wanting to be reminded of where she was.

Things fell into a familiar pattern until the day they heard the arrival of a helicopter at the main gate. The sound of it reverberated around inside the mountain compound. Nothing like that had been heard for a long time so everyone rushed to see who had arrived. A dozen or more people got out and rushed into the facility. Most were in suits and carrying briefcases, a couple in uniforms. They hurried by the civilians standing there, Cora included. The group all were hoping for some answers, but they would have to wait as the official looking newcomers were escorted to the Colonel's office. An hour later a notice went around that there would be an assembly of all military personnel at once, civilians would be briefed after that. That was disappointing to Cora, it was hard to wait and maddening to be the last to know anything new. She went back to Eve and the family.

The day drug on for her. Not even the cute antics of her little brood could make it better. Her small room was getting to be a tighter fit as the kittens grew and played more. It was a relief to get word that all civilians had been invited to the cafeteria for the news. Cora couldn't get there fast enough.

She hurried along and was joined by the other fifty or so people, all making their way to the dining hall. She had seen most of them at one time or another at meal times, and had heard their names, but there really hadn't been any socializing. Everyone just seemed to be in a sort of shock or despair. The family who had been in the tunnel, the Spears, usually looked sad. Mrs. Spears could be seen often in tears. The only one who seemed to still be able to smile or laugh was their son Eddie, especially when he was with Jake. The firefighters all ate together on a different schedule, as did the workers from Denver. This would be the first time they'd all be in the room at the same time.

By the time Cora arrived for the briefing, most of the seats at the front of the dining hall were taken. She hadn't really observed before that there were only about fifteen tables total in the room, with four chairs at each table, hence the need for the staggered eating times. The people who had just flown in were seated at a long table at the front. Cora took a seat at a table that was just two rows back from the front.

Beyond the serving counter, the cooks could be seen and heard getting ready for the evening meals to begin. They stopped to listen along with the civilians when the Colonel stood up and walked to a podium that had a microphone attached.

"Good afternoon everyone," Colonel Herbert said. "I wish we had more news than we are going to share with you this afternoon, but we feel that you need to know what little information we have so far." He cleared his throat. "You heard the arrival of the helicopter I'm sure. We were pleased to greet the Under Secretary of Department of the Interior, Janet Mannix, and the Secretary of Labor, Roy Michleson, Senator Robert Victor of Maine, and Senator Jacob Orwitz, of New Hampshire." The Colonel motioned to one of the two officers. "This is Major Eli Morgan, he will tell you the story of their travels and what they have learned." He stepped aside and let the officer in an Army uniform stand in front of the group.

The Major sighed, "Well, as you know this has been a unprecedented trauma to us all. Our country, actually the world, has experienced a frightening and unexplainable catastrophe. Captain Fowler and I," he indicated the other Army officer standing near him, "were in another facility like this one when it happened. We were near Washington D.C. at the time so we took a patrol out to see if there was any part of the government left. We were pleased to find several senators, as well as two cabinet members and some of their staff had been in the tram tunnel that runs under the Capitol building to the Senate office building. There were also many civilians in the subway in D.C. The trains had stopped when the main power went out. There were too many to take to the base so we established temporary camps for them in the underground mall where we found many other survivors."

He took a moment before going on. "There are small groups of people working on the answers, here and there in places like this that were spared. We have come to the conclusion, as you here, that those of us that are left were underground for many different reasons when whatever this is, happened."

He looked down for a moment. "Truth is, we don't know how we survived. The consensus is that the solar flares were bigger than this planet would have been expected to survive, yet some-how, it could be just by the grace of God, we did. Now we just have to figure out for ourselves where we go from here. Figuring it out is one thing, dealing with the loss of infrastructure is another."

He stepped back, taking a deep breath, "Then there is the real loss. All of us have family, friends, jobs, homes," he stopped. "Looking forward, the big question is how do so few rebuild or even survive without trees for lumber, dams are still there but how do we access the power they can make? The power poles are gone, the phone lines are gone as well as the satellites to use our cell phones. When our generators run out of gas, where's the nearest station?"

Mike put up his hand, "We found there is still gas in the tanks where there were gas stations. Just gotta know how to use a siphon hose."

Major Morgan nodded, "Even that will be gone eventually and who is there to refine more gas? What do we store it in? Nothing that was sitting on the surface is still there. We are fortunate that that little bit of New Zealand exists. They may become the saving grace of the world. We hope that we can somehow get seeds to grow plants and a few basics from them to start over if we have to. There are a number of submarines to navigate the seas and a few vehicles that were spared, but you can see the enormity of what we all face."

He glanced around, "I'd like introduce Professor Roy Michaels of Georgetown University, to speak to you now."

A man in his early fifties stood up and walked to the podium. He shuffled about uncomfortably while he gathered his thoughts and finally began, "Thank you, Major. I happened to have the good fortune to be on the Subway at the time. I'd been to the dentist. Who would have thought that would be a good thing." He looked around a moment, "It's hard to know if we have survived a crisis or we were lost in one isn't it? What happened to everyone else?" He paused, "I have to admit I wished I'd paid more attention to some of the theories my colleagues were tossing about over the years. Maybe one of them might have been able explain what has happened." He took a deep breath, "I teach an intro to physics class. There was never anything I read that could explain this really. We are in a totally new place. However, there are quite a few people who expound and give a lot of thought to the string theory that allows for the possibility of alternate universes. Are we in one now? Then there are those who believe in extra terrestrials, have we been attacked? Are we being invaded? Then there are those who think this is some secret government experiment. But for the life of me, I do not know how any of those wild ideas could apply to this situation. I'm afraid this is just something we will have to live with for now and explain later." He shrugged and walked back to his seat.

The Colonel looked around, seeing no one else step forward, he came back to the podium. "So there it is. We know that you and I in this country are not alone. We have no doubt that there are hundreds of people out there still waiting to be found. The main problem will be finding them and having enough supplies to face the coming winter. The military facilities that are underground have enough supplies normally for their personnel for a year at least, but can probably support a hundred more for a few months. The question though will become, what then?"

"We will be asking everyone to do their part. We will start interviewing civilians to see what skills or interests they have and assign them to work with our staff to help keep things running. For anyone not wanting or unable to be a part of this effort we will try to be accommodating as we can be. We are continuing to look for other survivors. Our patrol goes out each day in a different direction and uses the drone to search up to a hundred miles ahead of the patrol. We'll continue to do this as we can." The Colonel looked around at those at the head table. "Anyone like to say something else?" No one moved or indicated they had anything to add. "All right then, we thank you for coming. We are going to keep looking for answers as we work through this difficult time and as new things come up."

Cora thought of something and put her hand up. "Yes Miss," Colonel Herbert said.

She stood up, "I was alone for a few days and I found several storm cellars in my area. Some of them had supplies. In this area and anywhere they are apt to have tornadoes we might find some extra supplies and more shelters that could be used to house people. Also on our way here, we found a little valley that had water and trees still there. There were antelope, rabbits and snakes too. So there may be places like that to look for. They might make good areas for camps if we get too many people to be inside here."

One of the men that had come from Denver raised his hand, "Those tunnels under the airport are really quite large. If we had to, we could use those for shelters. The one we were in had been closed for painting." He shrugged, "The paint should be dry by now." He sat down.

The Colonel nodded, "Those are good suggestions, we'll be looking for resources and places that we could develop. Thank you. We need everyone to keep your eyes out for those kind of things. Please let us know if you know of something helpful or a resource." He switched off the mic and motioned for the head table people to follow him out.

Once the officials had left, the group of civilians just sat for a moment. Jake and Eddie got up and went out first. Most of the others followed, but Cora just sat, thinking over what she had heard. She hadn't been aware of it, but one of the men from Denver had remained seated across from her. When she looked up, she saw the same confused expression on his face. "Hard to fathom isn't it?" she said quietly.

He looked around, unaware of her being there until she spoke. "Yeah," he said hoarsely. "I was just thinking that I wasn't even supposed to work that day, but another guy got sick who was assigned to be with the painting crew. Normally I was in charge of the crew that repaired the doors and furnishings in the main concourse. I was asked to go help the painters. I didn't care; it was just something that needed doing. I could have said no, but I didn't." He put out his hand to her, "I'm Grady Lucas," he said quietly.

"Cora Mason," she took his hand gently and held it for a moment.

He looked around, "Odd what a simple little choice can do," he sighed. "You said you were alone for awhile?"

"Yes, I was a clerk in a clinic. We had a file storage area in an old tornado shelter. I had hauled a bunch of really old client files down there when I passed out." Cora glanced over at the man. Her guess was that he was about forty, muscular, but not overly so. He had a three day stubble that made him look older, but other than that, he was pleasant looking.

"Was that in Denver?"

"No, I was in eastern Nebraska. A couple days later I was standing in the middle of Highway 30, feeling completely alone, wondering if I'd ever see another person again when off in the distance I see this old truck coming towards me. It turned out to be Mike Spaulding, his friend Jay Breeden and Jay's grandson, Jake. I was never so glad to see anyone in my life. The four of us set out to find this base." She sighed, "I wasn't sure it even existed. I thought it was just made up for the movies. I'm glad I was wrong."

"I knew it was here, but I never thought of coming out here. I was really glad to meet up with their patrol and to have been brought back here." He shrugged, "I know things are not too bad right now, but I can't help but wonder what it's going to be like this winter or next spring. It may get pretty desperate."

Cora shuddered. She didn't want to think of that right now. She cleared her throat, "Did you have family in Denver?"

He shook his head, "No, my family, mom, dad and brother, Byron, lived in Boulder. I had a girlfriend though, Helen, we'd been dating about six months. I went by where her house was and it made me sick to see nothing there; it was just the foundation. Did you have family?"

"My mom and sister were in Austin, Texas. The only thing I had in Nebraska really was my job," she cringed. "Not much that I left behind. I guess we're two lucky people, huh?"

"Time will tell how lucky we are," he said as he stood up. He nodded towards the group of people beginning to cue up for dinner. "My group is in an hour, how about yours?"

"I think we're the last of the day, so probably be two hours."

"Think anyone would mind if I joined your group? Your company would be a lot better than those guys I came in with." He smiled at her, "At least you smell better than they do."

Cora chuckled. "I'm sure no one will mind, we're a pretty small group and a new person in the crowd makes the conversation more interesting." She got up and walked out into the courtyard with him.

Cora and Grady said goodbye and headed back to their own quarters. Cora was surprised to see another bag of cat food waiting by her door. She got a chill when she saw the note "last one" on it.

When she took the bag into her room she sat down on the floor and let the kittens climb all over her. Eve sat back and watched her growing babies with a disinterested look on her face with half-closed eyes. "Oh Eve, how am I going to feed you and your babies this winter? I hope that I can find more litter and food yet this summer or fall. Winter's in Colorado can be pretty brutal just like they were sometimes in Nebraska." Eve walked over and rubbed her chin against Cora's cheek. Cora and her little family sat on the cold concrete until the kittens had enough playtime and headed back to their spot on Cora's only rug for a nap. Eve opted to jump up on the bed and have a little time to herself.

Cora sighed and joined Eve for a little afternoon rest.

CHAPTER SEVEN

A couple of weeks passed. Cora found herself working as a clerk in the main office, their shelter had been tasked to establish a list of those who had been found around them and all the way to the Seattle area. Short wave and ham radio kinds of communications had been established between the several underground facilities like theirs around the country and the world. Cora thought it felt like taking roll call in school, but could see it was necessary. In a way, it was good to know that so many had survived. Already their list alone was up to eight hundred.

Grady and two other men had volunteered to go into Denver with a group to explore and see if there were any supplies to be had. He asked Cora if she would like to go along on one of the trips into town and she eagerly agreed to. It had been awhile since she had been out off of the base.

The young airman driving the truck dropped the four of them off at the edge of town and told them to be back to that spot in four hours when they would be going back to base. As they watched the Humvee head off, they started to walk, two men heading one direction, and Grady and Cora another. "We've been crisscrossing the town, taking a different section each time. We haven't found much," Grady said as they walked over and looked into an empty basement.

It was a fair day, the sun was out and there was a light breeze. It wasn't overly warm though, a sure sign autumn was coming quickly and the winter everyone was dreading would follow in a hurry. Cora took one side of the street and Grady the other.

They came to a corner and Grady called Cora over to where he was. Cora came across the street and looked into the basement that was in front of them. There in the corner was a wooden door. "How are we going to get down there?" Cora asked.

Grady looked around, then at her. "I think I can lower you down and then get you back up. Think you can get that door open?"

She looked down, "I don't see a lock on it. Yes, I can probably get it open."

Grady took her wrists, "Hold on to my wrists."

He lowered her slowly into the empty basement. She was about two feet from the floor when she let go and dropped the rest of the way, nearly falling over, just barely managing to stay upright.

With a sign of relief, she walked over to the door and was pleased that it opened easily.

She had a small pocket flashlight with her that she took out to look around. The room she found was a roughly hewn root cellar, it looked to be used mostly for wine storage. Several wine racks were against one wall and shelves of canned goods and crates of various household items. There seemed to be many useful things. Cora walked out and looked up at Grady, "Can you get down here?" There are some shelves that I think that we can use as a ladder to get the things up to the ground level."

"Why don't I get you up out of there so one of us is out of the basement at least if we need help?"

Cora went into the cellar and brought out a crate to stand on so she could reach Grady. In just a minute, she was back at street level and Grady was in the cellar. "Wow," he said as he brought out a bottle of wine. "We hit the jackpot. Wonder if they'll let us drink this at the base or we should leave it here and come back for it?" He smiled mischievously.

Cora laughed and shook her head, "That will make the food taste better. How are we going to get everything out?"

"There's a truck waiting on the edge of town waiting to see if we find anything. We have a ladder on that. What we need to do is put up a flag so the truck crew can find us. " He had a backpack with him and he got out a small walkie talkie to call the truck. After that he climbed up on the crate and, with Cora's help, got to the street level again.

Grady sat down on the curb to wait for the pickup. "Let's make sure this is worth hauling back to the base," he laughed as he pulled a bottle of wine out of his backpack. He quickly pried the cap off and offered the first sip to Cora.

Cora shook her head, "Not much of a wine person." She said waving him off. She started walking down the street. "I'll keep looking on my side."

Grady sat and sipped from the bottle a couple of times before putting the cork back on. The truck came within five minutes and he explained what they'd found. Three guys hopped out of the truck and began to retrieve the newly found supplies. Grady had put the opened bottle into his back pack before setting off to explore again.

Cora was almost a block ahead of him by the time he started walking up the street. She heard him whistle to get her attention. She looked back and he waved, but she kept on going. The neighborhood they were walking into had very few basements or anything else. Then she came to an intersection where the street they were walking on became four lane and crossed another four lane street. It was hard to imagine what had been there before without signs, businesses or signals. Cora waited for Grady to catch up with her. "Do you know this area? Any idea where we are?"

Grady shook his head, "No, but from the look of those foundations over there, I think that was a little strip mall. We're probably in a little commercial area. Might be one of the suburbs?" He started walking over towards what would have been a parking lot, from the lines on the asphalt. Cora walked along, "Amazing to hear nothing but the wind isn't it? Amazing and eerie too. Who would have ever thought we'd miss the noise of a city?"

"Yeah, and all the people," Grady answered. "I always liked to stop at a quick mart on the way home from work for a hot dog and a coke, sort of a treat before dinner for working hard. I miss those greasy, but tasty things."

Cora shrugged, "I miss ordering a pizza and picking it up on my way home at night."

There were some basements in the little mall buildings but they were all empty. "Looks like quite aways to the next residential area. Probably have better luck in those than the business area. Think we should start back to our pickup site?" Grady asked.

Cora looked around. "How about we go another block and then we can start back?"

Grady nodded, walking on. They had looked in several building basements before they came to one it what looked to have been a narrow business building. It had cement stairs at the back into the lower level and then it had a sub-level that looked to have had an escalator, which also was still there. Cora and Grady went around to the steps and went down.

The sub-basement was dark. Grady had a bigger flashlight in his backpack than Cora did, but even that didn't help much. As they peered around in the large dark room, they were surprised and pleased to see all kinds of furniture and bedding supplies. At the rear of the space, they found a break room with two fully stocked vending machines and a fridge full of soda with a sign saying "Soft Drinks $1.25 each." Cora reached in and got a coke, "I don't have the money but I don't see anyone to object."

Grady laughed and motioned for her to follow him out. "We're going to need a bigger truck for all that stuff."

"I think we should probably just take the food out of the machines and take the bedding. I'm not sure where the furniture would go, except in the new shelters they're developing." Cora said thinking out loud about how to use the things they'd found.

"That's an idea. We can suggest that to the Colonel." Grady called for the truck. Cora started walking back toward their pickup area, this time a block over from the last street they had come down.

After Grady had told the pickup crew what they'd found, he hurried to catch up with her. They slowly made their way through the barren neighborhood. They found nothing else on this leg of their search. By the time they reached the rendezvous spot, they were both tired and their feet hurt. They sat on the curb and waited.

The other two men, who had been dropped off at the same time, showed up within a few minutes and sat down with them. One of them leaned over, "I'm Joe Pena and this is Bill Wilcox, we're from Boulder. We were working on some underground utilities when this all happened. Real mess huh?"

Bill Wilcox looked at Grady, "You guys find anything?"

Grady introduced himself and Cora, "I'm Grady and this is my friend, Cora. Yeah, we did. We found a stash of wine and a few supplies." He unzipped his back pack and produced the bottle of wine. He handed it to Bill and smiled, "We had to make sure it was not spoiled. You want to test it too?"

With a chuckle, Bill took the bottle and took a good swig, then passed it to Joe. Joe tried just a sip, "It's okay, but I'd prefer a beer any day." He put the cap back on the bottle and sat it down on the curb. "What else did you and Cora find?"

Cora spoke up, "We found what must have been a furniture store. There were some used and some new things in a sub-basement. Might come in handy to set up a shelter here in Denver rather than at the base, if that gets too crowded. Sort of like what they've had to do in D.C."

"Hate to think of not being on the base, but more people are coming in everyday. I heard they found a whole group of people who were in a hotel that was built into the mountainside up north of here. Think I heard there was about thirty coming in that group." Bill sighed, "I think they said it was pretty high up, so wouldn't be able to be there when winter comes even though it was a skiing area usually. Just no way to get help to them if they needed it. Probably good it wasn't in winter when the place would be packed."

The Humvee arrived and they all got back into it for the ride back to base. Everyone was quiet as they travelled. The rig was too noisy to talk over anyway. When they pulled into their parking space they could see the truck with the supplies they'd found was already unloading the items. Cora felt good that they'd been able to contribute something. She saw the bedding and remembered how cold it was getting towards the late afternoon before they were picked up. Those blankets would be welcome. Dinner was more than an hour away, so she went to check on Eve and the kittens.

When she opened the door, she was surprised to see the kittens eating some of the dry food she had put down for Eve. Sitting down on the floor with a sigh, it was clear to her that now she would have to find food for four cats because Eve would soon be weaning the babies. Then another thought came, I wonder if there is a vet who could spay Eve and Spots as well as neuter BB and Gray? She would have to make some inquiries.

It was nearly a month later when the Colonel called another meeting this time in the base auditorium for all civilians. The place was packed. Cora had been working on the lists of incoming people and of other discovered shelters in Washington. She knew that over a thousand people had been found. Several other oasis had also been found. From the descriptions, they had been much like the one she and her traveling companions had found on their way out of Nebraska.

The base commander stepped up to the podium and the room went silent. "As you can tell by the number of people in this room we have reached capacity here on the base. We have set up a new shelter area at the Denver Airport facility. Our search teams have found quite a few resources to help us establish a fairly comfortable shelter for at least sixty people to begin with. Now, we have not noted any sun spot activity or solar storms out of the norm lately. And we are not sure if that had anything to do with what happened or if it was just a coincidence; either way the shelter there is not as far underground as we are here. Having said that though, many survived there when this all started. We would like at least fifty of you to voluntarily move to that shelter. We are sure you will be safe and as comfortable as you are here. We will continue to explore all areas for resources and share what we find."

He looked around the room. "I know that this will be a difficult decision for some of you. Those willing to go should let me know as soon as possible. We have gotten word that a new group will be coming soon from Idaho. Seems a full shift of miners were in a coal mine when things went crazy. They had a railcar in the mine so they are using the railroad tracks to get here, picking up a person here and there as they come." The Colonel shook his head, "Just let the Airman at the desk in my office know if you're willing to relocate." He nodded and walked away.

Cora sat for a few minutes thinking about what had been asked. She walked out into the courtyard and looked up at the rock above her head for the first time in a long while. It would be nice to not feel like it was bearing down on her, but on the other hand, she had felt safe in this place. And then there was Eve and the kittens. Would moving to the shelter in town be good for them? It was a hard choice.

She was jolted out of thoughts by a familiar voice behind her, "So what do you think? Want to go to the Airport? Those tunnels are not bad at all, sixty people will have plenty of room. It is pretty much an even temperature down there year round if the doors are closed. I heard that's where all that furniture we found wound up. There were several offices and meeting rooms, as well as storage areas for all kinds of stuff off those tunnels so we might find some good stuff to use down there if they haven't been searched yet."

Cora shrugged, "Oh Grady, what about Eve, my cat, and the kittens?"

He laughed, "There were always a lot of mice and gophers around the airport. She would have a field day hunting in the tunnels and in grassy areas around the airport, and so would the kittens. You said they are really getting too big to be confined in your room.

She had to admit she had thought that for some time and had been concerned about their future. "Maybe it wouldn't be so bad. Think we could go look at the place before we decide?"

"Sure, on tomorrow's run you can come with me and we'll go take a look." He smiled at her and gave her a quick kiss on the cheek. "See you at dinner." He headed for his quarters.

It sounded like he was going to be one of those going to the new place. Cora began to think that she would be too. She was looking forward to seeing what that would look like. It was a little scary to leave this shelter that had become home, but never quite comfortable. It could be the rock over head or it could be the formal military life they'd become a part of, but it was a bit lonely at times.

Other than meal times, she never saw Jake or the others she had met in Nebraska anymore. The people who worked in the office she worked in were military personnel and seemed indifferent to her. Grady was friendly, but he mostly hung out with the guys he had worked with before. She went with him several times on his searches and that was nice. They seemed to be good pals, but nothing more. There was nothing much for her in this cave of a place. Real sunlight more than twice a month would be a pleasant thing, she decided.

It was cloudy the next morning when they set off into Denver with a Humvee full of people wanting to see the new shelter. Grady had volunteered to be their tour guide. A couple of people were going to check on their offices, not that they had a business or were employed anymore. The place seemed unrecognizable without the planes, the hangers, the terminal, nothing denoting that it had been an airport. It just was a huge sea of concrete with a hole now and then. Down one of those holes, in the center of it all, was an escalator (now staircase) leading down to the tunnels.

There was a broad open space that had been the basement landing. Off to each side were still intact four large sets of double glass doors. Grady held a door open on one side of the courtyard looking place. "The other side was closed for renovation," he explained. Everyone followed him. Inside was a long wide hall, illuminated only by the light from the glass doors they had just come through. Grady walked a few feet ahead of the group and stepped into a utility closet and flipped on a row of switches. Immediately the hum of some emergency generators allowed lights to come on throughout the hallway. There was a collective happy murmuring from the group.

Cora could see that the furniture they had found had indeed been brought into this space. Couches and recliners as well as book shelves lined the hall. As they opened doors to offices they saw beds had been brought in and set up. Some rooms had queen sized beds, a few had king sized, but most had either a twin bed or bunk beds. The nice thing was that the offices had been carpeted. That was better than the cold concrete of the hallway or their rooms back at the base.

A meeting room that was twice the size of the base dining room was set up with a kitchen at one end and a variety of table and chair sets at the other. Some of the furniture was very fancy, Cora observed, seeing them in the light for the first time. There were communal bathrooms in the hallway, but there were several stalls in each. It seemed adequate for sixty people.

Grady led the group to the huge storage areas. Cora was surprised to see all kinds of things, golf carts type electric vehicles that were used to travel around the airport, all kinds of unclaimed luggage, boxes that had never been opened. There were discarded things from the shops that had been in the concourse. Cora saw some seriously usable things to sort out. Grady showed them the maintenance area next. The good news! There were two bathrooms with multiple showers. They had been installed for the workers, but now would be for everyone, as long as the generators lasted. Two large doors as well as a couple garage type doors lead out to the tarmac.

Once back in the main hallway, Cora walked out of the doors back into the light coming down from the opening above her. It was easy to imagine how nice it would be on a sunny day to come out and sit on the steps and feel the sunlight on her shoulders. They hadn't explored the other side of the tunnels yet, but she already knew she would be making the move. Just a little fresh air was all she needed to feel so much better.

She went back into the hallway and took one more look at the rooms. She chose one that had a twin bed; the room was about three times the size of her room at the base. Eve and the kittens would love having more space she thought. Almost everyone taking the tour decided to move to the new shelter. They found some paper and marking pens to put their names on rooms that they wanted. Grady and two others who had worked at the airport took a room with two sets of bunk beds.

Within three days, there were forty nine people in the new shelter and four cats. Since the airport was on the outskirts of the east side of Denver, there were still a lot of neighborhoods that had not been explored for resources, so daily crews from their ranks would go out in golf carts searching.

Cora and two others started going through the boxes and things in the storage area. Soon the hallway bookcases had lots of books and magazines, as well as a few souvenirs that hadn't sold in the gift shop. One great find were several boxes of clothing like sweaters and jackets, things that had small flaws or had been prior year fashions.

In the freight damaged and unclaimed luggage area they found more clothing too. The clothing was laid out on a couple of long tables so people could come and find what they could use. The real find were several boxes that had food stuff like fancy coffees, teas and cereals. Seasonal items like Valentine's candy, Christmas fruitcakes, chocolate Easter bunnies, and a wide assortment of snack foods for the vending machines that had been above in the concourse. Reminders all, how things had changed. The food was taken to the communal kitchen.

Cora couldn't believe it when one of the larger boxes that had been really battered contained gourmet cat food! She immediately claimed that for her little family. She sorted through the dented cans and found enough that were probably safe to last Eve and the babies for several months, probably the entire winter. Grady had told her there were bags of sand they used for icy walkways that he could get her for the cat's litter box, so, as long as there was water, she could take care of her cats. It was a relief for sure, the only worry was how they were all going to manage for themselves through the winter.

There was a sense of urgency as the group went out on their foraging trips. Not as much had been shared by the base nor found in town as hoped, by the time the first snow flake floated down into the outer courtyard at the bottom of the stairs. Winter was sending a calling card and it was time to be ready or else.

CHAPTER EIGHT

It had definitely turned colder. Two weeks after moving into the airport shelter, that the group now called "New Denver," the first real snow storm blew threw. It was short lived and the three or four inches of snow it brought was gone in a day; it was a clear sign of what they faced. A group meeting was held to plan an all out foraging effort. A few areas of the town and suburbs had been cleared, but the major part of the area hadn't been explored yet. A map of the entire area was laid out and anyone who could drive one of the dozen golf carts was given a sector.

Cora hadn't driven one of the little rigs, but it didn't take her long to figure it out. Jay and his grandson had moved into the shelter and so did Mike. When it came time to go out on patrol, Jake offered to go with Cora. She welcomed having the teenager with her. His friend Eddie had stayed with his parents at the base so he was by himself again.

As the pair reached the area they were to search, they got out and each walked one side of the street. They were in a neighborhood where the houses must have been large and spaced apart more than some of the other areas. Most of the homes here had basements. There wasn't anything to see in the first several houses they walked by though. It was starting to get discouraging.

It was about an hour later when they came to a house nestled back against a rock outcropping that they found the first sign of hope that day. In the basement was a large wooden door that was at the edge of the basement and obviously led to something beyond. In looking around, they saw that there were steps going down that probably had been a fire escape from the basement. Cora and Jake went down and up to the heavy looking door. It took both of them to get it open.

Cora gasp when bright lights momentarily blinded her and the smell of bacon came wafting out of the interior. She heard a shriek. Standing there open mouthed was a teenage girl, standing at a small grill, cooking.

Cora couldn't believe her eyes. She and Jake walked into a brightly lit, huge room completely stocked with food, clothing, books, a bed, couch and somewhere a generator powering everything. From another room a woman came out, "Who are you?" she demanded.

"I'm Cora Mason and this is Jake Breeden, we're from the shelter at the airport."

"Well, this is private property and you need to leave," the woman said stomping her foot. "What do you think you're doing barging in like this?"

Cora shook her head. "Have you any idea what has happened?"

The woman looked at her daughter, "No, we were in here putting bedding on this bed when the house disappeared." She rubbed her arms nervously. "Do you know what happened?"

"No one knows for sure. All we know is that there are people who were underground or under rock cover who are still here, like you. The base out of Colorado Springs is where most of the people in this area came to, but it got too crowded so other shelters like the one at the airport were set up. We've been going through the town looking for resources to help us get through the winter." Cora looked around. "What is this place?"

The woman's eyes narrowed, "This is ours. We knew something would happen so we've been preparing. It's too bad the rest of the world didn't heed all the warnings." She stood by the door. "Now leave and don't come back, you're not welcome. We'll be fine."

Jake looked at the girl who looked a little older than him, "We're at the airport, in the tunnels if you want to come join us."

The girl turned away, "We don't need your help. We'll be fine." She went back to stirring whatever was in the pan on the stove.

Cora took Jake by the arm and led him out of the room, back into the basement. They could hear the door being bolted behind them. "Did you see the guns mounted on the wall? Those people were prepared to fight to keep what was theirs."

Jake nodded, "I used to watch a TV show about doomsday preppers. They thought they'd need to be prepared for the end of the world. This isn't quite the end of the world though. How could they get ready for something like this? How could anyone be in the right place to survive this?"

Cora sighed. He was right. Why did she and the others survive? Was it divine providence or was it just dumb luck. And were they the lucky ones? The future would answer that serious question. "We need to warn everyone to be careful as they go on, there may be other people out here with guns."

The rest of the morning passed with nothing found. They were just about to head back to the shelter when they found themselves overlooking a lake. From the foundations it looked like there had been apartments or condos on the far side. They made their way around the small body of water to see if there was anything there. When they peered into the basement area they were surprised see several storage areas. They had been under concrete and roof with dirt over that. There were lots of things in the large cubicles.

"Oh boy," Jake shouted as he saw something special, "Look at the mountain bike!" He looked at Cora, "Can I take that?"

She sighed, they had been taking everything they'd found but after seeing the last people it did feel like they were stealing. But this was survival and something to get around on that didn't need fuel was a plus, "Sure, and I see several others stored down here we'll come back for."

They pried the lock off the gate and then took the bike and put it on the back of the golf cart. The rack for golf clubs became a sort of wonky bike rack. They would send the truck back for the rest of the things to be put in their storage area. They had a red flag that they put up on top of the foundation to show the location. With that, they headed back to the shelter. Even though the sun was shining, there was a bitter wind blowing that cut through their lightweight clothing. Both of them were chilled by the time they reached the airport again.

That evening when the group gathered for dinner, Cora told everyone of their experience with the woman and her daughter they'd found in a bunker. It was decided to just let them be and welcome them if they decided to come join "New Denver." It was a surprise to Cora that there were people who had guns within their ranks. One person had been a security officer and one had a gun permit.

After their meal, everyone gathered in small groups in the hallway for a while to visit and share experiences. It was warmer in the hallway than in the rooms. It had been decided at dinner how to best use their limited resources. The lights would be on from 8:00 a.m. to noon and 5:00 p.m to 10:00 p.m. The heat would only be on from 5:00 p.m. to 8:00 a.m., and that would only be as long as the generators were fueled up. Luckily they had quite a big reserve of fuel in underground tanks.

By the time the next snow storm rolled in almost half the city had been searched. Patrols were put on hold temporarily until it was safe to go on. Cora spent a lot of time reading and playing with Eve in her room. The kittens were now nearly grown. Cora had started letting them out into the hallway. Jake had talked his grandfather into letting him claim Gray as his. Another woman, Brenda Gonzales, who had a room at the far end of the hallway wanted Spots. Soon it was only Eve and BB with Cora. It made her little room seem strangely empty with the two cats gone.

It had been at least three weeks since Cora and Jake had last gone out searching. The snow had melted away to the point that the streets were clear when they set out again. There were still snow drifts up against the foundations and in the basement of most of the house sites they looked at.

They decided to go into one of the more downtown areas. There were lots of deep basements to look into. In an alcove under a set of stairs, they found a small room full of vending machines. They had a crowbar with them so they pried off the fronts of the machines and loaded the items into bags and boxes they had brought with them. It was a good find, but it was just snacks, no real nutritional things. Still in a crisis, anything to eat would be welcome.

The best find of the day must have been under a mini mart or small grocery store. They found four cases of canned soups, two cases of Spam, two cases of tuna, three boxes of assorted canned goods, several large jugs of laundry soap, two crates of toilet paper, various cleaning supplies, plus bags of dog and cat food in a side storage cupboard that had ran under the sidewalk above. They put a flag at ground level and called for the truck.

Everyone had a good day. One of the other foraging groups found a root cellar at one house and hit the jackpot with nearly a hundred pounds of potatoes, carrots, onions and garlic. They even found some apples that hadn't gone soft yet, not that would have stopped anyone from eating them, even if they were squishy. Fresh fruit was almost a distant memory by this time.

That night, everyone feasted on a hearty vegetable stew flavored by a dozen cans of chicken noodle soup. Cora could tell that the hot meal had lifted everyone's spirits. For a time, at least, people seemed to relax and laugh a little.

Here and there she could hear people talking and sharing stories as they ate. She had to admit it felt good to have a full bowl of food for a change. They had been trying to ration their supplies to the point that she always felt a little hungry. Looking across the table she was sharing with Jay and Jake and Brenda, Cora noted that they were enjoying their meal as much as she was.

Mike was sitting at another table with five older men, swapping stories and laughing. Grady was at the far end of the room with another group of people. Cora sighed, their relationship had cooled. They were still friends as were all the people in the shelter, but nothing more. That was all right with Cora though. It didn't seem the time for a romance. The world was just too uncertain.

That night Cora slept the best she had for weeks. She had enough to eat, she had warm blankets and both cats cuddled up with her. It was so wonderful that she overslept and didn't wake up until Jake knocked at her door. When she opened the door he rushed in with news, "The trucks from the base are here to check on us and bring supplies." He hurried out the door again.

Cora found her clothes, boots and jacket and went out to see what was going on. She was surprised to see Lieutenant Elroy in the hallway talking to Grady, who had become sort of the leader of the shelter. The Lieutenant smiled when he saw her. She waved slightly as she approached. "What's going on?"

Grady turned to her, "They are just bringing us a final load of supplies before the snow hits. They think this will be a major snow storm coming. It may be a long while before they can get back here." Grady looked grim, "We'll be on our own."

The Lieutenant shrugged, "If anyone wants to come back to the base we can take them."

The whole group of New Denver residents were now in the hallway listening to what was being said, passing it back to those who couldn't hear. The Lieutenant continued. "We've developed three more shelter areas to the south of the base. There are nearly three hundred people now housed in those three shelters. Do you think you could take any more here?"

Grady looked around, "We haven't opened the rest of the tunnel system because that part was undergoing renovations. Its still pretty torn up. I doubt if it would be suitable, but we can begin working on it. There are some large basement areas in the downtown section of town that if we could cover over, might make suitable shelters. Maybe in the spring we could work on making those habitable, but for right now we're almost at capacity here. I think we could probably take at the most, possibly up to twenty more, but we'd have to double up." He looked around at the people. He could tell they were all questioning whether they could share with that many.

The Lieutenant nodded, "There is another matter. We would like to station at least five military men with you. We have found several people that have reported some militia people that are armed and raiding shelters for supplies. We'd advise that when you go looking for resources you have someone who is armed with you, in case you run into these supply raiders."

Grady looked at Cora, "Thank you Lieutenant, I think we've already run into some of those folks with that mind set." Cora nodded. "We have two rooms that are currently available if your men wouldn't mind bunks."

"We're used to bunks. I'll be deployed here with the detail of men." He stepped aside as four soldiers came in carrying boxes of supplies. "Do you have a freezer? This is all frozen proteins. It is all we could send at this time so we need to stretch it as much as possible."

"We do have a freezer, it's in the maintenance area in the back. It's a walk-in, the airlines kept their food for the flights in it." One of the men who had been a worker at the airport led the way for the supplies. Grady motioned for everyone to go to the dining hall.

It only took a few minutes to find seats and wait. Grady and the Lieutenant stood in front of the gathering. "I think most of us remember Lieutenant Elroy from the base. He and a few other soldiers will be joining us here at the New Denver as protection. There have been reports of thugs raiding shelters for supplies. As winter comes on harder, the situation is apt to become more desperate, so we might be at risk. I, for one, welcome having the added security." A small smattering of applause could be heard for a minute.

"We've brought some extra supplies and we have been allowed to bring one additional truck to help with your foraging. We also found some coal resources and have brought a supply of that for heating as well as two coal burning stoves. We'll have to figure out how to set them up, but they are usable. We also found some wood stoves that we can use if we can find fuel."

Jay stood up, "We used to roll newspapers up and soak them in water, when they dried you could burn them like logs."

Grady nodded, "We have a lot of materials we could use to burn around here." He looked around for a moment, "We've also been told that there are three other shelters now, south of here. There was an invitation made for anyone who would rather be back at the base to go there." He looked around, "Anyone want to go back?" No one moved or said anything. "Guess that's your answer," he said to Lt. Elroy.

"Okay then, I will be back tomorrow with the truck and the men who are going to be stationed with you. We may have some other civilians coming within a few days too. In the meantime, I have a treat for you to enjoy. He motioned to a young man standing by the door. With a motion to someone outside, things started to happen. The first was a large double layered cake that was brought in, it was decorated in a soft looking white icing. Then a soldier carrying four, one gallon bins of ice cream came in and put them down on the long serving table. "We were down to the last of the ice cream and there looked like there wouldn't be any for a long time so we decided to bake a cake for each shelter and divi up the ice cream with everyone. So this may be the last party until spring so enjoy this!"

Several of the ones in their group who had taken on the responsibility of doing the majority of the food prep got up and put the table service out as well as bowls for everyone. It was bitter-sweet for Cora. The cake was wonderful and the chocolate ice cream was beyond what she remembered it tasting like. Still, thinking about how long it might be before anyone had time and resources to have a relaxed, safe moment with cake and ice cream again was sad. It was a difficult time and a different world that she was now stranded in.

The group only used two of the gallons of ice cream so they, as a group, decided to save the others for Thanksgiving or Christmas. It might be the only present they would have.

Everyone sat around discussing what they would have to do to find make room for twenty more people in New Denver. Brenda looked across the table, "Would you like to move in with me? Or I could move in with you."

Cora sighed, Grady had said they might have to double up, but she hadn't thought about what that would mean. She looked at Brenda. She looked to be just a few years older than Cora and seemed pleasant enough. One thing in her favor was she had Spots, the cat that Cora had originally thought about keeping herself, besides Eve. "That might work. Let's compare our two rooms and see which would be a better fit." Cora got up and followed Brenda to the end of the hall where her room was.

Cora could see one advantage to Brenda's place immediately. It was closer to a set of bathrooms. It was also closer to the front entrance. Cora walked into the room and looked around. "I think my place is bigger. Once we move my bed in here we wouldn't have much space to put a dresser or all the stuff for the cats. Come to my room and see. It has a little alcove that had a desk in it. I've moved the desk against the wall and use the area for the cat box and their supplies." Cora motioned for Brenda to follow. Cora noticed as they stepped into the hall there was a slight breeze coming in under the doors that was cooling that part of the hall. "I think that my room is apt to be warmer."

In just a few minutes, they were standing in Cora's room. They could see it was twice the size of Brenda's space. "Oh yes," Brenda said, "I can tell this is much bigger. I think I could put my bed over against the wall and we could have a little sitting area right here." She looked to Cora for acceptance of the idea.

Cora nodded. She wasn't fond of the idea of sharing her room, but if others were coming they'd all have to make some sacrifices. She reminded herself that the goal was to survive this incredible situation. "Sure, sounds good. I think the guys will be happy to help move you to this room."

Brenda shrugged, "Okay, I'll talk to Grady and get it done." She smiled and left the room.

Eve came out from under the bed and begged to be petted. BB had also sought the safety of the bed. He came out and jumped up on the bed, ignoring his mother and Cora entirely. "Well, my little friends, we are going to have a family reunion of sorts. Spots will be moving in with us and her new mom, Brenda." Cora looked at the room as she petted Eve. She got up and shoved her bed against the wall opposite of where Brenda was planning to put hers. It allowed at least eight feet between the beds.

Cora remembered seeing two tall thin bookcases in the storage room. She went to look at them again. Several men were working on projects in the maintenance room so she asked them to move the bookcases to her room. They didn't hesitate to help out. Once the furniture was in her room, she placed them in the center of the space between where her's and Brenda's beds would be. She faced one towards her and one towards Brenda's side of the room, allowing them each to have some storage area as well as a little privacy.

When Grady and two others brought Brenda's bed and the suitcases full of her personal things, she seemed pleased to see what Cora had done. Cora had also found a padded bench that she had brought from storage that she sat along the wall just inside the door. With the addition of a couple of TV trays, it almost seemed homey.

Even the cats seemed pleased with the arrangement. Spots, who was now called Sophie, claimed Brenda's bed to stretch out on and Eve, with BB, curled up on Cora's bed.

Out in the hall there was a flurry of activity. Some of the extra furniture that had been stored in the unfinished area of the tunnel was brought over to furnish the rooms for the new people and the military men that were being assigned to them. Several people besides Brenda and Cora had agreed to share quarters. They found enough room and beds for about twelve more people, plus the five military personnel, to begin with. Everyone agreed to help, repairing the renovation area into a livable space. If they could work on that through the winter, perhaps they would have enough room for up to forty or so more.

Cora listened to the people making plans for a place to house more survivors. She couldn't help but wonder how the group they had now would make it through this first winter, let alone all the winters to come if they kept doubling their numbers. It seemed a daunting task as it was. Maybe Jay's suggestion of going where it was warmer, perhaps by the ocean, wasn't such a bad idea.

It was night time, just before lights out, but Cora wanted one last breath of fresh air. She walked out into the courtyard. It wasn't snowing. Looking up, she could see a million stars. Without the city lighting up the sky, the velvety blackness of space seemed to reflect all the beauty of the points of light. It was breathtaking, but the night air was so bitingly cold that it became hard to breathe. Pulling her jacket around her to take it all in as long as possible, it became too much and she had to retreat to the safety of the warmth inside.

74

It wasn't terribly warm in the hallway, but at least not freezing like it had been outside. Most people had already returned to their rooms in anticipation of the lights being turned off. She just made it inside her door when the lights went down. She got into her pajamas by the light of her little penlight. Eve and BB were waiting for her as the snuggled down for the night. Cora had forgotten that she now had another roommate until she heard Brenda softly snoring from across the room.

Cora had almost fallen asleep when she felt a soft thud at the foot of the bed. She turned on her little flashlight and found herself starring at a pair of familiar eyes. Sophie had come to curl up with her mother and brother. It was pretty hard to twist around so all the cats could lay together, but within minutes, everyone on the crowded twin bed was fast asleep.

CHAPTER NINE

Eldon and the other soldiers moved in the next day. They brought eight other people with them, including the Spears family. Cora had been just coming out of her room when the new group came. She walked down the hall towards the main doors. Grady was standing there giving them directions to their new quarters. Cora smiled, she could see that he enjoyed being the captain of their little lifeboat.

Cora saw Eldon. He smiled at her and made a gesture as if tipping his hat to her. It was hard not to laugh when she saw Grady frown that little interplay. Cora turned and walked back to the maintenance area. She and Brenda were going through another dozen or so unclaimed suitcases they'd found in a backroom. From the dust on the bags, they'd probably been there for a very long time.

Brenda had already brought three of the suitcases out and had them on the sorting table when Cora got there. "Hey girl, it is cold in here. Hope we find some wool underwear!"

Cora laughed, "That would be an itchy prospect." Cora walked over and scooted a suitcase in front of herself. "Shall we begin?"

Brenda nodded, "Okay." She made a face, "This always seems like such odd thing, going through someone else's stuff. I know we need clothing and supplies but still, kind of creeps me out."

"Yeah, I know what you mean. Me too," Cora opened the suitcase locks with a screwdriver, something she'd become pretty good at. "Well, let see what we have?" She began gently lifting things out. "Oh, this was a man's suitcase." She took a suit jacket and matching pants out and laid them on the table. "Oh Lord, look at these!" The suit was a red and green plaid.

Brenda chuckled, "That's straight out of the 1980s. I think I saw a guy wearing one of those when I was a kid. It was a Christmas suit. Can you imagine anyone wearing that? Wonder if any of our guys will claim it for themselves?"

Cora shook her head. It would be a stretch of the imagination to see any of the men in this decade wearing that. She continued respectfully lifting things out of the case; belts, socks, underwear, two or three dress shirts, pajamas, and a small photo album of a family from years ago. Cora gasped when she saw a small wrapped package, clearly a present that never got delivered. It was almost heartbreaking to think of the disappointment someone must have felt not getting that present. Cora couldn't open it. She just took the tag from the suitcase and put it with the gift back into the suitcase and put it behind the other already processed suitcases. No one would ever look in that case again.

Brenda hadn't found too many usable items in the first case she'd gone through. It was mostly snacks that were long past their use by date. There were some socks and undies, both adult and child's. Children's clothes and a few of women's tee shirts and shorts in a very small size were the bulk of the items that she found. There were also three pairs of children's sneakers, various sizes, and two pair of women's loafers in a very small size. "I don't think I've seen anyone in our group with feet as small as this," she said to Cora holding up a pair of the shoes. "We don't have any little children here either. It might be one of the other shelters have kids." Brenda moved the stuff to the table marked, "Not for New Denver".

Brenda went to the storage room and brought out three more suitcases. She handed a large one to Cora. "This one might be a good one, it's really heavy." The suitcase she put on her side of the sorting table was about half the size as the first one.

The case was heavier than any of the others Cora had opened. She really had to pry to get it open. A terrible stale smell assaulted her senses. "Oh my gosh!" She held up a bag, holding it at arms length, "What is in this?" Cautiously she peeked inside. "Yuck, someone had packed wet dirty laundry and it's all moldy." She took the bag across the room and tossed it into a garbage bin.

Coming back to the table she looked inside the case. Everything touching the bag was ruined, stained beyond cleaning. Cora took an armload of clothing to the bin without even looking at what it was. Halfway down into the bag things looked more salvageable. "Another man's case," she said, piling things out on the table. There were several pairs of hardly worn jeans, sweatshirts, socks, underwear, leather belts, and then it was without a doubt what had made the case so heavy. At the bottom of the bag were three boxes, two with new looking cowboy boots and one box of heavy silver belt buckles. In a side pocket was another heavy object. Wrapped in a towel, there was a hand-gun with a long barrel and a box of bullets. "Whoa,

77

this must have been before the age of airport scanners. Can't imagine this getting checked through." She laid the gun on the table. "I'll go get Grady. I think we ought to give it to the army guys."

Brenda nodded, "That's kind of scary actually. Wonder what that person was doing or planning to do with it?"

Cora shrugged and went to find Grady. She saw him still talking to Eldon when she walked back into the hallway. She hurried up to the two men. They saw her coming and stopped their discussion until she got there. "Hi," Cora said quietly, "Brenda and I were emptying the unclaimed luggage and we made a find that I'd like the two of you to see and advise us what to do." She motioned for them to follow her and they did.

Once back in the maintenance area, the men looked the gun over, "What do you think?" Grady asked Eldon.

Eldon picked up the gun and looked it over then gave a little low whistle, "This is nice. I think it's a very expensive Colt 45. This is nothing we use in the military, but my dad was kind of a gun buff and we went to a lot of gun shows. He always wanted one of these." He laid it back down on the table. "Another gun isn't a bad thing to have around here, but we'll have to find someone who really knows how to handle these and make sure it's stored safely. I'll keep it in our gun locker until we find the person that we can trust with it."

"I can do some asking around. We do have guys with gun permits and their own weapons. I've heard them talking guns with some others so it might be we'll find that person quickly." Grady nodded to Cora and smiled, "Good find."

The two men took the gun and left. Cora shrugged to Brenda, "Guess we get back to work. Let's do the remaining two suitcases and break for lunch okay?"

Brenda nodded and opened her next suitcase. It was pretty usual stuff, shirts, shorts, a couple long pairs of slacks, some kids' clothes, kids' flip flops and adult sandals, men and women's. "I guess these people were headed to Florida or something."

Cora was just finishing her case, "I found pretty much the same stuff. I wonder if a whole flights luggage was misplaced and presumed lost."

"Could have been," Brenda gathered up all the items from the two suitcases and put them on the "not for New Denver" pile. "One thing for certain, we're not going to need these shorts and flip-flops for a long while." She pointed to the window to the outside in the shop office. It was snowing, hard and fast.

Cora shivered. "I hope they have something hot for lunch today." They walked out into the hallway, which was better a better temperature than where they'd been working.

Lunch was at least warm. The cooks had made a potato soup flavored with the leftovers from a beef roast. There was enough meat to almost flavor the broth. They'd had enough potatoes and onions to make a pretty good bowlful for everyone, which was nice. At best, they went away feeling almost full.

Everyone had eaten, the ones assigned to washing dishes and cleaning the dining room for the day took over. It happened to be Cora's turn, although it was a task she didn't mind. The four of them assigned to the duty made short work of it. One of the men on the team was one of the firefighters who'd come into the base just after she had. She'd not seen him up close before but now that she did, it surprised her that he looked to be about her age, if not a little younger, very muscular and quite good looking. They were the dish washing team, him washing, her drying.

He saw her glancing over at him. Extending his hand he walked over to her, "Hi, you know I don't think we've been really introduced. I'm Boyd Harms," he looked around. "Want to get a cup of coffee and sit down for a few minutes when everything's done."

Cora nodded, "Sure. I'm Cora Mason," she went back to drying the dishes he was handing her. "So where are you from?"

He kept on working, "I'm from Boise. We'd been called in to help with a nasty, wind driven fire." He looked at her, "Where are you from?"

"Well, I was born and raised near Austin, Texas but I got a job offer in Nebraska and I'd lived there for the last eight years, just after I got out of secretarial school, when all this happened." She looked at him, "Got any idea what's happened?"

He shook his head, "Not a clue. We were just about to be overrun by the fire, when we found and went into that old mine shaft. Figured the smoke might kill us anyway. We all felt dizzy, passed out. Then when we woke up, the noise had stopped, we got up and went out and there was no fire, no nothing. Just a lavender sky and silence. For a minute, we thought we might be dead and this was what comes after."

Cora shook her head, "It was pretty bizarre, first of all faint, then wake up to all this." She looked at him for a moment, "Did you see anything odd before you went into the mine?"

With a shrug, he stared at a coffee cup he was cleaning for a minute. "I didn't see anything, but I did hear a real funny sound. The guys told me it was just the chaos of the fire, but I heard something that sounded a little like a someone blowing a whistle." He chuckled, "I guess I was just wishing it was someone was coming to rescue us."

"I heard a sound like that before I passed out," Cora said quietly. "I have no idea what it was."

Boyd nodded and looked into space for a moment, "I wonder what happened to all the others?"

Cora put her hand on his shoulder, "Did you have family?"

He nodded, "My parents lived in Boise, across town from where I lived. My brother, Andy, lived with me. He was going to Boise State College." He sighed, "We both had dogs, I had a lab and Andy had a border collie. Great dogs, great lives together." He didn't look at Cora, just went back to washing dishes.

"I had a mother and sister in Austin," Cora said as she dried the last dish. "Let's get that coffee and go out where it's a little warmer. They got that coal stove going at the end of the hall and it's made it pretty comfortable in the hallway. At least it's well above freezing. I guess we have to be grateful for that, the way it's snowing outside."

"Is it snowing? I hadn't looked out at all yet today. Been working in the other part of the tunnel making rooms out of what materials we could find. Really cold in that part of the building."

Coffee in hand, the two went to the hallway. Almost every couch or recliner was occupied except for a few near the front doors which was furtherest from the stove. But with their coats on, it wasn't too bad. From that perspective, they could also see the snow beginning to drift into the courtyard at the bottom of the stairs that lead up to ground level. It was pretty, but there was no doubt, winter had served notice that it was arriving.

There was a fairly large knitted throw on the back of the couch that Boyd and Cora sat down on. He scooted over next to her and put the robe over both their laps. They sat quietly, sipping their coffee, watching huge flakes drift down from the sky, occasionally turning into almost a white-out blizzard, then backing off into the lazy pinwheels that were so big you couldn't tell one from another. It was almost hypnotic. It was at least fifteen or twenty minutes before either one of them spoke.

"I've never gone skiing," Cora said absently. She realized what she'd said, a little embarrassed, "I guess all this snow got me thinking about things I've never done."

"I went a couple of times, but it wasn't for me. I'm not a big fan of running into trees with my face, which happened more than once." He smiled at her, "We may both need to learn how to ski if this keeps up."

Cora shuddered, winter in Colorado! She had never dreamed that's where she would find herself. Jay had been right, they needed to go south. "We'll see in the spring, perhaps we can head south, to Texas where it's warmer."

"Who knows what it's like anywhere right now."

Cora nodded, he was right. How would anyplace be with no resources, fuel or power? Humans had become so dependent on so many things. Even the preppers and survivalists would have a hard time with nothing to hunt, grow or cut down. How could anyone prepare for the world that they now had to contend with?

"I've finished my coffee so I'd better get back to work." Boyd said, handing the cover to her. "Been nice visiting with you. Maybe we can do it again soon."

Cora smiled at him, "Yeah, I liked talking to you. I'll look forward to seeing you around now that we're friends."

He gave her a thumbs up and walked away. She decided to sit for a few minutes more looking out the window. She drew the robe up around her and began to feeling drowsy. That was until Brenda came looking for her. "Ready to get back to work?"

81

Reluctantly Cora nodded. She threw the warm lap robe aside and walked with Brenda back to the sorting area. Once inside, she was jolted awake by the cold. "What say we just do four more cases and call it a day?"

"I'm all for that. It is so cold that this little jacket I have on feels like its made out of paper." She grabbed two cases for her and two for Cora.

Opening the first case was disappointing. It was empty except for some papers and magazines. Cora put those on the pile of papers that were being saved to burn in the wood stove that was being installed in the remodeled side of the building. Her other case was more rewarding. She found some toiletries and bars of good smelling soaps, probably being taken home as souvenirs. There were some small toys and a few child sized sweatshirts with a local attractions gift shop name on them. Again something that was never given, and probably a big disappointment to the grandma as well as the grandkids. The clothes in the case said older lady for sure. There were support stockings, large underwear, flannel nightgown and a terry robe. There were two sweaters, two pair of slacks and an empty hot water bottle. "I think these things might be good. I'll put them on the table for people to look through."

Brenda had found several things for that table too. She brought them over and put them down with the things Cora had added. "Okay let's get out of here. My hands are numb." She held up her hands, "Did find one good thing though. There were two pair of mittens in that last case. They might be for kids, but this pair fits me so I'm claiming them. There were three other pairs of gloves too. You want to try them?"

Cora looked at the gloves and then her hands, "I've got long skinny fingers." She tried one of the gloves, but they were way too small. "No luck. Let's go. Got to check on the cats."

"I fed them after we had lunch and cleaned the litter box."

Cora laughed, "I knew I liked you!" She patted Brenda on the back. "You're a great roommate."

"You too," Brenda said as they stepped back into the warmth of the hallway. "Oh, yes, this is so much better."

Grady saw them and walked over, "All done for the day?"

Brenda answered him before Cora could, "Yeah, it was really cold in there, but we were able to find some additional clothing and things. There's a whole box of silver belt buckles if you're into that kind of thing."

He laughed, "I might just be. Want to show me where the box is?"

Cora couldn't believe he was flirting with Brenda, but he was. And Brenda seemed to be going with it. Cora chuckled and walked on down the hall towards her room. She wasn't aware that Jake had come up behind her until he tapped her on the shoulder.

"Hi," he said once she turned to look at him. "Want to go out foraging as soon as the snow stops?"

"Oh Jake, those little golf carts can't go on the snow. We have to wait until it melts off the streets."

"Who said anything about golf carts?" He looked smug, "Over in the other side's storage area we found two snow mobiles and some cross country skis. We are set for this kind of weather."

Cora shook her head, "A little mouse of a golf cart is nothing like a roaring lion of a snow mobile. You can really get hurt if you don't know how to handle one of those. Have you ever driven one?"

"No," he admitted, "but Eric Ward, one of the guys from the fire crew was from Steamboat Springs, owned one. Said he'd teach me how to drive it."

"Okay, after you've learned how to drive the thing and I'm sure it's okay, we'll talk about it okay?"

Jake nodded, "It's a date." He turned and hurried down the hall.

Cora laughed as she watched him excitedly talk to someone at the other end of the hall.

"So you've got a date?" a voice behind her said quietly.

She was still chuckling when she turned and found Eldon standing behind her. "Oh, Lieutenant, I didn't hear you behind me."

He smiled, "I was in stealth mode. And my friends call me Eldon, remember?"

Cora nodded, "I remember. So how's life at New Denver for you? Do you have a good room?"

"Like all of them here I suspect. I share with the unit sergeant. He snores; he tells me I do too, so I guess that's okay. The other men I brought are in one large room with two sets of bunk beds. It's a little chilly in my room, but we're making do."

"I share with another woman too. And she snores sometimes, if she's really tired." Cora hadn't thought to ask Brenda if she snored.

"I was on my way to get a cup of coffee. Are you in the mood to share a cup with a friend?"

"Always," Cora said as she turned and headed for the dining room where a big pot of coffee was always brewing, or at least would be until they ran out of grounds. "I saw a case of tea bags. Some day when the coffee is gone I imagine we'll all have to learn to love that if we want hot drinks."

Eldon laughed, "I actually like tea. My mother was English. We had tea a lot when I was growing up. She missed it a lot. It was a sacrifice she made to marry my American father."

Cora looked at him, "Did you lose a lot of people?"

"Just my dad. He was in Michigan, where I grew up. It's hard not knowing what happened to the people in your life. I had an ex-wife too. We'd only been for married three years while we were in college. Big mistake on both our parts. Her career took her to New York and mine to the military. We parted not quite friends, but not enemies either. She was still in New York. She may have been lucky enough to be on the subway. I heard there were lots of survivors there" He looked at her. "What about you? Husband, family?"

"No husband, just sister and mother still in Texas. No subway where they lived," she said sighing. They'd reached the dining room. It only took a couple of minutes to get their coffee and go back out into the hallway to find a seat. They were fortunate this time to find a seat in the middle of the hallway where it was pretty warm, no need for a lap robe. They found two folding chairs and sat almost knee to knee.

They spent a pleasant half hour talking about their childhoods and career choices. Both tried to avoid talking about the future. That was a thing no one could imagine at this point. The immediate elephant in the room was just their survival of what was promising to be a pretty brutal and cold winter with limited resources. Outside, there was already upwards of eight inches of snow and the temperatures were plummeting. Without trees, the winds whipped over the naked mountains, without the heat of traffic and houses that kept the ground warm, everything was ready to freeze. No one in the shelter doubted that they were facing a fight for their very lives. All they could do was wait and see.

CHAPTER TEN

Luck was with the residents of New Denver. The storm that had come in cold and hard, passed within three days, though it stayed cold. It was bracing to go outdoors, but at least the sun was shining.

The work on the renovated part of the shelter continued well. By Thanksgiving, it was ready for at least twenty to thirty more people. They'd stretched the resources at hand though, to finish the work. Furniture became an issue, they had more bunks than single beds. There were mostly folding chairs and office chairs that would be for the folks in that section, although they could come into the other part of the building anytime they wanted to sit on a couch. Another wood burning stove had been jerry-rigged into the end of that part of the shelter's hall.

Since wood was scarce, Jay's rolled up paper idea was employed. It worked pretty well, but it was a big job, rolling the paper, soaking it, and drying it. They had to work at it everyday to just keep enough paper logs to heat the place during the night. With that they were able to keep most rooms above freezing.

The newer side of the building was only carpeted in the rooms. Mrs. Spears showed several of the others how to make rag rugs out of the unusable clothing they had found in the suitcases. There had been a small snack bar type coffee shop in that area so it served as a second kitchen.

Cora and Brenda had finished the job of sorting through the unclaimed luggage. When they were done, everyone had come in and picked out what they could use. The rest was left for whoever came next.

Cora had found herself two sweaters and a pair of tennis shoes, as well as a down jacket with a hood.

Brenda had found five skeins of red yarn and some knitting needles. She knew how to use those so she set herself the task of knitting up as many mittens as she could from the yarn. They would come in handy as winter wore on. As they sat just outside their tiny one-room apartment, Cora watched Brenda's fingers fly over the work and decided it wasn't something she could learn easily.

It wasn't anywhere near lights out, so Cora put on her coat and went outside to look up at the stars. She liked doing that if it wasn't snowing or blowing. When she walked to the middle of the courtyard, she stood looking up at the dazzling array of stars. It was cold but without the wind to drive the frigid air through her coat, she could bear it.

Upon hearing the door open, she turned to see Eldon coming out to join her. "You're a brave soul," he said as he approached her.

"Just love seeing the stars on a night like this. They look like you could almost touch them."

He chuckled as he stood beside her and looked up. "I used to like to drive up to this one lookout spot above the base in the mountains. You could camp up there but I usually just went up during the day, staying until it got dark just to see the stars."

"I never really looked at them until I was alone."

He put his arm around her shoulders, "Well, you're not alone anymore."

She smiled at him, "I know that now, but I have to tell you when I was standing there in the middle of the Highway all by myself and couldn't see a house, tree or car, it was so overwhelming. First time in my life I was so utterly alone. It was awful. I thought I could die right there. Then like an answer to prayer, off in the distance I saw that old pickup of Mike's, getting closer and closer." She shook her head, "I didn't know whether to be afraid or overjoyed. Would it be friendly people or wackos." Cora looked at him, "What was it like for you when you realized what had happened?"

Eldon sighed, "We knew about the sun spots, flares and the potential for solar winds. There was even some talk about it wiping us out, burning the earth to a crisp. Scientists have been watching the sun for years and there have been many flares in the past. You kind of get used to everyone predicting the end of the world. Who really takes that kind of talk seriously after awhile? The activity lately had been really worrisome to many of those folks. But when it did happen, it was faster and more violent than anyone expected. We really had no time to react, the alarm went off, we felt dizzy for a bit but those of us inside the base didn't pass out. By the time we realized anything was wrong, everything outside had changed. Whatever the event was, it was over."

"Or just begun," Cora said with a shrug.

"Yeah right. We were blind for awhile on the base, our satellite connections were gone, communications were down. The only way to learn anything was to take a patrol into town. When we got there, we were shocked to see what was left of a town of over a million people. No one, no debris, no sign of fire, nothing, it was just gone. I was horrified, wondering how all those people could have disappeared in an instant. There were no bodies so we couldn't even tell if they were dead or how they died, like in a normal disaster. Then I thought of my family. That hurt too much to contemplate so I just put it on the back burner until I knew for sure. My hope was to wake up and find it had all been a bad dream."

"Is there such a thing as a group dream?" Cora wondered aloud.

Eldon stamped his feet, "I don't know about that, but I do know that if we don't go in soon I'm going to have frostbite. I hear that's pretty painful."

Cora laughed, "Okay, I guess you're right. I can't feel my lips anymore."

Eldon sighed, "Oh, I know how to get feeling back in those." He turned her around to face him and kissed her gently, "Better?"

Cora gave him a playful shove. "Nice move, fella." She walked back into the hallway. The warmth of the heated space almost felt like it was burning her skin. "I guess we were out there a little too long."

Eldon was taking his coat off as he came in beside her. "Yeah, but it was worth it." He winked at her and walked on.

She couldn't help but smile. It was the highlight of her day to have someone flirt with her. In these strange times, it was a respite from worry to have something pleasant to think about. It couldn't mean anything, it wasn't a time to think beyond the moment, but it was a welcome break from the bleakness they faced. Cora chuckled to herself, "It was a nice move. With a little luck, he'll find a reason to do it again." She took her coat off and walked to her room before the lights went out.

Thanksgiving day came and the turkey the cooks were saving was brought out and a slightly scaled back traditional meal was prepared. There were now seventy people at the New Denver shelter, thirty coming from one of the other shelters. Everyone did get a nice slice of turkey, a serving of mashed potatoes and gravy and green beans. For dessert there was the ice cream saved. The coffee was gone so they all had tea and some of the leftover Valentine candies. It was a feast enough to feel almost full and content.

Brenda had volunteered herself and Cora to be on the cleanup crew that evening. Cora wasn't as happy about that as Brenda, but it was okay, she'd do her part. "You want to wash or dry?" she asked her roommate.

Brenda pointed to the sink area, "Neither. Two of the guys from the other side have already started washing and Jake has roped his friend, Eddie into drying. Eddie's dad is putting the dishes away. There weren't any leftovers so nothing to put away."

Cora knew with a group as large and hungry as this one there would probably never be leftovers again. She fell into step with Brenda as they washed the table tops and put the tables back into separate sets as they had been. It had been nice to have the room arranged with two long family style tables. Everyone got to sit and visit with new people or ones they hadn't really talked to before. It had been interesting to hear their stories of what they had been doing at the moment things changed. They finished up by sweeping the floor and then taking the two small bins of trash to the dumpsters.

When they were done Brenda headed to find Grady. They had found another couple that liked playing gin rummy. It had been their good fortune to find a few decks of cards in suitcases as well as some boxed games. Several little groups had developed to play various games. It was a great way to pass the time on very cold days that kept everyone inside.

Cora spent a good deal of time reading in her room and playing with the cats. Eve and Sophie had come into heat so Cora asked one of the other people to keep BB until their season passed. BB didn't like the arrangement and when someone was going out the front door he saw his opportunity, and he made a mad dash for freedom. The person tried to catch him, but he was fast and though they alerted everyone to watch for him no one saw him again. Cora stood outside two or three times a day calling for him, to no avail. After two weeks she decided he wasn't coming back until he wanted to, and she stopped looking.

It was just a day or two before Christmas when the cat returned and waited at the door until he was let in. Cora and Brenda were so glad to see him. Only slightly thinner, he appeared to be in good health. He was happy to sleep on Cora's bed again like nothing had ever happened. As she sat next to him petting him, tears were rolling down her face. "You scared me so bad. I love you BB and I just hated the idea of losing you. I tried not to imagine the worst but it was so hard. We've lost so much, I couldn't think of life without you." She kissed the cat on the top of his head. "You just went hunting didn't you? Found some mice and things I bet. A hunter like your mom, Eve."

Cora looked at the older cat laying on her pillow. BB's sister, Sophie, was using the litter box. "My sweet little family. Now if Gray was still with us we'd be complete." She sighed. Jake was taking good care of Gray and it had been a positive thing for him to have something to be responsible for. Jake was growing up fast.

Without meaning to, Cora fell asleep with the cats. When she awoke all three of them were curled up around and on her. It was a sweet moment, one that she enjoyed often and loved. Upon standing, she realized that her room was pretty cold. She stepped out into the hallway and was surprised it wasn't much warmer there.

Grady was coming down the hall speaking quietly to a few people at a time. When he reached her he smiled, "Hey gorgeous, we're asking everyone who can drive a golf cart to make a run through town to some of the unsearched areas to see if we can find any coal or fuel. We're down to just a little coal for the stove so we're trying to burn as little as we can to stretch it. I know it's cold out, but at least the sun is shining and we've got five or so hours of daylight. Are you game to go?"

Cora nodded, "I'll get Jake to go with me." She headed off to find the boy.

"Take a walkie-talkie in case you find something," Grady called after her.

Jake was excited to be going out again. Cora wished she was as enthusiastic but she would do her part. They'd been given a set of blocks in the northwest corner of the city.

The roads were still icy in spots so it took some careful driving on Cora's part but they finally made it to their assigned neighborhood. There had been enough days that temperatures were above freezing that the snow had melted everywhere except in shaded places.

After parking the cart, they started off on foot looking at each home that had a basement. Per usual, most were completely empty except for some small snow drifts that remained from the last snowstorm.

Jake, of course, with his young body and long legs could cover more ground than she could so he was two or three lots ahead of her. As long as they could still see each other, Cora didn't mind. She was looking into one basement when without warning she heard Jake scream.

Looking around she didn't see him, but she knew he had been just a few hundred feet ahead of her. She began calling and running at the same time. "Jake, where are you. Jake, what's happened?" She was out of breath, hurrying, looking in the two or three basements on the other side of the street that he might have gone to. Finally she found him.

He was laying in a shallow area that must have been a daylight basement at one time. He wasn't moving. She grabbed her walkie-talkie and called the truck for help as she jumped down to him. "Jake, honey," she said, approaching him fearfully. "Are you all right?" She was bending over him when some movement caught her eye in a nearby corner.

She jumped at the sight of a small dog huddled against the wall. She took a deep breath and returned to Jake. He was breathing and still warm to the touch, but she didn't dare move him in case he'd broken something. The men on the truck arrived within minutes. They gently lifted the unconscious boy and lay him in the back of the truck. Once he was out of the basement Cora went over and picked up the shaking dog, that looked to be an older Jack Russell terrier. "You're all right fella," she said as she climbed out of the basement and hurried back to her cart. She put the dog on the seat next to her and he didn't move, still seeming to be in a state of shock.

Once back to New Denver Cora hurried inside to find Jake. She carried her new find in and handed him to Brenda. "Where did they take Jake?"

"There's an EMT among the new group of people in the other part of the shelter," she said as Cora headed off to find her young friend.

Jake was sitting up on a table when she found him. He had a bandage around his head and his face was pale. "Cora, did you find the dog?"

"Yes, he's here. Where did you find him?"

Several men, including Mike, Jay, Eldon and Grady were standing near Jake. He looked at them and tears began to roll down his cheeks. "I didn't find him. He hit me."

"Hit you?" She looked at the men who looked worried. "How did he hit you?"

Jake shook his head, trying to remember it exactly as it happened. "I was just approaching the basement to look into it. I heard the dog bark, but I didn't see it." He swallowed hard. "At least at first. I had just turned a little to try and see where the dog was. The bark seemed to be coming from above me. I looked up and, just for a second, I thought I saw a house with a tall porch right next to me. I mean it was just the blink of an eye. The next moment, the dog came out of nowhere hitting me right in the chest and both of us went falling backward into the basement. Then there was nothing until I was on the truck on the way back here."

He looked at the men standing beside him. "I don't think they believe me, Cora."

A man who Cora didn't know stepped up beside Jake. "Well, I know these things; he has a slight concussion and he has a pretty good bruise, right where he says the dog hit him. And from the angle and the height of it, it had to have come from above him and it was a very hard blow. It would be hard to explain a bruise on the front of him like that and a bump on the back of his head anyway, except how he describes it." He extended his hand to Cora. "I'm Al Benton, I'm an EMT for the city of Colorado Springs." He shrugged, "At least I used to be."

"I'm so glad to meet you and know we have someone with medical training with us," Cora responded.

"Where's the dog?" Grady asked.

"He's with Brenda. I think he's in shock, like all of us were when we wound up here," Cora said. She turned to the medic, "I know you deal with people, Al, but could you look at the dog?"

"I can do better than me. We have a veterinarian among us. She had a practice in Pueblo. Let's go get her. Jake will be all right with rest. He can go with his Grandfather as long as they keep him awake for several hours and keep an eye on him."

In a few minutes, Cora had been introduced to Marla Houston, the vet. Brenda was still holding the dog when they found her. They took the dog into one of the unoccupied rooms and Marla gave the dog a physical exam. "Well, nothing seems broken. I think he's just scared. He has a collar. There's a name scratched into the side. I think his name is either Tiny or Toby, little hard to read. I think we'd be safe to call him Toby." She looked at his eyes and ears as best as she could without all her instruments. She felt safe saying there was nothing really wrong with him except he was frightened and was an older dog, probably at least eight to ten years old. "One thing I can tell you is that he's a well fed dog, might even be just a tad overweight. He's been eating regularly and has had a bath recently. Wherever he's been it has more resources than we have here."

Grady and Eldon came in and looked at the dog. "He's the first dog I've seen in a long while."

Eldon sighed, "My dad had a Jack Russell. They make good pets."

Grady laughed, "I guess we need someone to take him. You want him?"

Eldon shrugged, "Sure, if no one else wants him, I'll take him."

"Wish he could talk and tell us where he come from," Cora said absently.

"Do you believe what Jake said?" Eldon asked her.

Cora thought a moment, "Jake has never lied about anything since I've known him. I really can't imagine why he'd tell such a story if it weren't true."

Grady sighed, "I've sent a few guys out to see if there are any clues out there where you guys were. No one has ever reported anything like that before. If we can't find a reasonable explanation, then we've got one heck of a mystery on our hands. One that will raise a lot of questions."

"Just thinking about how hard this year has already been," Eldon said shaking his head. "How many more things can go wrong?"

CHAPTER ELEVEN

Christmas came and seemed so odd. Other than a few outbursts of singing of the few carols that anyone could remember the words to, there wasn't much of a celebration. They had beef stew for their dinner, which everyone ate, grateful to have it, but almost everyone was missing the traditional feasts with their families. There were no presents to exchange so that part of the normal festivities couldn't happen. A couple of people had bibles, so there was an informal Christmas Eve service in the dining hall, just as those in the group who celebrated Hanukkah had done earlier in the month.

After eating her meager meal, Cora sat on a couch near the coal stove sipping on a cup of tea. It had become a luxury to have heat. They had found a little more fuel for the fire, but were having to stretch what they had in hopes of getting through until April. They had agreed that they would only light the fire at dinner time and use two buckets of coal per night. That seemed to have become the only goal, stay warm and stay alive. It meant that they wore their coats most of the day.

Eldon saw her and came, sitting down beside her. "Feels good here, doesn't it?"

"Yeah, although when you walk back down the hall you really feel the cold. I'm not sure being this warm then getting so chilled is good for the body."

He nodded, "We do the best we can. Isn't that our motto in this place? I hear someone say that almost everyday."

About that time, the Jack Russell, came running down the hall and jumped into Eldon's lap. "I think he wants out. He's been pretty good about asking," Eldon got up and headed to the door beyond the storage area that led out to the tarmac. "Less wind out this way," he said to Cora. "Want to go with us?"

Cora thought a moment, she loved the fresh air, but she was enjoying the few minutes of being warm. In the end though, she chose the bracing night air. It hadn't been too awful during the day, well above freezing so she agreed and got up to walk out with Eldon and Toby.

The storage room area felt more like a meat locker. It wasn't being heated at all so they hurried through that to the door. When Eldon opened it, Toby shot out and started running around, barking and looking for "just the right spot." It took him a few minutes to find his quest and do what he needed to.

Eldon and Cora stood just outside the door waiting for the dog. There was a cold, white sliver of a moon and the ever present stars that were so brilliant against the blackness of space.

"I love that you can see everything so clearly here," Cora said.

Eldon nodded and looked at her, "I like what I see too." He reached over and pulled her to him, "I wouldn't want your lips to get cold again." He kissed her, looked at her, then repeated his actions.

Cora didn't resist, in fact she was surprised that it was so enjoyable. It was a little sad when the dog came back and wanted to go inside. She laughed and opened the door for the dog and Eldon.

Once back inside, they headed back to reclaim their warm seats but someone else had taken that spot. Eldon shrugged, "I think I'll take Toby back and put him in my room. He'll probably be willing to sleep for awhile." He nodded to Cora, "See you soon?"

"Sure, I'm not going anywhere." After she watched Eldon walk away, she went to her room to read. She was surprised to find Grady and Brenda sitting together on the bench in their room. "Oh hi," she said.

Brenda hopped up and came over, throwing her arms around her for a hug. "I'm glad you're here. You'll be the first to know. Grady and I are going to get married."

Grady got up and joined the hug. "Can't believe it took this catastrophe to bring us together." He leaned over and kissed Brenda on the cheek. "Something good will come out of this after all."

Cora laughed, "Wow, a wedding. Do we have a minister?"

Grady nodded, "One of the people staying in the renovated side is a retired justice of the peace. That will do for us."

Brenda was smiling, tears welling in her eyes, "We're not going to wait. We're going to go talk to him about marrying us on January first. A great way to kick off a new year."

Grady stepped back and drew Brenda to him, holding her as she wept happily. "I am one lucky man." He was obviously as happy as she was.

Cora bit her lip, remembering how sweet it was to have Eldon kiss her. She hadn't even thought of them as a couple, though. Despite that, she was truly happy for Brenda and Grady. At the moment though she felt like a third wheel. She stepped out of the room quietly.

Jake was coming towards her on his way to his own room. "Are we going out searching tomorrow?"

Cora nodded, "Sure. You still feeling okay?"

"I am. Haven't had anymore pain and my bruise has even gone away." He hadn't seen any other things appearing so had begun to think it was just an illusion, although there was still no explanation of where Toby came from.

"Good. I'll see you in the morning after breakfast." Cora watched the boy walk on down the hall with a wave. It was great to see him growing into a young man from the boy he'd been when they'd first met months ago.

The next day promised to be a sunny day. As Cora and Jake set off in their golf cart, the temperature was hovering around thirty, but there was no wind so it didn't really feel all that cold.

They took another section in the northwest side of town to scour for resources. It had been quite awhile since it had snowed so that made the work easier. The problem was that nothing had been found in a long time and they had nearly canvased an entire section of town.

The neighborhood that they were in for the day seemed to have been on the edge of town. There houses had been further apart. Most did have basements so it meant walking up either walking or driving the distances between each house. It was tiring; even so, they chose to walk, at least in the beginning.

The first three basements yielded nothing. But the next one that Jake came to had a few interesting things. There was a doorway under the cement steps on the outside of the building that led to the basement. Jake called Cora over before opening the door. "Should we wait until more people are here? Remember that woman and girl with the guns?"

Cora nodded and put her ear to the door. "I don't hear anything. Can't smell anything either." Cautiously she opened the door just a crack and peered in. "Smells musty." Motioning him to step back, she swung the door open and stepped aside. She froze for a moment, waiting to see if anything came out of the room. Seeing nothing, they both moved towards the opening.

It was dark and unmistakably some sort of storage area. The light from the doorway didn't do much to illuminate the space. Using her small flashlight, Cora stepped into the room. "Well, it's dry in here. Got cement walls and floor. Lots of shelves, lots of old magazines, newspapers, boxes of Christmas decorations, a couple of electric fans, a high chair, crib, old frames, mostly unusable stuff." Then she looked on the floor at the end of the shelves, "Oh here's a real find. There is a stack of pressed logs for a fireplace. I'm sure we can burn these in the wood stove." She motioned to Jake, "Go call the truck. I think we can burn the papers, the frames and, of course, these logs."

He nodded and headed towards the ground level. Cora continued looking at what had been stored by the family that had lived in the house above. There was a box of holiday table place settings that hadn't even been opened. It had twelve plates, cups and more. That would be useful, it didn't matter if it had holly as the decor. There were also some vases, some votive candle holders with candles still in them. Cora began sitting things they could use out into the basement. On top of the shelves, Cora spotted two pair of cross country skis. She had to stretch to reach them. She added them to the pile outside the room.

By the time the truck arrived, she'd amassed a nice little stack of things for them to take back to New Denver. At least there were some things that would help keep them warm for a little longer.

She left the basement and headed on down the street with Jake. They spent an hour or so walking. As it reached one o'clock the temperature had risen to almost fifty although the wind had come up, making it seem much colder. At that point, they opted to continue on, using the golf cart. They'd gone about two miles when Jake asked Cora to stop and back up. When she did he got out. "I thought I saw something," he said. Hopping out, he headed over and looked into the gaping empty basement of what had been a very large house. He looked back at Cora and shrugged, indicating that he didn't see anything.

97

Cora watched as Jake went around to the back side of the place, then walked up and over a small hill. He disappeared for a moment, then came back, waving excitedly. She hurried to join him. "What is it?" she asked.

"I think this is something," he said pointing down the backside of the mound they were standing on. He ran down and waited for her.

When they were both at the same place, they were standing in front of a large metal door that was under an overhang of sod. Cora studied it for a minute. "I think this is almost some sort of garage with a living roof. I've read that people do that to insulate houses and other kinds of buildings." Looking down at the ground, she could see they were standing on a driveway. "Yeah, I think it is a garage." Taking a few steps back, she could see that it was a large one if that is what it turned out to be. "Call the truck. We may need help getting the door open and there might be a lot in there to search."

Jake made the call as Cora felt around the door to see how it opened. There wasn't a handle or any visible sign of which way it opened. There was a small key pad at one side but without the code or electricity, there didn't seem to be a way to use that. She was still looking for a way in when the two men in the truck arrived.

Cora stepped aside as Dave, the older of the two men, easily used a screw driver along the sides of the door breaking its connection with the wiring. She couldn't help wondering how he'd learned how to do that. Soon the door was open and they were staring at a dazzling sight. It was a garage and inside, at the back of the cavernous space, were three mint condition vintage cars from the 1990s. Even Jake was impressed.

The men went immediately to examine the cars. Cora could hear them discussing the value and what kinds of vehicles they were. She was more interested in what they could use so she began opening cupboard doors and looking around. Jake came to help after a few minutes.

The cupboards held a lot of tools and car products, that might be good to have, but since this looked like an auto shop she suggested it would be better to leave the repair equipment here and bring their vehicles here to fix. The two men agreed. They also felt the show cars wouldn't be practical for what they needed now so it was best to leave them where they were for the time being.

There was another room off to one side of the show room/garage. It was set up as kind of a party space. It had three leather couches and three high tables with tall stools. There was a dart board, a digital jukebox, and a snack bar with a soda vending machine that had three or four extra cases of assorted soft drinks next to it. The furniture and the soda were about the only things that weren't really heavy that they would be taking back with them. One exciting find for Jake was a big jar full of beef jerky sticks on the snack bar's counter. It got even better when he found another three boxes of twenty four under the counter. The shelves behind the bar netted them some large commercial packages of individual serving sized chips of varying kinds and several boxes of cookies.

Watching Jake savor one of the beef sticks made Cora chuckle. She hadn't realized how much she, too, had missed junk food. It wasn't hard to see that the boy had really been missing some of the treats he'd known. The food stuff would make a welcome break from all the bland, same food that you could survive on, but wasn't much fun. She could see this causing quite a stir. It was good that there would be at least one of each thing for everyone in New Denver, if Jake didn't eat it all on the way back.

They loaded the truck and then closed up the garage again. They all headed back to the shelter with the load of supplies. It had turned out to be a good day of foraging.

Cora had been right. Everyone at dinner that night really enjoyed the chips, soda, beef sticks and cookies. It brought a lot of laughter and good memories. Everyone was in a happy mood for a change. In the midst of that good time, Grady and Brenda stood up and he announced proudly that they would be the first to be married in New Denver. There was cheering and clapping as well as a few funny jabs about them, but it was all joyful.

Cora couldn't help but feel a bit of hope. They were planning a future, something no one had been brave enough to even think about before. It was certainly up-lifting. She looked across the room and saw Eldon. He was smiling and clapping for the happy couple just as everyone around him was. It made her strangely happy to see him joining in the festive mood.

At that moment, Jake came rushing into the room. He went straight to Eldon and whispered something. Eldon's happy mood disappeared instantly. He motioned to the soldiers in the room and they all went out into the hall. Grady saw them and followed immediately. Several other men got up and went out. Cora wasn't about to stay behind. She and Brenda ran out into the hall just in time to see the soldiers getting their weapons and heading for the storage area.

"What's happening?" she called as one soldier went by her.

"Someone's trying to break in," she said breathlessly. "Stay back and out of the way."

Brenda and Cora more or less froze in place. Others came and stood in the hall. Within moments, the people who had guns were armed and standing by the doors. It was a tense few minutes after they heard several shots fired. Then silence.

It seemed like an eternity before Grady and the others came back into the hallway. He went straight to Brenda, who wept as he took her in his arms. "You won't believe what just happened," he said loud enough that not only Brenda, but everyone in the hall could hear. "Our marauder turned out to be a hungry black bear. He must have smelled some of our food scraps."

Eldon came into the hall. He looked at Grady, "Well, he's scrawny but we'll have bear steaks for a few days. The men are dressing it out now." Eldon smiled and walked over to Cora. "Like wild game?"

She laughed, "Never tried bear."

"You're in luck. I think you'll get your chance." He walked on to put his weapon away in the gun locker at a center point in the hall. He saw the folks with guns guarding the entrance door. "Good job. It was just a bear," he said to them. Cora heard a collective sigh from the guardians.

Cora took a deep breath, the good time that they'd all been experiencing was gone in a moment, reminding all of them that they were living in perilous times. Nothing was for certain. She felt like she needed to spend some time with the cats; they always helped her find peace.

Once back in her room, she lay down on her bed and was immediately joined by her three little friends. Eve seemed to sense Cora's need for comfort. She crawled right up next to Cora's face and lay, purring, cheek to cheek. Cora loved the sound and fell asleep easily.

Strange thoughts were floating in and out of her mind, a big house, Toby the dog, nothing made sense. Then there was the sound of her name being repeated, her arm being touched, she wondered if she was being attacked by a bear? Cora sat up, knocking Eve off her pillow. It took a few moments to focus but she finally could see Brenda sitting on the edge of her bed, smiling at her.

"You were really snoring," Brenda said, chuckling.

"Sorry, didn't know I did that."

"You don't very often." Brenda took Cora's hand. "Can you get up and come with me? Grady and I want to get married today. The Judge is ready and we're going to have the ceremony in the courtyard. I'd like you to be my maid of honor."

Cora reached out and hugged her friend. "Of course, but I don't have anything to wear but what I have on or something like it."

Brenda stood up, "Me either. I never dreamed I'd be married in jeans and a tee shirt, but I don't really care. I'm just happy to have found the right man for me."

Cora stood up, "I'll comb my hair and be right with you."

Brenda shrugged, "Got to go tell everyone to meet in the courtyard in an hour."

Cora smiled. She looked at Eve, "Well, I guess today is a good as any for a wedding. I think that Sophie may be leaving us though. But I'm sure your daughter will come back and visit now and then." Cora put on her heavier coat, the wedding would be in the courtyard and it would still be winter. It might not be below freezing that day and the sun might be out, but it still was cold to her, especially if there was any wind. Best be prepared.

Nearly everyone gathered outside in the space they called the courtyard. The Justice of the Peace stood on the stairs, halfway up to the ground level. Brenda and Grady stood a few steps down, but still up enough so everyone could see the services. Cora, the maid of honor, and Mike, the best man, were on the next to the bottom step. It was a simple wedding, the most common vows were read, the couple recited what they were supposed to and with a "I now pronounce you man and wife," it was over and sealed with a kiss in front of witnesses. Cora and Mike got out of the way so the bride and groom could come back down.

Cora stood beside the stairs and watched as Grady and Brenda made their way around, thanking everyone for being there. It was a nice wedding despite the circumstances of their lives now. For a few moments, it was nice to get lost in the pleasantness. Then a cloud cut off the streaming sunlight that had been making being outside bearable. It didn't take long for everyone to choose going in.

Later that afternoon, Brenda and Grady moved her stuff into the other side of the shelter, into a large room of their own. Brenda left Sophie behind until they had everything in place. Cora didn't mind; she knew Eve had gotten used to having her now grown son and daughter with her.

After they had left, Cora sat on her bed trying to decide how to arrange the strangely empty room. Brenda's bed was still there and one of the bookcases. They had taken her bench and one of the TV trays. It would be worth making a trip to the storage area to see what she could find to fill out her space.

Her planning was interrupted by a knock on the door. "Come in?"

A familiar face appeared, peeking around the edge of the door. "Hi. I was wondering if you had a minute to talk?"

"Sure, come on in." Cora recognized Lois Wilkerson, the Sergeant who had been in charge of the barracks at the base. "What brings you here?"

"The base commander has stationed several more people at each of the shelters. The supply raiders have become more organized so he wanted a few more military people stationed at each site. I came with about five others. There were three of us women who were going to share a room, but it was really tiny. Someone told me your roommate just moved out so I thought I'd see if you'd consider me as a new one."

"Well, remember I have cats," Cora looked around. Eve and the two others were under the bed. "I have two that I'm keeping and one I'm babysitting."

"I love cats and I remember the ones you had at the base," she shrugged. "I used to have a dog, but he was staying with my mom in Jackson Hole."

Cora nodded; she understood that everyone had lost someone. "If you like cats, you're in the right place. You can have that bed," she pointed to the vacated side of the room. "I was about to go see what kind of furniture I could find to make this a more homey space. Want to come with me?"

"Sure," Lois put up a finger indicating Cora should wait a minute, "got my gear in the hall." Lois stepped out and back in quickly, hauling a duffle bag over her shoulder and a rifle in her hand.

Cora shuddered at the sight of the weapon but knew it was probably good that her new roommate knew how to use one. Such were the times.

CHAPTER TWELVE

There wasn't much left in the storage area as far as furniture went. They did find one of the high tables from the fancy garage and two of the matching stools. On the miscellaneous table they found two souvenir placemats and a dice game. They kept rummaging through the things they'd found until they came across an old radio/CD player. In a small box near it they discovered ten music albums on CD. The collection was a pretty eclectic collection, but no one had heard music being played for a long time. Anything would be welcome. By the time they had finished their search they had an armload of small things that they carried back to their room and then asked a few of the men to bring the table.

Once everything was in place, Lois laughed, "This looks like a college dorm. Not that I was ever in one for more than an hour. My sister went to Colorado State and I visited her a few times." She looked away, "I miss her. I didn't see her much after she finished school but we kept in touch. Just thinking I'll never see her again really leaves an empty place in my being, you know?" She looked at Cora.

Cora nodded, "I know exactly what you mean. I have a sister too." Cora picked up Eve and sat down on her bed. BB remained under the bed and Sophie jumped up on the other bed as she always did.She stopped and froze when she saw Lois.

"Oh, aren't you a sweet baby," Lois said as she held out a hand to the cat. Sophie cautiously approached the offered hand.

"Sophie is the cat I'm babysitting. I used to call her Spots, but I gave her to my last roommate, Brenda. Brenda is on her honeymoon, such as it can be in a place and time like this."

"Well, Sophie can stay with me if Brenda doesn't come back for her."

Cora sighed, "If she does take Sophie you can have BB. He's a bit of a hunter, but very sweet. He likes to snuggle just like Eve does."

"I'm okay with that too," Lois answered. She was now holding Sophie and the cat was purring loudly. "Oh, I could get used to this," Lois said as the cat rubbed chin to chin.

Cora hadn't actually thought about another roommate, however already she was glad to have one, especially one who loved cats. It had been a good day.

Later that night, just before lights out, Lois played a couple of the CDs. Cora began to move to the music. "You know this would make good dance music. I think it's from a decade or so ago, but who cares. What do you say we organize a dance?"

Lois laughed. "I'm not much of a dancer, but it sounds likes something fun to do on a cold winter night. We've got another month or two that it's going to be too cold to do much out of doors."

Cora nodded, "When we have a nice day at all we have to really get out and forage. Our supplies are getting pretty limited. I think the soup is getting thinner all the time."

"Yeah, back at the base they were worrying too. They had enough for a year but with so many extra coming in, we were stretching it." Lois turned off the music. "I think a dance would at least be a diversion."

Cora agreed. Things could get grim.

In the morning, they woke up to a new snow storm. Within three days, they had almost a foot of snow and below freezing conditions that lingered for three weeks.

It was well into February before they could go foraging again. They were going into the suburbs and small towns around the Denver area now. They had scoured the greater Denver area pretty thoroughly.

Lois was now going with Jake and Cora on their ventures out of the shelter. She was armed, which was a reminder of the dangers, not only from bears that might be coming out of their dens, but the raiders.

It was a very crisp morning. The sun was shining, promising a day that would warm up a little by afternoon. Everyone was in a cautious, yet optimistic mood. Jake, as usual, was well ahead of Cora as they walked along, seeking out houses that had basements or underground shelters. The first few blocks provided nothing encouraging.

It was kind of a hilly area. Cora went up a fairly steep hill and stood for a moment looking back at the neighborhood they'd just combed. When she turned to look ahead, she gasped. "Jake, Lois come here," she called.

Her companions ran to join her. Jake was the first to arrive. "Wow," was all the breathless boy could say.

105

Lois was close behind him. She too was astonished at what she saw. At the bottom of the hill they were standing on was a car. Out in the open and in the middle of an intersection. Laying the way it was, on its side up against a snow drift by the curb, it looked like there had been an accident.

The three of them approached the car. There were no skid marks or any sign of anyone being there. Just the car. Lois climbed up and looked inside. "The front windshield is gone and there looks to be blood on the dash. I'd say someone was thrown out of this." Getting off the car, she continued to walk around it. "There is snow under the car, but not in it. So it wasn't here when it snowed last. It's too cold to have melted anything." She motioned to the drifts of snow around them.

Jake looked around nervously, "Think it could have been the looters?"

Lois shook her head. "This car has Colorado plates and it's got things still in the back seat." She called for the men in the truck to join them.

In a few minutes, the men with the three of them were able to sit the car upright again. They pried the trunk open and found several bags of groceries. Obviously someone had been shopping. They started to carry the food to the truck to take back to the shelter when one of the paper bags broke and the contents spilled out onto the ground.

Cora went to help pick things up and then just stood there amazed. Laying on the ground in front of her was a bag of small oranges, a bag of romaine lettuce, and several tomatoes. Jake and Lois came to look at what had stopped the other three from picking up the items.

Lois was the first to recover, "My Lord, how could this be? This looks like whoever was in that car was in just their way home from grocery shopping! Like it used to be. " She looked around, "Where are they?"

The men quickly picked up the precious items they'd found and put them into the truck. There were more things in the back seat that they took too. Cora was grateful to see that whoever the groceries belonged to at one time had pets. They found a case each of cat and dog food cans. She knew who would appreciate that.

Lois stood in the intersection and looking around. "There is absolutely no sign of any car being here, except that one!" she said as Cora joined her. She was right. There were no tracks in the patches of snow on all the roadways except those of their supply truck and the golf cart they were driving. There was no evidence of any accident, no broken glass, bits of metal or other vehicle. The only thing they had was another mystery. How could there be an accident like that? How could anyone have fresh vegetables?

"Maybe it's another survivalist somewhere who's got a greenhouse," Cora said, thinking out loud. "That woman and daughter we found last fall seemed pretty prepared."

Lois shrugged, "Maybe. But it would have to have been underground."

"That garage was big enough to house all those cars remember? I think it's possible." Cora sighed and looked around. "If it was them, they might be coming back for their stuff. We should get out of here. They'll know it was us that took it."

Lois looked at the golf cart, her guns were there. "You're right. Let's go. I need to report this anyway." Cora looked surprised when Lois took a couple of photos with her small cell phone. "I don't have any service but I can still take photos with it," she explained to Cora.

The drive back to New Denver felt like it took more time than ever. The minute they arrived Lois jumped out and headed to find Eldon. She was very much back in military mode, not in the relaxed civilian lifestyle she'd displayed in the last several of months.

Later that morning, Grady called for a group meeting in the dining hall. With the seventy nine of them who were now housed at New Denver, it was standing room only. "My friends, I think we all need to know what happened today." He held up a tomato. "This is absolutely fresh. Somehow, somewhere, someone is able to grow things. We have to find out how and where. Of course we will save the seeds from this little beauty for growing some ourselves, but right now we have a mystery to solve." He stepped aside and Eldon stepped to the podium they had.

"As most of you have heard, one of our foraging teams came upon a car that had the tomatoes and other things in its trunk." He looked at Lois. "Sergeant Wilkerson came back with some photos that frankly are hard to explain. Just like my dog, Toby, just showing up out of the blue, this car and the apparent accident it was in has no explanation, at least at this time. We need to be documenting these phenomenons. I will be traveling to the main base to report this and see if anyone else has experienced these anomalies. I think there is no need to be concerned, but it will cause us to be on the lookout for unusual things. I will keep you informed of anything I find out." He turned and left the room. The Sergeant followed him, as well as two other soldiers.

Cora had watched Eldon leave. He'd not looked to find her in the crowd. She wished he had, but he didn't. He was first and foremost a military man, that would always be his primary concern and duty. She thought about that all through the morning.

It was warm, at least bearable, so she took a walk out on the tarmac in the early afternoon. She wandered to the far side of the paved area. The wind had created snowdrifts and had left cleared patches of bared ground here and there. It brought tears to her eyes to see a tiny fringe of green starting to show. The seeds of grass and weeds that were under the dirt were fighting to survive just like everything else. She hurried back inside to tell everyone.

In a few minutes almost everyone was outside looking at what she had found. It was the best moment they'd had in a long time. Cora was among them, taking another look at the hope of spring. It was the first snow flake hitting her eyelashes that reminded her that winter wasn't over yet. Within five minutes, the first flake had been joined by millions and everyone was driven back inside.

At least the soup for dinner that night tasted better than it had for weeks. Among the groceries found was a pot roast, more potatoes, carrots and garlic salt. The soup was thin but very tasty, certainly better than the bear stew had ever tasted.

Eldon and Lois didn't come back that night, nor the next day. Cora missed her new roommate almost as much as she missed seeing Eldon, though they hadn't been alone together for a few weeks. He hadn't tried to kiss her again, which she found that she regretted. But she knew he was worried about their situation and what might happen.

When Eldon did come back, he brought four more soldiers, all of them looked heavily armed. Grady called for a group meeting within an hour of their arrival.

Eldon was the first to address them, "We found out that one of the crew scavenging in downtown Aurora was hit and seriously injured by something falling out of the sky. It turned out to be a piece of metal, looked like the cover off an air conditioning unit. It was too heavy to be blown about by the wind. Another mystery. So we need to be extremely careful when we are outside the shelter. There's no telling where these things are coming from." He coughed a little,

"Excuse me," he continued. "There was also an attack on the shelter we set up in Pueblo. They were nearly stripped of their supplies. So the folks from Pueblo will be moved into Colorado Springs as soon as we can develop a place for their hundred or so folks. We may have to house more people here too. We may have to reorganize the storage area into some type of dormitory for the single people. We won't start moving people until the weather improves, probably late April." He looked around, "I know this is not good, but we are trying to do the best we can for all survivors." He nodded to Grady and walked out of the room.

Grady stood a moment at the podium. "We'll need to post watchmen from now on. We can take four hour shifts, day and night. We can park those fancy cars we found outside of all the entrances to sit in while we watch. It will be warmer than just standing out there. See me to sign up for the time you're willing to be on lookout."

Cora had wondered about what would come next. Everyone would be running out of supplies and eyeing what little others had as a prize. She'd even worried that if they ran out of food at New Denver, someone might start looking at Eve and BB as a potential meal. She kept a close watch on her beloved animals, never letting them out of the room if she wasn't with them.

* * *

Late in February, the snow was heavy in the mountains, but not in town. Grady and several other men decided to go hunting. If one bear had been left, maybe there were others. Mike offered to be the driver in his old pickup, two soldiers went with him. Grady drove one of the supply trucks with Jay and another armed man.

Mike took the lead as they headed out of town on a clear and bright morning. They'd gotten about two hours away from New Denver when he stopped. He was in the middle of the road so Grady had to stop too. Grady got out and walked up to Mike's rig. "What's up?"

Mike pointed ahead. "Look over there at that snow drift."

Grady could see why he'd stopped. There in the snow that was piled up was the unmistakable sign of something big crossing it. "Should we follow that trail?"

"Get your guns," Mike said as he swung out of his pickup. He walked over to the snow drift analyzing which way the tracks led. "They go that way," he called to the other men who were gearing up. He started off, not waiting for the others. The tracks were easy to follow in the deep snow, but walking wasn't. He'd wished he'd thought to bring the cross country skis they had in the storage area. It was exhausting work.

Grady was quite a bit younger than Mike. Despite that, he had trouble keeping up. The others were further behind. Mike stopped when he came to the edge of a cliff. He motioned for the others to be quiet, but hurry up to join him. When they were all standing there, the others were astonished. Below them was a small valley, teaming with life. Trees, water, it was too much to take in at once. "This is like a place we saw on the way here. A narrow canyon that was spared from whatever happened. I suspect there are many places like this," Mike said, then he pointed to an area just beyond the small lake at the far end of the gorge. "I saw something pretty big and brown moving in those trees." Let's divide up, half go down this side of the valley, the rest down that one. See if we can get a clean shot."

Quietly the men worked their way down the steep side of the canyon. Three, including Grady went to the left. Mike and the others stayed on the first side. It wasn't easy to move quietly through the underbrush and drifted snow as they made their way around the small, long lake.

They'd almost reached the far side of the lake when Grady and his team were surprised and nearly run over by a small herd of elk bolting out of the woods towards the far end of the valley. They didn't even have time to fire a single shot. Luckily the animals dashed back towards the other group. Mike didn't hesitate. He was able to bring down a large bull.

It took all of them to get the animal dressed out and back to the truck. Grady drove their treasure back to New Denver. Mike and a couple of others went back to the lake for an hour or two of fishing. By the time they were ready to leave the valley, it was beginning to get dark. The day had been profitable though. Besides the elk, they had caught seven trout. The little lake had clearly been stocked at one time.

They had just got back to the truck when they heard gun shots off in the distance. As quietly as they could, everyone got in and Mike started the old pickup and headed out. It was troubling to realize they weren't the only ones with guns out there.

When the men got back to the shelter, they shared the news with Grady and Eldon. Immediately the soldiers took the place of the civilian volunteers to stand watch. The tension level was raised.

The new food was welcomed by the cooks. At least for the night, the stew was out and steaks were in. The fish were saved for breakfast.

That night, the delight of fresh, tasty meat for dinner was tempered with the knowledge that no one felt safe, and the raiders might be closer than they had suspected.

CHAPTER THIRTEEN

March came in like a lion and stayed. The snow came and went, but the cold weather persisted. During the month the hunting party went out several times, but only got a few rabbits. It wasn't as good as the elk had been, but somehow it sustained them all. By the end of March everyone was talking about moving south before the next winter.

There had been no new unexplained things happening, which was good. They hadn't figured out anything about the car they'd found or the dog, Toby. Days passed and everyone, including Cora, was getting tired of being in the shelter, day after day.

Then it happened, it was the second week in April and the sun came out. The snow was gone and a warm breeze broke over the once frozen ground. The revitalizing breath of spring caused a carpet of green laced with splotches of color to appear. In the neighborhoods, long forgotten bulbs of daffodils and crocus brought touches of life and color everywhere.

The foraging teams started their searching outlying communities again. The need was urgent. Supplies were on the edge of being completely exhausted. It wasn't just to supplement their rations, it was survival.

Cora and Lois took a car to a small community about thirty minutes from New Denver. This time Jake had gone with his grandfather, Jay, and Mike in the pickup to another community.

The city center netted them nothing, but on the edge of town they found a basement with a storage area. Upon closer investigation, they could see that it had been recently been ransacked. There were muddy footprints, indicating several people had been there before them. Lois made sure her rifle was loaded and they quickly left that area. Although the raiders hadn't tried to hit them at New Denver, it still wasn't a good idea to be out on their own. They headed back to take another look around the suburbs nearer the city.

Their efforts that morning turned to be in vain. Some of the others had better luck, finding a root cellar with some still usable vegetables among the rotting things. With garlic, onions, and ginger, their thin rabbit stew would at least taste better. The fishermen had some luck and had caught several good sized fish to add to their stores. A smoker to preserve some of their catch was gerry-rigged on the tarmac.

A team of people began preparing a plot of ground to start a garden. Cora had brought the bottles of seeds she'd found with her so the people who were going to be the gardeners had started all kinds of things indoors before the frost had left the ground. Those along with the seeds from the tomatoes had been planted in pots inside and were pretty well established. They erected wind breaks around the garden area to protect the tender young plants and built a temporary greenhouse structure over the area out of PVC pipe and plastic. It took several days to get the ground prepared and the structure up sturdy enough to withstand the wind that could get pretty strong and be damaging to the plants.

By the end of April the garden was planted and doing well. It was hard to keep the rabbits and other ground dwelling critters out. Toby and BB were helpful in that respect. Toby lived up to his Jack Russell rep and BB was a natural born killer of mice and rats. Even Sophie and Eve lent a paw now and then.

Word came from the Colonel that three representatives from New Denver, as well as Eldon, should come to the base for a new briefing in two days. Grady called everyone together in the dining room immediately. He and Eldon stood at the front of the room. Grady went to the podium, "We need to pick three people to go to Crystal Mountain. It seems there is some new information to hear. Who would be willing to go with me and the Lieutenant?" Hands immediately went up all over the room.

"Thanks everyone," Grady said. "Obviously we're all anxious to hear what's going on. I wish we all could go, but we just need two more." People looked around at each other.

Mike stood up, "I'll go." People around him applauded.

Cora took a deep breath, "Me, too." Again applause.

Grady smiled, "Thanks, we have our representatives. We'll go tomorrow and come right back and tell you what was said. Write down any questions you have and give me your lists before we leave in the morning. Hopefully we'll be able to get more supplies too, so we'll take one of our trucks." He nodded and walked away from the podium.

Eldon came over to Cora. "I'm glad you're going with us tomorrow. I don't have any idea what is going on, but it must be something big if we've been summoned for a pow-wow."

Cora smiled, "Hopefully it's good news, not bad."

Eldon sighed, "Yeah, something positive would help." He nodded towards the door, "Want to go for a walk? I was out earlier and it's a pretty day."

Cora agreed and fell into step with him. He was right, it was a bright sunny day. It wasn't hot at all, but at least, almost warm. The sweater she was wearing was enough as long as the wind didn't start to blow.

They walked along the tarmac to the end. Here and there, the weeds and grasses were poking up through cracks in the paving. It wouldn't take long for nature to reclaim the land once things weren't being maintained. It would, however, take a long time to build up their world again to where it had been. Would they have the skills and people to do that? No one really knew just how many people were left on the planet. Communications were very limited and everyone knew how short supplied anyone was.

"So what about us?" Eldon said quietly as they stood looking at the fields beyond the runway.

Cora was surprised, "I didn't know there was an 'us.' Is there?"

Eldon laughed, "Yeah, I guess I'm not very good at courting am I?"

"Well, under the circumstances, what does that look like anyway? You're not going to be taking me out on a date, going to dinner or a movie. I'm not taking you home to meet my mom and sister. We all eat together, live in the same place, and are displaced from our old lives. Nothing is the way it used to be. Grady and Brenda getting married was the only recognizable thing that's happened since last summer."

He walked over in front of her. He took her face in his hands and kissed her. She responded and put her arms around him. "Okay, that's nice," she whispered as they stood in each other's arms. "What prompted you to ask about 'us' today?"

He nodded, "What if my unit is being called up to go somewhere? Would you go with me? Or would you wait for me, knowing I might not come back? There are still those we have to fight to keep our freedom."

Cora looked deeply into his eyes, "Would you resign to stay with me?" She shook her head, "No. I wouldn't ask that of you. I know you serve with honor and pride. We need our soldiers, it comes at the sacrifice of many things. Intellectually, I know that and will abide by your choices, but forgive me if there is a tiny corner in my soul that resents that I would not be the center of your world. The thing is that I will have to struggle with is what kind of person am I? Am I willing to rise above my pettiness because I love you, and love what you're willing to do for not only me, but the country?"

Eldon sighed, "Military wives, and sometimes husbands, have to be pretty tough, like their soldier. But it is because our loved ones are the center of our world, we can face what comes. Nothing is better than when we have that support." Eldon smiled, "Did I hear you say you loved me?"

Cora looked down, slightly embarrassed, yet smiling to herself. "I guess I did."

He lifted her chin and kissed her again. "I love you, too." He kissed her again and then stepped back and got down on one knee. "Marry me?"

Cora laughed and pulled him to his feet. "I know a retired justice of the peace."

Eldon laughed and kissed her several times before they started to walk back to the shelter. "So when?"

"Let's see what tomorrow brings. We can be engaged for a day or two. We have to line up a bridesmaid and best man."

"I'm sure Grady and Brenda would be happy to stand up with us."

Cora sighed, "So would Jake and Lois."

"Who said we only have to have two? All of New Denver would be happy to serve. I think everyone already knows we're a couple. If they don't they soon will."

"How's that?" Cora asked.

"I'm so happy and you're glowing, it's like a strobe light in your eyes and I'm sure mine." He grabbed her hands and they danced around for a moment, laughing and enjoying the moment. The gardeners saw them and laughed. There was no denying that was a moment neither of them would forget. Cora was so happy, it was a great day.

There was a light rain falling as they headed out for the base the next morning. Everyone was quiet as they drove. Usually the trip would take just over an hour in a car, but the lumbering old truck they had, added an extra thirty minutes. They were all anxious by the time they arrived.

115

There was a surprising number of vehicles in the parking area outside the base. They had to park outside the base entrance and take the shuttle in from the main gate. There seemed to be many more people walking around too. Cora thought they might be the survivors from Pueblo. They headed for the auditorium.

Eldon went to join the other officers who were on the stage. He stood at his seat and waited until the Colonel came to the microphone. He was joined by another officer. Cora didn't know how to tell the rank of Army officers, but from where she was seated, she could see the man had two stars on his uniform. Her question was answered when the Colonel introduced "Major General Harrison Vela."

The General stepped up to the podium. "Good day, everyone. I am glad to be here today to let you all know what we have discovered to this point. First of all, I want to acknowledge how difficult the past few months have been for all of you. Needless to say, it's been a devastating time. We have, however, passed the first test. We have survived the winter. Now is the time to reassess our resources and make plans for rebuilding the future. We have approximately five hundred thousand people accounted for at this time, including you who are here in this room. Canada has nearly that many also. Much of the rest of the world hasn't been tallied, but it is reasonable to assume they have as many. The part of New Zealand that was spared has nearly a million people too." He took a sip of water. "So we have people and as always, our people are our greatest resource."

Cora was surprised at the numbers of survivors. She wondered how so many had been spared. Must have been a lot of people in the subways and other underground places in the big cities.

The General continued, "We would like to have an inventory of skills that people possess. We are in need of all kinds of professions, from farmers to engineers. We have several stations at the back for you to register how you can help with our rebuilding effort. Of course our first priority is establishing a supply chain to house, feed and protect our population. As you probably heard, there are roaming bands of people, raiders, looters, marauders or whatever you want to call them, that think it's easier to steal provisions than to forage for them. We will be asking people to stay in their designated shelters and will assign military personnel to be on guard at all

116

times until this crisis is resolved. We are committed across the country to protecting the civilian population." He looked around. "I know you are all brave men and women. I applaud your efforts and your being here after such a trying time. It speaks to that American spirit of pioneering. We are pioneers. This is a totally new frontier. I'll let the Colonel tell you what the latest thoughts are about what happened." He turned and went to sit down.

A grim faced Colonel Herbert took the microphone, "As it turned out several scientists from MIT were in New York at the event time. They were attending a conference and just happened to be on the subway that day, headed for lunch downtown. They have been in touch with other scientists that were spared and been having chats via our systems across America and Canada. What they think at this moment is that the unusually large sun flare or solar storm that hit the Earth, was only a glancing blow, which is why it didn't burn off our atmosphere. Many of us saw a sort of lavender colored sky for a little while after the event which probably means we were close to becoming extinct. But why so much and so many disappeared is still a mystery. We have been monitoring the sun's activities and it seems to have settled down. Can we expect it to happen again? We always knew it was possible, but nothing in Earth's history had ever been recorded like that. And it wasn't what we expected either, it was faster than we thought it could be, it apparently wasn't a direct hit. That's the only explanation for why we're still here. There are many questions to ask yet, and answers we may never know. But here and now we have to prepare to live and grow again what was lost. To that end we are organizing shelter zones. We have established them around bases that survived by being underground. So there will be shelter areas near underground bases in Arizona, Arkansas, California, Kansas, Georgia, New Jersey and New York City as well as here. Satellite shelters will be established within close distance to the nearest hub. Regular transport of personnel and goods between the bases will be maintained to man and supply equally each site. Civilians will be able to choose where they want to be."

He looked around the room. "I know this is a lot to take in at once, but be assured we are working hard to come up with plans that will start us off on the right track to help us continue to survive. Most areas already have their shelters in place so if you want to transfer, just sign up and you'll get on the schedule. There are several tables at the back of the room for you to sign up for skills or professions. If you want to transfer, there are clerks back there to help with that." He nodded to the General, who got up and led the way off the stage.

Cora saw Eldon and the other officers that were seated on the stage get up and follow the General. She wondered if he would be going back with them. She sat a for moment, thinking about what she could offer as a skill or profession. She was a secretary by training, which didn't seem all that important at the time, but someone had to take notes. She got up and went back to the tables to sign up for what she could.

There was no way to know what was happening for Eldon at the moment. She thought about their conversation around being a military wife. It was something to think seriously about. Lois carried a gun and was trained to use it. Would Eldon ever have to do that? She had always thought she could never date a policemen, being a little leery of men who weren't afraid of carrying weapons. Just something about someone capable of shooting someone else, or being shot themselves was unsettling. The chances of winding up a widow popped into in her mind. All of a sudden, she felt chilled. Did she have the right stuff for that life?

They had waited by the truck for nearly an hour before Eldon came back to them. His grim face told Cora it wasn't to be good news. He didn't say anything just helped her into the truck. They had to sit to the side of several boxes of supplies they were taking back. It gave them a chance to be alone and huddle together to stay warm and a little out of the wind. "So?" Cora finally said over the roar of the old truck's engine.

Eldon sighed and leaned over close to her ear. "There are only so many officers so they are deploying us as evenly as they can to each of the bases that will serve as shelter hubs." He kissed her and looked into her eyes. "I asked to stay here, but I don't have seniority so I am being reassigned to Atlanta. Would you go with me? I leave in ten days."

Cora looked at him. She was hoping not to have to face that question just yet. She pretended she couldn't hear what he'd said. "I can't hear you. Let's talk when we get back."

He nodded and cuddled up to her with his arms around her.

It felt good to be in his embrace but Cora knew she would have to have an answer for him when they did arrive back at New Denver. In a little over an hour, she would have to choose being fearful and staying behind or being brave and moving on with her life. Could she love him that much?

CHAPTER FOURTEEN

The old truck lumbered along at a slow, but steady pace. They had been traveling for about half an hour when Cora heard a loud pop above the roar of the engine. She looked up and saw the back window of the cab had been shattered. Looking around she saw nothing. The next second Grady was pulling the truck over to the side of the road, rolling to a stop.

Everything that came next seemed to be in slow motion, Eldon jumped up, grabbing his firearm as he went out the back. He turned and pushed her down hard against the floor of the truck among the boxes of supplies. Cora wasn't sure, but the screams she heard might have been her own. There was the sound of gunfire all around, echoing off the cliffs and mountains. It was deafening. She froze, feeling totally immobile as she lay on the rough bed of the rig for a few minutes as the battle raged on.

When she lifted her head to take a quick peek, Eldon was standing at the back of the truck. She couldn't see what he was aiming at, but he was fully engaged in a firefight. It seemed an eternity until all at once he fell back against the truck. He turned to look at her just before he slid to the ground. This time she knew it was her screaming as she crawled out of the truck to Eldon's side. He'd been hit at least two times. There was a bloody gash on his head and one on his side. Cora took off her jacket and put it under his head. Applying pressure to his side stopped the bleeding, but she wasn't sure what to do with the head wound. He didn't respond at all to her calling his name.

Cora was so intent on tending to Eldon she hadn't seen that Grady had picked up Eldon's weapon and gone on the offense. He and Mike had joined the fight and within minutes, the firing stopped.

Mike came over and helped Cora get Eldon back onto the bed of the truck. They turned around and headed back to base. Cora had never been one to do too much praying, but she did all the long way back to the safety of the underground refuge. As she sat beside the man she loved and watched him bleed all over her hands, she suddenly realized how real the danger was now. Mike sat with her, helping keep Eldon from moving around.

Eldon opened his eyes for a moment, "How.." he tried to say.

Mike patted him on the shoulder, "We got them, Sir," Mike said. "Turns out Grady was a Marine and so was I." Mike smiled, "Mission accomplished."

Cora was numb as they drove into the mountain and right up to the infirmary entrance. Several corpsmen ran out to help get Eldon into the building. She just sat and watched as they lifted him onto a gurney and whisked him inside. Without her jacket, she was so cold she couldn't even feel her arms anymore, but the shock of what she had just been through had left her unable to realize that.

Mike came back out of the clinic and helped her out of the truck. He put a blanket around her shoulders. "They think we got here just in time. He's going to make it."

Cora looked at him, "Who were those people?"

Mike shrugged, "Who knows? They were just waiting for us to head back to New Denver with supplies. Why they don't come and join us rather than try to take things by force is the real question. Since history began, there's always been the element who wants to hurt others and just be mean. My mother always used to quote the Bible and said something like 'the devil is always looking for those he can devour. Once you allow him a foothold, you'll be lost bit by bit.' I think she was right. Those three men we killed back there probably were cute little kids and grew up like the rest of us, but, somewhere along the way, got lost."

She shuddered, "You killed three men?"

"Hey, they were trying very hard to kill us! Not rob us, they could have stopped the car and held us at gun point to take our supplies. But they were not going to leave us alive, that's why they were in hiding behind the rocks and they fired first. We were lucky, Eldon got one of them before he went down." Mike turned as Grady came out of the building.

"We can go back to New Denver now. Eldon's in surgery to remove the bullet. It went through the upper parts of his stomach. spleen, and into his liver. He's going to lose his spleen, but the rest they can patch up and it should heal. Might be a long process. This afternoon he's being air-lifted to Arizona where they have a team of surgeons that can do more complete reconstruction than they can here. He has a fractured skull too, so they're not sure what damage he'll have. They've got to make sure his brain doesn't swell so he's being kept sedated. They've asked that he have no visitors."

Grady looked at Cora, "I'm sorry. I know the two of you are close. Hopefully he'll get to come back when he's better." He walked over and hugged her. He didn't move as she wept silently onto his jacket.

Mike stood quietly by until Cora moved a foot away from Grady. "Let's head back to the shelter. Cora you ride up front with us. We're going to have an escort home this time," he motioned to a humvee with four armed soldiers waiting for them.

Cora looked at the clinic and then got into the center of the bench seat. With a deep sigh she leaned back and closed her eyes. She hardly noticed the long road back to the shelter. The joy she'd felt the day before seemed like a fantasy. For a moment, she had been the princess in a lavish movie. But the lights came on and the curtains closed, she had to walk out into the daylight of reality. Life was never going to be the same.

Then there was the question she never got to answer. As she rode along with her eyes closed she was glad for one thing, at least she didn't have to give Eldon her decision. Before the attack she might have said yes, but after seeing him have to kill someone to save her and the others, she wasn't as sure. Would he be the same gentle man he'd been? Does killing someone, even in the line of duty, change people? How could it not? In her mind she could see her blood covered hands. She would live with nightmares the rest of her life.

It was nearly dark when they reached New Denver, Grady sent for Brenda to stay with Cora for awhile. He and Mike helped put the supplies away, then went around telling everyone what had happened. They'd been a little relaxed in their vigilance, only making patrols around the perimeter a few times a day, but now the guards would be posted day and night at the entry points. Assignments were made by the ranking military person which happened to be Lois.

Brenda helped Cora gather what she needed and take a shower, then wash the blood out of her clothes. Cora hadn't realized how stained she was until she was watching the water run off her hair, arms and face. She could only vaguely remember hugging Eldon or throwing her body on top of his to protect him as bullets flew around them. The people firing at them must have had some pretty high powered automatic weapons. "Thank goodness for Mike and Grady," she thought.

When Cora finished dressing, she came out to where Brenda was waiting for her. "Now, you look like the girl I remember," Brenda said as she put her arm around her shoulder.

The two of them walked back to Cora's room. Eve was waiting on the bed, meowing to be loved. Cora rushed to her and picked her up. It was sweet to hold the warm, loving body and feel the comfort of the familiar. She couldn't help it. She began to sob and had to sit down on the bed.

Brenda came over and sat down next to her, "I know what happened. Grady told me. You and Eldon were very good friends, everyone knows that."

Through her tears, she looked at Brenda. "He asked me to marry him just yesterday." Looking away for a moment, "I said yes, but then, when we got to the base, they told him they were sending him to Georgia or some place, anyway he asked me if I'd go with him. I told him I'd tell him when we got back here." She shook her head. "I never got to tell him."

Brenda sighed, "He'll be back as soon as he's able, he loves you."

Cora nodded, "I love him too." She couldn't think anymore, she lay down with Eve and BB. Within a minute or so, she was sleep. Brenda tiptoed out of the room, switching off the lights as she went. Lois had taken one of the first watches so there would be plenty of time for Cora to rest.

When Cora did wake up, it was already after the time breakfast was normally served. She got up and saw that Lois had fed the cats. After dressing, she headed to the bathroom to wash her face to help her wake up. The mirror told her what she knew, her eyes were swollen and red from the crying and her face was puffy. It was a day to skip breakfast. She went without looking up at people as she passed through the hallway to her room. She couldn't help it, the tears continued to drip off her face. She looked toward the wall when she heard the door open.

Brenda came in with a tray that had some toast and coffee on it. "Hey, you have to try this. Remember bread?" She sat the food on the bed next to Cora. Eve immediately came to investigate, Brenda pushed her away. "This is for your momma." She rubbed Cora's shoulder, "You have to eat something, just a little. I know you're upset, but we still have to be ready for anything. So you need to keep your strength up. Eldon would want you to."

Cora nodded and turned to look at the things Brenda bought. It struck her so odd that it had been at least three months since they had real bread, real slices of bread. The best they'd had were some homemade tortillas. They had been good, but not bread." She reached down and took a piece of toast. It was buttered and bore a thin layer of jam. She bit off a small corner. It felt alien in her mouth, she had almost forgotten the rich, crunchiness of a simple thing like toast. Even better, was toast with grape jelly. She just sat with her eyes closed, just for a moment savoring the food in her mouth. Slowly she made her way through the piece of bread. When finished with the one she handed the other slice to Brenda. "That's all I want. Thank you. That was really good." She sipped on the coffee until the cup was half empty and then she handed that back to Brenda too. All she wanted to do was sleep, so laying back down, she did.

It was late in the day when Lois came in and sat down on the bed next to Cora. "Okay, it's dinner time. The cooks have promised a great meal. So come on, get up, brush your hair and let's go."

Cora looked up at her, "I'm so tired," she said quietly.

"Yeah, but you got to fight it. There are always hard things we have to deal with. You are a strong person. I know you're a survivor and resourceful. We all grieve for things, our families, our pets, the world we knew, lots of things. But we're alive and we have to keep going. It's all a matter of taking life one day at a time and doing the best you can with what you're facing." She sighed, "I know you're worried about the Lieutenant, but he's in good hands. He'd want you to be brave and taking good care of yourself."

"Yeah, I know he would." Cora ran her hand through her hair. She stood up and stretched. "Do I look awful?"

Lois laughed, "You're asking someone in combat clothes and military boots how you look? Ah, you look fine. You can tell you've been crying, but no one is going to fault that. You had a rough couple of days." She put her arm around Cora's shoulder, "Come on, we'll go together."

Cora felt wobbly so the support was welcome as they walked towards the dining hall. No one said anything, just nodded and let them pass. Word had gotten around that she and Eldon were planning on getting married. They made it to the dining hall and Lois sat her in the back. "I'll get you something to eat."

Cora started to protest, but instead just nodded. Her body felt like it weighed a ton and her head hurt. It was a good thing that she didn't try to carry a plate or anything else at the moment. Lois was back in a just a minute with a bowl of soup and a dinner roll on a plate with some steamed carrots. Cora sat looking at the carrots. It had been quite a while since anyone had fresh anything. They had been cut in to tidy little slices. It was all she could do to pick up a fork, however it was hard to resist the succulent dish. The vegetable simply seemed to melt in her mouth as she deliberately chewed each slice until the last bit of flavor was gone. She hadn't realized it, but there was also butter for the roll. This truly was a feast, she only wished she felt better to enjoy it.

"Pretty good stuff isn't it?" Lois said as she sat down next to Cora.

Cora nodded, "I had forgotten the taste of carrots. I've always loved them."

Brenda and Grady came with their tray of food and sat down across from Cora and Lois. "Good to see you here," Brenda said. "You feeling better?"

With a sigh, Cora nodded, "Some."

Grady waved to someone across the room. "We've gotten a new man to be in charge here. Arrived this morning," he nodded towards a tall, thin man who looked to be in his late forties. He looked at Lois, "Do you know him?"

She looked up and then went back to eating, "Yeah."

Grady looked at her, "So?"

"He's not an Air Force guy, just happened to be temporarily assigned to a project at the Arizona base at the time of event. He's Marine, Sergeant Major Virgil March. Tough, no nonsense kind of man. Not terribly friendly."

Cora glanced at the man. He was taking the position that Eldon had occupied. She suddenly felt a little guilty that she had not fought to go with Eldon. He would wake up alone in a strange place. She excused herself from the table and hurried back to her room where she could cry herself to sleep again. It was a long night.

When Cora woke up, she dressed and went to shower. It felt good to feel the water running down her body, it seemed to revive her at last. She redressed and went outside before going to breakfast. It was a cloudy day, but not too cool. Her light jacket was enough for a small walk to the edge of the tarmac. She could see the garden that was coming along nicely. There were well established plants growing and the greenhouse was still standing well. It was a very hopeful sign. She smiled as a prairie dog sprang up out of its burrow and looked at her from fifty feet away. Several others appeared quickly and ran to another hole in the ground. It made her laugh. It hurt to think she could still laugh despite what happened to Eldon and the attack. "Life truly does go on," she thought sadly to herself. "Lois was right, we all have hard things to deal with. Eldon is still alive and going to be all right. He's not like the millions who have disappeared."

Drawing a deep breath of the clean, unpolluted mountain air, she turned and went in for breakfast. It surprised her how hungry she was.

CHAPTER FIFTEEN

A few weeks went by without incident, for which Cora was grateful. There had been no more attacks on those on the foraging teams or on the main highway to Colorado Springs. The little garden had begun to give the cooks a few fresh vegetables like carrots and radishes so meals were enhanced, at least taste-wise. They were still on pretty severe rationing. The cooks were now just fixing a mid-day light meal and soup again for dinner. Usually the soup was either rabbit or an unknown something else, everyone guessed it might be ground squirrel or possum. No one really wanted to know.

There were several cleanup crews, doing building maintenance. Cora chose to be on one of those rather than going out on supply hunts. She was sweeping off the tarmac just outside the back door of the shelter when she looked up. There was an odd noise. It wasn't a bird or anything she could see in the sky. But the sound was certainly above her. There were several people working in the garden across the way. She saw them stand up and look skyward too. Then in one second, they heard what sounded like a jet plane flying very low. Then the sound was gone with no evidence of an aircraft of any kind. Two of the gardeners came running over to her.

"Did you hear that? Did you see it?" the man she knew as Barry asked.

Cora shook her head, "I heard it, but didn't see a thing. I didn't know anybody had any jets. Did you?"

He shook his head, "Let's go find Sergeant Marsh. He might find out about that." The two gardeners rushed inside to find the Sergeant Major. Cora stayed outside leaning on her broom as she scanned the sky and listened intently.

In a few minutes, Sergeant Marsh came and found her still watching the skies. "They said you heard a jet plane?"

She nodded, "Sounded like it was right here. I was expecting to see it land it was so close, at least, seemed to be."

He looked around, "That's odd, I radioed the base and they didn't see anything on their equipment, nor did they have anything scheduled to come in. The majority of what they have to fly is helicopters in this area, and not many of those."

Cora watched him as he looked back and forth, "I know three of us didn't just imagine that at the same time." He turned and looked at her. She hadn't been this close to him before to really see him in detail. One thing she noted were his eyes, they were a shade of brown with flecks of green. She had never seen a man with such beautiful eyes before, not that she'd seen a lot of men up close. She looked away, embarrassed that she might have been staring.

"No, of course not," he answered. "Just damn strange." He walked over to the garden area and looked at the sky from that angle, then shook his head and started to walk back to where Cora was. Before he reached her though, out of nowhere, the sound began to build again. He was looking around furiously trying to see what it was, but just as it was for the first three who heard the sound, there was nothing to see. Sergeant Marsh began to run as the noise reached a crescendo almost on top of them.

Cora took a deep breath as he came up beside her and put his arm in front of her in a protective move. "Did you see anything?"

"Just like before, there wasn't anything to see." Cora stepped back. "You know about the other things don't you?"

He looked at her, his brows furled, "What things?"

"We've had two other incidents that were unexplained. We were out on a foraging trip in one of the suburbs and we came upon a car that looked like it had been in an accident. It looked like there had been someone thrown out the front window. It was laying on it's side, oddly though there were no skid marks nor sign of any other vehicles, and even though it had been months since we all woke up here, there were fresh vegetables and fruit in the trunk, not a day old." She could see that he was listening intently. "Then there's the dog, Toby. He came flying through the air and knocked Jake, one of our teenage boys who was on a forage trip with me, into a basement. The boy got a concussion and some sore ribs from the encounter." Cora shuddered when she thought about the dog, Eldon had taken him as a pet, now Jay had him. "We weren't able to explain either of those events."

Sergeant Marsh nodded, obviously thinking about something. "We had an unexplained thing happen in Arizona just before I left to come up here. We found a car at the bottom of a canyon, looked like it had been caught in a flash flood. It was mired down with mud and debris.

The odd thing about that was the motor was still warm, like it had been running when it was lost. The other thing was that the river bed was dry and hadn't seen water in a very long time."

Cora felt a chill, "What is going on? Are we all dead and this is a nightmare?"

He reached out and put his hand on her shoulder, "You feel pretty alive to me. We can't all be dreaming the same dream." He shook his head and started to go in, but stopped and motioned for her to follow him. "Let's go have a cup of coffee and talk to folks. We'll see if others have some stories to tell."

The Sergeant went to find Grady, who sent word around that there would be a meeting that evening after dinner to let everyone hear what had happened.

Cora went on into the dining hall. She welcomed the cup of coffee. It seemed to steady her nerves, which seemed to be on edge at the drop of a pin anymore. In a few minutes, the Sergeant Major came in to the room, got a cup of coffee, then joined her.

"Feeling better? You looked a little pale when we were outside." He looked concerned.

"I don't know if it was shock or surprise I felt, but it was unsettling. To hear something so familiar yet not being able to see it."

He nodded, "Rattled my cage for sure, I thought the thing was going to land right on top of us. I swear I could feel the air being displaced around the plane."

Both of them shrugged almost at the same time. What can you say about what you can't explain? They sat quietly until the last of their coffee was gone. The Sergeant Major got up and smiled, "Glad you're better. I will probably call on you tonight to tell what you experienced. Will that be all right with you?"

Cora nodded. He turned sharply and walked away. It was time for her to get back to her cleaning detail. She would do her sweeping to keep the dust from being tracked inside, all the while would also be listening and watching, just in case something really did land. A strange thought crossed her mind, if something did land, would it be one of their planes or would it be an alien craft? Could this all have been some attack from outer space. She'd seen enough science fiction movies to know others had thought that might happen someday.

Lois came out to stand guard at the back door. She waved at Cora who was on the other side of the old runway by the garden area. She motioned for her to come back to where she was.

Cora nodded and after looking both ways, she walked across the way to Lois. It struck her that she'd not looked out for traffic in a long time, why did she now? It sent a chill up her spine, what they had heard was so real. She really thought something was landing.

"I heard what went on out here," Lois said. "That was just plain scary. The Sergeant said it was so close, whatever it was, that he felt the turbulence like you would if you were too close to a plane taking off on the runway." She looked up and down the area, they scanned the sky. "And you didn't see anything at all?"

"Nothing," Cora said shaking her head. "It was eerie."

The two women stood for a few minutes and silently listened, but heard nothing except the wind blowing through the grasses that had grown up around and in the pavement.

One of the men came out to stand guard over the garden, which had been raided regularly by the neighborhood varmints, much to the peril of some of them who wound up in the daily soup. Cora tried not to think of Disney characters when she was having her lunch. Cora sighed, then waved to Lois. "I think I've swept enough for today out here. See you later."

Lois nodded and kept watching the skies and listening. Cora saw her turn quickly at every new sound. This latest mystery had everyone wondering what was next?

That night at dinner the discussion over the vegetable soup was all about the events that morning. Cora got tired of saying, "Yes, it's true. We heard a plane, but saw nothing." She finished her dinner in less time than most just to not have to talk about it anymore. She put her jacket back on and went for a walk around the front of the site. The huge area where all the cars used to park seemed vast. She tried to imagine just how many vehicles of every kind would have been there on a busy weekday.

Cora saw the door guards and waved to them. They returned the wave after they recognized her. On the other side of the several acres of pavement, she saw Mike and Jay walking Toby in the fields just beyond the parking space. It was a cool evening, but the wind wasn't blowing so it was not too bad. She walked across the open area to join her friends. Just as she was within fifteen or so feet, she heard a familiar sound. She saw that Jay and Mike heard it too and were looking around. There it was again, the unmistakable sound of a plane, probably some sort of jet, coming their way.

130

Mike and Jay hurried to her side, "Oh God," Mike said breathlessly. "What is happening?"

Toby was dancing around, barking. Cora looked at him and then touched Mike's arm, nodding towards the dog. Toby was intently watching something as the noise came over them and then passed into the distance. The dog watched every moment. "Did he see something?"

Mike shook his head, "I think his hearing is so much better than ours, probably like radar."

Cora wasn't convinced the dog had just heard the sound; he looked like he'd seen something they couldn't, but she'd have to accept that now several people and Toby had witnessed the phenomenon. It wasn't just a fluke, it was real. But what did it mean? Why was it happening? They stood scanning the sky for a few minutes, then Toby ran off into the field.

Jay went running after him, "Darn dog, get back here! Toby!" he called after the dog.

Mike laughed, "I bet he doesn't catch him."

Cora watched as Mike started walking in the direction the dog was leading Jay. He stopped when he saw Jay stop and bend down. Toby was standing over something. Then Mike broke into a run. Cora was curious so she started jogging over to see what was going on.

Jay had been holding something, transferring it from one hand to the other quickly. "What is that?" Cora asked.

Mike was now holding the item. "I think it's something off a plane, might be a piece of a wing flap."

Cora shrugged, "Well, this was an airport."

Jay sighed. "Yeah, but this piece was still hot when I picked it up." He looked around. "And it was above ground, not under it. Everything still here was underground or under pavement remember?"

Cora nodded. "Yeah." She looked up. "More mystery."

The three of them walked back towards the main door of the shelter. The guards were visibly shaken too. They were talking rapidly to several others who were outside looking at the skies, hoping to see what no one had seen yet, the source of the sound. Cora was more convinced than ever that Toby had actually seen something, but she would keep that to herself. She was tired of being questioned. All she could hope for was that this would just go away, like questions about the dog and the car had, at least until something new came along. She hoped that whatever was to come, she wouldn't be among the only witnesses.

Enough people had heard what she had witnessed, that at breakfast the next morning no one bothered her. Others were more than willing to share their experiences so Cora was left in relative peace. She finished her scant meal and cup of tea then went on to her cleaning duties.

About an hour later, Lois came looking for her. She was sitting on a bench in the work room rolling newspapers into logs to soak. They had found a large supply of old editions on a foraging run. They were to be used for the wood stove once the logs were dried out. "Hey girl," Lois said as she approached Cora. "I got some news."

"Oh, what news?"

Lois sat down next to her, "Got an update on Eldon. Thought you'd want to know. It's some good news and some bad news."

Cora put down the work and looked at Lois. "What's the good news?"

"He's doing really well. Healing, able to get up and move around. He's able to eat and his speech is coming back. I guess the part of his brain that got injured really messed him up for a while. It affected him almost like a stroke," Lois said.

"What's the bad news?"

Lois sighed, "He has amnesia, or something like that. He doesn't remember anything before waking up in the hospital. He didn't initially know his name. He's having to learn to do a lot of things like it's the first time. He'll going to be in rehab a long time. They're not sure at this point if he'll ever get everything back."

Cora sat in shock. "He doesn't remember me," she said absently. "Oh poor Eldon. I should have gone with him. Seeing a familiar face when he woke up could have helped him."

Lois put her arm around Cora's shoulders, "We don't know that. He didn't remember himself, hard to think he would have recognized anyone else." She sat a moment, "Best thing for you I think is just to try and put this behind you. Someday you may see him again, but the chances are slim in a time like this. They may take him to New York. They've got a bigger clinic set up there that can deal with cases like his. He's probably never coming back this way." Lois got up and left Cora alone.

Cora wept into the pile of newspapers. Moving on seemed an impossible task. How do you find something to hold on to when something like this happens? She walked outside and stood on the tarmac. She looked down at the cracked but still visible lines on the pavement.

It was an odd place she now found herself in. Cora remembered how alone she felt standing in the middle of that empty highway in Nebraska. Somehow, this time in her life was even lonelier.

CHAPTER SIXTEEN

The spring passed quickly into a hot summer. The water truck had to make its run to the base almost every day to keep New Denver supplied. Lois and Cora had been going with Jay and Mike to the outlying communities to forage. They were all glad nothing unusual or unexplainable had happened in the last few of months.Things seemed to be settling into a routine as the entire community went about preparing for the winter to come. There was a sense of urgency as they worked from daylight to dusk.

It was just before mid-day when the truck rolled into what had been Golden, a community northwest of Denver. It was hilly where they began their search so it took a little longer to go from foundation to foundation. They'd only gone a couple of blocks when they came to a basement that had a large set of metal doors with a padlock. The forbidding looking doors were set back under an overhang of rock. There were no stairs so Jay brought the ladder from the truck. He had a pry bar to work on the lock. Mike climbed down to help him. It took a few minutes, but they managed to get the chain off and the doors open.

When the two men looked inside with their flashlights they almost fell over backwards. Mike looked grim as he turned to call up to the women. "Lois, make sure you keep an eye out. We could be in trouble here." The men put the lock back on the door and tried make it look as it did before they pried it open. Then they came up quickly, looking around as they stood on the ground. "That obviously was a stash for some of those raiders. I never saw so many guns. Looked like they could outfit an army."

Jay looked around, "Let's get out of here. I doubt if we'll find anything but trouble in this town. If there's that many raiders hanging around here, we probably should report this place as off limits, at least until we hear from the military people. Maybe they want to come in and get those weapons."

The four of them headed for the truck as fast as they could, all the while, keeping a vigilant watch around them. There weren't many hiding places with no buildings, trees or shrubs. Nevertheless, they didn't want to take a chance. Besides, it was such a hot day that any little extra effort was exhausting. They all agreed to head back to New Denver and report what they'd found.

On the way back, they were close to a creek so they stopped long enough to take turns spending a quick few minutes in the cool water. The women went first while the men stood guard, then while the women stood by the truck to dry off, the men got their turn. After that refreshing dip, everyone felt better. Everyone felt better as they headed home.

Lois and Mike told Sergeant Marsh about their find. He called the base on the shortwave and the next morning, a troop of soldiers came to get Lois.

She lead them to the cache of weapons. They had initially seen the guns, but beyond that they found a many months worth of canned goods and other supplies. It looked like no one had come into the vault since the event occurred, which was a relief to everyone. Probably whoever had put the stuff in there was among the missing and no one else knew about it. It was providential that Lois and her team found it first.

Half of the weapons were taken back to the base, but the others were left for the people of New Denver who wanted to be armed. Rumors of the raiders massing to do harm were always swirling about. Ten more soldiers were stationed with them, which lent some credibility to the rumors. They now had a platoon of about twenty or more soldiers guarding the community.

As Cora sat sipping her tea one evening after dinner, Brenda came over to sit with her.

"Hi, my friend," she said as she leaned forward.

Cora could see she was excited about something. "What's up?"

Brenda smiled and motioned for her to lean forward so they could talk quietly. "I wanted you to be the first to know. Grady and I are going to have a baby. That will be a first for New Denver!" She smiled, "I know I'm a little older, but still, at thirty-three everything works and I'm healthy."

It surprised her that Brenda was younger than Cora had originally thought, even though she was still a couple of years older than her. Cora had never expected anyone to be having babies during this time in the world. It was hard to imagine for Brenda or for that matter, herself. Was it the right thing to do? Brenda looked so pleased. She tried to be happy for her friend. "That's such wonderful news. When will the baby be born?"

Brenda sighed, "About Thanksgiving is my guess. We're going to move back to the base where there's a doctor and a regular infirmary soon. I'm a little apprehensive about leaving everyone here. With luck we'll come back in the spring and be able to help out." She looked around and saw someone else she knew. "I'll see you later. I've got a couple of other people I want to tell, but I wanted you to know first." She hugged Cora and moved on to a table across the room.

Cora heard the happy chatter and squeals of delight from the other table. She smiled and walked out into the hallway. It wasn't too late yet so she went outside to walk a little. Somewhere off in the distance she heard a coyote; this time another off in the distance answered its plaintive call. "At least it knows it's not alone", she smiled sadly.

It wasn't quite dusk yet, but the sky on the eastern horizon was growing dark. Heavy, ominous clouds were moving quickly towards the northeast. "Wow, someone's going to get rain," Cora said to herself. "Glad it looks like it's maybe twenty or thirty miles from here." Here and there in the far off scene, there were small flashes of light, undeniably a serious thunderstorm was brewing. She watched the storm intently, so much so that she didn't notice Sergeant Marsh come out and stand near her, watching the same thing.

"Looks like a bad one," he said quietly.

Cora jumped a little, "Oh, sorry. Didn't know you were there."

"Didn't mean to scare you."

Cora shrugged, "Did you hear that Brenda and Grady are going to have a baby?"

"Yeah," he looked away.

Cora saw his reaction, "Do you have kids Sergeant?"

With a surprised look on his face at her question, he nodded. "You?"

"No, I'm not married," Cora swallowed hard, "I wasn't before and most likely won't be now."

"I've been divorced for almost seven years. My boy was fourteen, and my Julie was twelve when the wife left me, didn't want to be "married to the service" like I was. My kids were with their mother in Salt Lake City. The first three years I got them for the entire summers. But as they got to be older teenagers, the kids got so involved with their own lives that I only got to take them to California for a week after school got out. Now Fred is in his second year of college and Julie is about to start college too."

136

Cora could see the pain on her companion's face. What could she say that would make any difference? She put her hand on his shoulder, trying to think of something to comfort him. Before she could open her mouth, a distant clap of thunder caused them both to look at the horizon. "Oh my, would you look at that!"

Miles away in a really dark area of the sky, the unmistakable shape of a huge tornado was tearing across the open plain. It was so big; it looked closer than the original storm she had been watching just minutes ago. As it undulated in an almost sensual way, Cora began to observe bits and pieces of something? "What is that? In the funnel, do you see debris?"

"Yeah, I do." The sergeant was holding his hands up, shielding his eyes to see better. "As soon as it blows itself out, I'm going to get a team and so see what it left behind. Might have to be tomorrow though, it's getting late. It may have blown across one of those little oasis places like you found on your way here."

Cora nodded, "Yes, it could have. I hope you find a valley with life in it. We could use a place with game in it."

The sergeant didn't say anything, he just turned and hurried into the building. Cora stayed outside and watched the funnel cloud dissipate and finally retreat back into the clouds it came from. The storm had moved on to the edge of what she could see as the day transitioned into night. Finally a breeze started to cool the air around her and she decided it was time to go in.

The next morning Sergeant Marsh left New Denver with several soldiers in one of the trucks to investigate the twister they'd seen the night before. They were gone most of the day. Cora kept watching for their return. Finally, just before dinner, she saw the truck pull into the parking lot by the maintenance doors. She walked out to the tarmac to see what they'd found. It was surprising to see the back of the truck filled with wood and various kinds of debris.

Several men from inside the building came out and were looking through the things that had been brought back. Grady was among them, "What is all this?"

Sergeant Marsh walked to the back of the rig, "This is from the path of the tornado we saw last night," he nodded towards Cora. "We saw stuff being whirled around in the funnel even from where we were standing. It had to have been forty miles from here." He pointed in the direction they had been looking. "Darn thing must have traveled twenty or more miles on the

137

ground before dissipating. We only had time to go into less than few hundred feet of the debris. There is a trail of this kind of stuff the whole way." He shook his head. "The land was just like it is in Denver, nothing above the ground. Nothing! Which begs the question, where did all this come from? It looks like the twister was at least a five, tore through a neighborhood and some stores, just like you'd see in Oklahoma or Kansas. But there were no neighborhoods or businesses anywhere."

Grady walked over and picked up a board and then reached into the pile and pulled out a garden hose. Water ran out of the hose and dripped on his shoes. "This was being used just before it got sucked up by the storm." He shook his head, "What is going on?"

"Well, that's not all we found," Sergeant Marsh motioned to one of the men still in the truck. The man got out and walked to the back of the truck where everyone was standing. He was carrying a small bundle. The Sergeant took the bundle from him and unwrapped it. There was a round of gasps as a small baby was revealed. It was moving and started to cry.

Edna Spears was among those outside. Without hesitation, she went to the Sergeant and offered open arms for the baby. She held it tenderly to her chest and rubbed its back. "Is it hurt, did you look it over? This baby doesn't look more than three months old."

"Yes, she is very young and no, she's not hurt. She looks like she made it through just fine. She was still in a very sturdy, carved bassinet. We brought that along for her." He motioned to the other soldier who went to fetch the bed at the front of the pile of debris. "Could you look after her until we can find a permanent solution for her?"

Mrs. Spears nodded and moved the child quickly inside. The soldier with the crib followed her in. The crowd silently watched the woman with the baby until they were out of sight, then the murmuring started.

Grady put his hand up. "Okay, I know this raises more questions. How could all this stuff appear out of nowhere?" He looked at the Sergeant. "I guess we should go back out there and sift through it for more answers and since we found one survivor, there might be more."

"I agree. We should take three trucks out tomorrow. At least ten or more men too. Some things may be usable even if we don't find another survivor. Let's plan on leaving at first light so we have the day to look."

Grady nodded and turned to the men, "We'll talk this over at dinner." He turned and walked back inside. Cora stood and watched as the remaining men stacked the lumber and other things they'd found just outside the shop doors. She could see among the tangled mess of lumber and unidentifiable things were personal things; photos and even a tennis shoe. She walked over and picked up one of the photos. It was of a teenage boy on a four-wheeler. She wondered if it had been a gift or a special occasion for him. A tear rolled down her cheek, she would never know him yet he was someone's child. Was he lost to the wind or to the event? It hurt to even think about.

The next morning Lois was going out on one of the trucks so she invited Cora to join her. Cora saw several other civilians, including Grady, were already in their assigned places to go, so she felt better about accompanying the others. It felt like a long ride in the lumbering old truck. This one was an old "deuce and a half" WWII vehicle that must have been in storage. It still had its canvas cover on the back and benches around the sides. Cora could only imagine the men who'd had to sit in the thing. It was hard to sit for very long on the rock hard seats. It was a mercy when the truck finally came to a stop.

Once on the ground everyone stood out in front of the truck and looked around at the mess. Sergeant Marsh had a megaphone, and stepped out in front of the trucks. "Let's divide up into two groups. Grady you take half the team and go to the left. The rest of you come with me to the right. If you find something, make a note of where, mark it somehow, and in an hour we'll come back here and talk about our findings. Make notes on what you see so we can discuss it later. Clear Grady?" Grady nodded and four soldiers, along with two civilians headed off.

Lois, three other soldiers and Cora went with the Sergeant. It didn't take long to see the enormity of their task. To find anything of use in the twisted piles would be a challenge, let alone looking for someone else alive in the violent scene. Cora had been given gloves and a paperboy type bag to pick up small items that might be useful. It was unquestionable that this was dangerous work. Climbing over nail ridden lumber, looking under debris where snakes could be lurking; any number of things could be hazardous to one's health.

Morbid as it was to be picking through the remains of homes and lives, it was, nevertheless, intriguing. She found bars of sweet smelling soap, then a half empty tube of tooth paste, a smashed jar of peanut butter that was unusable, a golf club, an unopened deck of cards. Then, in the middle of everything sitting seemingly untouched was an old piano. She marked that location with a flag from her bag. That would be worth having. By the time she'd gone the equivalent of half a block, her bag was full of things to take back.

The hour passed quickly and they all returned to the truck area. Grady was already there when Cora's group reached the place. He motioned for everyone to gather round. "So what did you guys find?"

Lois stepped up to speak for their team. "We did pretty well. We found a tree that was uprooted. It will probably provide fuel for the wood stove for half the winter. With the lumber we found and other things, we'll probably be able to get through the winter pretty comfortably." She looked at Cora and smiled, "Cora found a piano. That will be good for morale on cold winter nights." She looked at Grady, "What did you see?"

He sighed, "We found most of a house. It was in pieces, but the roof was over on the driveway, some of the walls were gone and most of the interior spread far and wide, but the people, an older man and woman must have stayed in a basement bathroom, in the tub. Unfortunately, that the tub ended up with most of their kitchen on top of it. They didn't make it. We're going to form a burial party this afternoon." He swallowed hard, "It is hard to get our minds around, but this was probably bare ground just like it is on either side of this mass of destruction, until this twister came through. Now the debris looks like it's from what was here before the event. This tornado made it seem like nothing had changed. This looks like normal damage a storm like this would leave in any town in tornado alley." He shook his head, "The old couple had a thermos of coffee with them, it was still hot." He lifted his hands to the top of his head, "I wish someone could explain what is going on here."

Sergeant Marsh stepped up and put his hand on Grady's shoulder. "We all wish for that, but we have to focus on our job today. Let's have a bite to eat then let's go back to where we left off and search for more. I can see this will take several days. We'll do another hour, load up the trucks with what we've found so far and then we'll come back tomorrow and the next day if need be. Maybe we'll find some answers in our search.

Cora dreaded the idea that she might find a body as they resumed their picking through the remains of peoples homes and lives. She found hints of those who had just hours before called this mangled scrap heap home. It was hard to fathom what had happened, not the tornado itself but the whole thing, everything familiar gone, then these occurrences out of the blue, hinting that there was something else going on. But what?

She was very glad when she heard the truck horn signaling it was time to return with whatever they found and go back to New Denver. She needed a bath and some time to think about all she'd seen.

There was a lot to talk about and plenty for everyone to express an opinion on. People had such wild imaginations about what had actually happened to them. Some often discussed theories ran from "they were actually dead and this was one place or the other" to they'd been "abducted by aliens."

Cora listened but couldn't believe any of them. Nothing made sense and she felt it just didn't seem to make a difference what had happened. She had come to realize, at least in her mind, this was a test of will and resourcefulness. Could they stay alive in a world that was not full of modern conveniences? This time last year she'd had a car, a large screen TV, a cell phone, a microwave oven, a job, any food she wanted, money and places to spend it. Now she had nothing, just things she'd found, a family of strangers, two cats, a meager meal or two a day, and a bed in the basement of what used to be an airport. To her, the future was something to endure not look forward to, and the past was just gone and best not thought about too much.

Cora decided she wouldn't go out the next day. She didn't want take the chance of being the one to find more bodies. She retreated to her bedroom and the only comfort that was hers alone, sharing her bed with her two cats, Eve and BB.

CHAPTER SEVENTEEN

The trucks were gone most of the day. Cora had busied herself with her normal duties of keeping the areas outside the doors clear of weeds and dirt that were blown in by the constant winds that stirred the air across the open land. She was about done for the day when she saw the three rigs coming back. They pulled in not too far from where she was standing, leaning on her broom, to watch what they had brought back.

It was a relief to see that there were no bodies laying in the back of any truck. Instead they had brought back a full load of logs from downed trees to make wood for the fires and one truckload of boxes. From where she stood, she couldn't see what the other vehicle had in it so she walked up to the area where they were unloading. She saw Grady and two other men rush big boxes of things inside. Lois was in the back of the last truck. "Hey, Lois, what did you find?"

She smiled when she saw Cora, "Must have been a convenience store out in a neighborhood. Part of the store was still standing. We found all kinds of food. We salvaged what we could so that will be real helpful this winter."

That seemed like very good news at least for them. Cora couldn't help but wonder who owned that market. Where were they? She walked inside and put her broom away. Down the hall, Grady and the people in charge of the food supplies were storing the food that had been brought in. Dinner wasn't due for an hour so Cora walked on by the dining room and went to feed the cats. They had been going outside with her in the mornings. The mice they caught was a good deal all around, they keep the building and surrounding grounds clear of things that would eat their crops and infest their living quarters. The side benefit was it supplemented the cat's diet that was often as slim pickings as their owner's.

When Lois came in she brought a fair sized box. "This is for you," she said as she handed the box to Cora, "or rather for the kids."

Cora looked and saw two or three bags and several cans of cat food. "Oh the cats will be happy tonight!"

Lois smiled. "I gave several cans and a bag to Brenda for Sophie, as well as about the same to Jake for Gray. Now everyone has something to eat. Oh and, by the way, we did find one live thing today. We found a big male cat. Sweet boy, I think he's what they call a Maine Coon. He looks to be young. I took him to the vet we have. She said she'd keep him."

"Are you going out again tomorrow?"

Lois nodded, "Yeah, we've only scratched the surface of what's out there. We probably will need more than a month to sift through everything. We're just trying not to think too hard about how that all happened. It's the biggest mystery yet. Virgil sent word to the base and I think they're going to be joining us to look through the stuff."

Cora hadn't thought about the base in a long time, but suddenly the moment she met Eldon flooded back into her mind. She felt a pang of longing for what might have been. Nothing seemed right anymore. It was easy to feel like giving up, but that wasn't an option. She had always considered herself a fighter and a survivor.

She looked at Lois as her room mate changed from her military clothes into a teeshirt and jeans. Her Beretta M9 pistol, as Lois identified it, was never out of reach and her M4 Carbine was not far away. Cora imagined until this event, Lois probably never thought of using those weapons while in the States. Now she carried them all the time and needed them from time to time. She was a fighter for real.

"I have a feeling we're going to have a different kind of dinner tonight," Lois said with a smile. "We found some interesting stuff." She motioned for Cora to follow her. "It's time to see what the cooks have for us."

Cora was intrigued by the idea of something besides their normal watery soups. She didn't hesitate. The cats were fed quickly, each getting a half can of cat food and then Cora followed Lois to the dining hall.

Lois was right, it was a different meal. They were having hot dogs! It had been more than a year since anyone saw this once all American classic. As the line began to cue up one of the cooks explained that a case of the dogs had been found. Since they were partially thawed, they needed to be eaten right away, so everyone was getting one bun with two hot dogs. A cheer went up from the crowd. There would be no soup that night, but no one minded that. There were a few bags of potato chips to make it almost a meal. Several bags of broken up cookies were laid out so people could take a handful.

Cora got her plate and was thrilled to see two beat up looking squeeze bottles of mustard on the table. As she took her food to a table, she couldn't believe how her mouth was watering at the sight of this rare treat. It struck her funny because, in normal times, she didn't even like hot dogs, but now she could hardly wait to sink her teeth into one of them.

Lois joined her within a minute. "Told you this was going to be good!"

Cora tore her bun in half long wise and held a hot dog on the first half. It wanted to slip around because of the mustard, but, by holding it with her fingers wrapped around the whole thing, she was able to get into her mouth without losing it. It didn't matter if she had mustard all over her, it was worth it. She ate the first hot dog in a hurry, but was able to control herself better with the other half, savoring each mouthful. When it was gone, Cora sat back and took her time with her handful of chips. Once the chips were done, it was time for her pieces of cookies. She'd gotten two pretty sizable pieces of what seemed to be chocolate chip and a few smaller pieces of what might have been an Oreo. Whatever they had been, they were wonderful.

Lois wiped her mouth with the back of her arm, "I can't remember anything tasting that good in so long."

Cora agreed. "That was amazing. It has been so easy to forget what things tasted like. Who would of thought I would be grateful for a hot dog!" With a laugh, "It took all this for me to realize that they taste better than I remembered."

They were just sitting there, lingering over their cups of tea when, all of a sudden, a huge yellow and white cat jumped up in Lois's lap. "Oh, hello fella," she said as she began to pet the newcomer. "This guy rode back in the truck with me. I guess we sort of bonded over being rescued and fed."

Marla, the vet, came in. "There you are," she walked over to Lois. "I'm sorry. I forgot and left the door open. He's a wandering boy I'm afraid." She sat down next to Lois. "He seems to like you more than me."

"Must know you're a vet," Lois answered.

Cora smiled, "Marla, I want to thank you again for spaying Eve and neutering BB. I think they've been a lot more willing to stay close to home since that. Did you get to Gray and Sophie?"

"I was able to get Gray, but Sophie has been in heat for the last few days and I'm afraid the first thing this cat did was go find her." Marla shrugged. "I suggested to Brenda that we do both cats ASAP, but Brenda said it might be a good thing to have at least one more litter of kittens for the good of the shelter. There are plenty of mice and things to control." She shook her head, "Maybe it's because she's pregnant herself. I am reluctant about another batch of cats, but it's her choice. As for this big dude," she smiled. "I plan to change his mind in the morning."

"What are you going to call him?" Lois asked.

"I'm thinking he is a Maine Coon, probably purebred. So I was thinking of calling him Leo because he was found in July." She looked at the cat, "He kind of reminds me of a lion anyway. I think he weighs about eighteen pounds." She reached for the cat and he jumped down and ran for the door. "I'll get him, he'll be all right."

Lois laughed as Marla ran out after the cat. "He's going to be a handful. But he's a nice guy, just young and feisty."

Cora finished her tea and policed up her area. "I'm going to see if Brenda is up for another knitting lesson. She's trying to teach me how, which is no easy matter. Just can't seem to get my fingers to do what I see."

"I was never good at that kind of stuff," Lois said as she too prepared to leave the dining area. "I'm going to clean out the the truck beds for tomorrow's run. See you later."

The next morning, Cora got up and was delighted to find that there were corndog pancakes for breakfast. The leftover hotdogs had been cut into thin rounds and put into a batter with cornmeal in it. It was a strange thing for breakfast, but that didn't keep it from being one of the best things they'd had. Everyone got at least two good sized pancakes, which was one of the most ample meals they'd had in a long time. It was truly a treat!

As she finished her breakfast Cora could see the cooks putting on the big kettles of soup for their next meals. It was a little disheartening to think things were going back to their new normal. But it had been wonderful to have a break, however short, from that routine.

Once she got outside, she saw that the trucks were already gone. Off in the distance, she could see a caravan of trucks headed towards the wreckage area. It was her guess that the extra vehicles must have been from the base. It was a partially cloudy day so it probably wouldn't be as hot as the last couple had been so that would be good for those having to dig through the rubble. Secretly, she hoped they'd find more hotdogs, or at least some more bread products. With a sigh she began her job of sweeping dirt away to keep it from being tracked indoors.

After she'd had her bowl of soup for lunch, Cora returned to work. She noticed that it was cloudier than it had been that morning. The air felt heavy and threatening. The dust was being blown toward the west this time. The wind continued to pick up and small things were flying about. A few yards from the tarmac, a dust devil played across the land in an undulating dance. In the distance, it had become quite dark, obscuring the horizon. All of a sudden there were flashes of light in those dark clouds.

Cora gasped as she recognized the same shape she'd seen just a few days before, in a slightly different place, nevertheless close to where the first storm had been. She was concerned for Lois and the others out there. She called to several people who were working on making firewood out of the logs that had been brought in. When she got their attention, she pointed to the storm. Everyone dropped what they were doing and watched with her. It was terrifying to see the funnel cloud become very visible. Just like before they could see things imbedded in it.

This time, however, the tornado had a different destination. Ever so slowly, it began to twist its way to the northwest. It was plain to see that, if it kept on its present course, it would come very near to them. One of the men ran into the shelter to alert everyone else about the danger that might come their way. Within moments, nearly all the eighty or so residents of New Denver were on the tarmac watching the storm.

It began to rain lightly as the clouds ahead of the tornado began to spread across their piece of the sky. It was no more than ten miles away. Hasty plans were being discussed about the safest place in the shelter for everyone, what needed to be brought in, all kinds of other details. There was a feeling of panic and danger as everyone tried to think of the right things to do.

Then as quickly as it had developed, the storm seemed to shift more to the north and dissipate. Within a few more minutes, the rain had stopped, the sun came out and the funnel cloud was just a swirling mass of fluff in the sky.

Cora breathed a sigh of relief, then thought of Lois and Grady. Had they been caught in the tornado? She scanned the horizon and was pleased to see the caravan from the morning heading back towards the shelter.

Lois saw Cora waiting and headed for her the minute her truck pulled to a stop and backed in to unload. "That was a close one!"

"We saw it from here. How far away from that tornado were you?" Cora asked.

"We couldn't have been more than five miles. Some of the debris whirling around was from the stuff at the western edge of what we were sorting through. We saw it turn more this way so we started back right away in case it hit you here. We were all relieved when we saw it finally play itself out."

Cora nodded, "We were glad too. Did you find anything interesting today?"

Lois shrugged, "A few things. We'll have a lot of sorting to do, there's a lot of trash of course, but some useable things. Found lots of clothing for you to sort through. One odd thing, that new tornado didn't leave any wreckage behind like that other one. I still can't quite figure out how all that rubble was left behind with that one in a place where nothing existed before." She fished around in her pants pocket for something, "I did find something for you though."

She laughed and handed Cora a key on a keyring. "You don't have the car, but at least if you ever find the one that goes to that you'll be happy."

Cora looked at the souvenir that Lois had found. She shrugged, "I don't know what this is."

Lois sighed, "I think that's as close as either of us will ever get to owning a Ferrari." She shook her head and walked off to help with the unloading of the trucks.

Cora stood and looked at the key. Somewhere, someone was missing their very expensive car! She slipped the trinket into her pocket and went to help with the new things that had been found. Lois was right, it looked like they'd have to dig through a lot of trash to find anything of value to the shelter. But they all knew this winter would probably be even harder than the last had been.

There was a lot of clothing, it was true, but most of them had been in mud and rain. There was more washing and mending than could be done in a week! It would be a big project for several of them, but again, everything they could gain helped.

The trucks were going back out the next day. Sergeant Marsh reported that they still had several miles of remains to pick through. It was slow going because of the devastation they were getting into. The tornado must have intensified as it got nearer it's end. He also reported one more interesting observation. The twister of today had picked up some of the stuff they'd gone by earlier, but when it left their area, the twister didn't drop the material. When the storm disappeared, so did the items it had picked up. Another mystery to wonder about.

One of the other soldiers who'd been in on the searches came into the maintenance bay where Cora was sorting. He was carrying an unconscious dog. "He's breathing okay, I think he's just weak from dehydration. I'm taking him to the vet." Cora watched him walk on by. She'd seen that kind of dog before, it looked like a border collie.

Another survivor, Cora thought to herself. Would they find others? How can things like this be still happening after a year? That dog looked well fed and it had a collar on it. It was someone's pet, how did it wind up out there alone a mile from Leo, the cat they found on another trip out to the site?

It made her head hurt to try to sort through the myriad of possible, but not probable, answers to her questions. She would wait until someone came up with a plausible theory. It was easier just to forget it all and throw herself into to the work at hand. She'd have another winter to listen to everyone's ideas on the predicament they and their world was in.

It was an odd moment. It sounded like someone was stomping on the lids of the garbage cans outside or fireworks at a distance? Cora tried to identify the sound. She stood still and listened, the sound continued as she turned to hear better. Then the window shattered and she realized it was gunfire. Outside, she heard shouting and the sounds of orders being given, more gunfire. Cora crouched down and made her way into the area where the large walk-in freezer provided some cover. There were two other women working in the sorting area that followed her lead and joined her. It was a harrowing few minutes.

Finally, there was silence. Then two more shots, and then quiet voices sounding urgent, but controlled. The back door to the room opened. Cora pushed the other two back as far as they could go as not to be seen. There was no way of telling who would be coming through the doorway. She breathed a sigh of relief and cautiously stood up when she saw it was Sergeant Marsh.

"Are you all right in here," he asked when he saw her.

Looking at the other two with her quickly she answered, "Yeah, is everyone out there?"

"We got two wounded. They're being transported back to the base. Go get Brenda. She'll want to go with the truck. Grady will be fine, but he did get shot in the crossfire. Just a leg wound." One of the others nodded and headed for the hall, the other worker in the room left too.

"What about Lois? Sergeant Wilkerson?" Cora was afraid to hear the answer.

He nodded, "She's fine. Best shot we have here I think too. She nailed two of the raiders and wounded another. They're taking the wounded one back to the base too. I think they were trying to steal the trucks. They were just driving old cars. I counted six men. Some of them were pretty young. But when they're carrying something like an AK-47 their age doesn't matter." He shook his head. "We'll know more when we question the one of them that Lois hit. The others got away so we may have more trouble, although I think they were surprised that there were as many soldiers here as they found. I'm requesting the base send even more troops." He walked on into the hallway.

Brenda hastily packed a bag, brought Sophie to stay with Eve and BB, then left with the truck to go back to the main base. It was a very tense time. At dinner, Sergeant Marsh explained the situation to everyone. By lights out that night, twenty more armed military personnel arrived with some heavier equipment in case there was an even more serious attack.

Armored cars now sat at all the entrances to the shelter. The guards were outfitted with night vision gear and they were armed to the teeth. That, however, didn't make anyone feel safer. It just brought home the fact that things were getting pretty hard for everyone. This coming fall and winter would be a challenge like none other.

CHAPTER EIGHTEEN

Several weeks passed without any thing new happening, much to the relief of everyone in New Denver. Word had came from the base that Grady was doing fine. He and Brenda would continue staying at the main base, at least until their baby was born.

The man that Lois had only wounded, was also doing fine. He had recovered and had come back to New Denver. His name was Clay and it turned out he was just fourteen years old. He claimed he had been alone and found by the group of armed men and forced to join them to survive. He was claiming sanctuary with the shelter.

Sergeant Marsh had asked if Jake would keep an eye on the boy in case his story wasn't true. He had said might it be easier for him being just a couple of years older than the new kid. Jake seemed a little hesitant, but had agreed.

A month passed easily and without much change. Clay, had been with them now for over a week. Cora had seen him at dinner, but didn't know him yet. He really did look young for his age. He seemed nervous.

Cora had felt sorry that Jake seemed to be enlisting in the service. In a way now, he was a spy. It was hard not to feel that something was being lost. Even she felt like a prisoner at times and when she looked at Lois, it was almost scary. There were fully loaded weapons were just a few feet away and someone always a little on edge, at the ready in case. Lois had the skills and knew what to do if she needed to "grab and go."

It took a little bravery on her part to volunteer to go out on another scavenging run with the trucks, but the morning was beautiful and the fresh air was beckoning. It was the end of summer and there wouldn't be many more days like this one so Cora chose to go.

The tornado debris field had been pretty well gone over. The storage room was almost overflowing with clothing, wood for their stove and a variety of things. They were down to the last half mile of rubble to search through. After they arrived, four guards stood watch while the rest of them donned gloves, face masks and headed into the mess. Cora hadn't been out in quite a while and had forgotten how heavy the work was, shifting boards full of nails, picking up bricks and shoving appliances out of the way, all the while watching out for snakes or broken glass.

It had been almost an hour when Cora overturned a pile of crumbling sheetrock when she saw the corner of a blanket. Hesitantly she moved the last piece of wall and saw a baby sized form wrapped in the cover edged in pink satin. She involuntarily let out a scream. Three of those closest to her came running over and around the wreckage.

Cora stood back as one of the men bend down and unwrapped a corner of what lay before them. She saw him relax and heard him laugh. He stood up with the bundle and took the blanket off of it. It was a large doll. Cora thought she might faint from relief.

"I think you should keep this," the man said as he tossed it to Cora.

She would never hear the end of this, but she smiled and nodded. "I will. It nearly scared me to death." She put the blanket down and laid the doll on it. She would take it home as a reminder that things might not be what you think they are.

Once her heart rate came back to normal, she resumed her work. Things went smoothly the rest of the morning. The bag she carried for small stuff had to be emptied many times during the six hours they worked. It grew really warm during the late afternoon so they headed back to the shelter. The trucks were full enough that it was hard to find places to stand for some of the soldiers on the trip home. There were also six people crowded into the cab of the trucks meant for five. It wasn't a pleasant ride for anyone.

When they pulled into the yard, Toby, the Jack Russell and the fully recovered border collie, they'd named Speedy, were running big in circles, chasing things in the field next to the tarmac. Speedy was a camp favorite, he sort of adopted everyone and was fed right in the dining room with the rest of them. They'd made him a bed in the hallway and he became the night watchman. All the animals they had seemed to have adapted to their new situation with no issues. The cats tolerated the dogs and the dogs left the cats alone. Although, all of them seemed a little leery of Leo, the Maine Coon. He was bigger than Toby, and had an attitude that made even Speedy give him way when they met in the hall or outside.

Cora saw Jake and Clay waiting by the door for the trucks. She waved at Jake when she got out of the rig.

He came right over. "How was it today?" He looked back to make sure Clay was following him. The new boy was, just shuffling along slowly. He made a face of disgust that only Cora could see. It said to her this wasn't a match made in heaven.

Cora smiled at Clay, "I don't think we've met. I'm Cora Mason. I know your name is Clay. Are you liking New Denver so far?"

He shrugged, "It's okay." Stoically, he walked on by her and started helping with the unloading. Jake sighed and walked over to do the same.

Cora stood watching what was being taken into the storage area. As the trucks were being emptied she did see that Clay kept glancing off to the east, scanning the horizon. It was more than a casual look. He was definitely expecting to see something. Just as they were finishing up on the last load, Cora walked over to Clay. "What were you looking at? I saw you looking over that way." She pointed towards the east.

He sighed and looked down. "I was from Bennett. On a clear day you could see the airplanes landing and taking off from here. I thought I might be able to see Bennett. We had two grain elevators and a water tower that were all pretty tall. I kept looking to see if they were still there. Guess that's foolish 'cause when I came out of the storm cellar, there wasn't anything left but me."

Cora saw the pain on the young man's face. "What were you doing in your cellar?"

Clay smiled sheepishly, "It had just been me and my dad on our small farm just at the edge of town. He'd been divorced for years, can't say as I remember my mother. She never came back after moving to Arkansas, where her people were. My uncle came to live with us three or four years ago." He sighed, "My dad didn't know I smoked. I went down in the root cellar once in a while when I took one of my uncle's cigars. Wasn't very often, but it just happened I had one for more than a week that I'd been saving for when my dad and uncle were away. They'd gone into Aurora for some fertilizer. So I had a whole morning to myself." Tears were forming in his eyes as he looked again off at the horizon. "Guess this's what I get for doing something I shouldn't have."

"How did you wind up with the raiders? The ones you came here with when you got shot?"

He shook his head. "There were some deer out in a canyon not to far from my place. I was trying to figure out how to get one. We always kept a few tools in the cellar for an emergency in case we had to dig ourselves out of the mess a twister might leave. So I had a saw, hammer and shovel. When I went out looking for food. I had taken the hammer and shovel with me. A couple of those guys were out looking for food too. They shot the deer that I was after. When they saw me, they almost shot me too. One of them wanted to, but the other said they needed men and I would have to go with them if I wanted to stay alive." He shook his head, "I was so weak from hunger, I think I would have agreed to anything. I told the people back at the base what I knew about the ones who took me. There were only about eight of them, but there are plenty more in the hills over by Grand Junction. All of them were as mean as a rattler. A few of them laughed as others told stories of robbing and killing people. They just foraged off the land and stayed out of sight. Said they didn't believe in religion or the government. They'd been living in the woods, had a mine they'd been working." He looked at her, "I feel so lucky to have would up here even if I had to get shot for it to happen."

Cora put her arm around the boy's shoulder. "I haven't decided whether this is punishment or a reward. Don't be too hard on yourself. All of us have questioned why we're here at one time or another. The best thing we can do at this point is look out for each other and do the best we can everyday. You are now a part of this family and we love you." She felt him relax. "Let's go in and see what's for dinner."

As she turned she saw Jake standing there, waiting. "Hey Jake, let's go eat." She walked into the building with her arms around both boys, one on either side of her. "I won't be able to get my arms around you boys much longer, you're both going to be much taller than me at any minute. In fact," she moved her arms down and took the boys by the arm, "you're already so tall it makes my arms ache to have them that high. Wow, when did you grow so much?" That made both boys chuckle. "That's great," Cora thought to herself, "Clay is coming out of his shell."

The next morning, Cora opted to stay and help with the sorting out of the things that had been brought back. She picked up her picking bag and dumped it on one of the tables. It was full of small things, combs, brushes, packages of toothbrushes, various items that were still intact enough to be usable.

Then she saw it, the envelope. It wasn't from a business, it was more the size of a greeting card. Something had obscured the name of who it was to and the part where the sender's address would have been was missing. Cora opened it and found that it was indeed a greeting card, a birthday card. Looking around, she saw a chair at the side of the room. She walked over and sat down. There was something almost surreal about seeing a birthday card. In the last year the only birthday anyone had celebrated that she knew about, was when Jake turned sixteen. They'd had a cake and sang happy birthday, off key of course, like everyone always sang that. It was followed by laughter and good wishes to the boy, but there were no cards or presents.

With a sigh, she looked at the card. It had a simple message on the front, "Happy Birthday to Someone Special." Opening the card to the inside, Cora found that it had been a blank card to write your own message in. She nearly fell off the chair when she saw the date at the top of the page. She got up and went to find Sergeant Marsh.

It had been raining since early that morning so the salvage crews were waiting a day before going back out to the debris site. She found the Sergeant having coffee in the dining room. There wasn't anyone sitting with him so she sat down across from him. "I want to show you something I found yesterday." She handed him the card.

He looked at it and shrugged, "I saw a few pieces of mail and things like that laying around too. Didn't think we would waste space and time picking it up."

"Look at the date written on the inside of the card Sergeant," Cora said.

He smiled at her, "Hey, we've known each other quite awhile, it's okay for you to call me Virgil. Almost everyone around here has gotten to know each other well enough to be on a first name basis, at least with civilians." He opened the card and his eyes went wide open in surprise. "This is only two months ago, isn't it? I know we don't have current calendars, but we kind of have made up our own."

"How can that be?" Cora said in disbelief. "How could someone have sent that card two months ago?"

Virgil shook his head, "And how did it get here?" He put the card into his jacket. "I'm going to keep this and read it to everyone after dinner tonight. Then we'll talk about what this could mean. Best not say anything until we have an open discussion."

Cora shrugged, "Okay." She got up to leave, "Thanks, Serg..Vigil."

Cora regretted that she hadn't read the whole letter before she gave it to the sergeant. Now she had to wait like everyone else to see what news it contained. It was very puzzling how that letter could have been written just months ago when it had been well over a year since any town out that way had existed. Dinner time seemed a long time away as she threw herself back into the sorting process.

There was nothing unusual in the stuff they'd brought back. They had enough hair brushes for everyone in the shelter, plus the animals. A few more food items were found, most likely from someone's kitchen. There had also been one house partially whole under a heap of rubble. There was also some furniture that had survived. The trucks would be concentrating on what they could salvage out of that, if the rain hadn't ruined what they'd had to leave behind for another day.

Finally it was time for dinner. Their garden had done pretty well, tonight they were having baked potatoes with steamed carrots and a slice of fried canned ham. Three sizable cans of the tinned meat had been found and was being used for their dinners. With more than eighty people, the portions had to be conservative; nevertheless it was a good meal. One thing about the meal times was that there hadn't been any leftovers for at least the last year. People ate their share to the last morsel, even the once picky eaters.

Sergeant Marsh got up in front of the room at the podium when everyone was almost through eating. "I want to share something that we found, actually Cora found, from the last trip to the debris site." He took the card from his camo shirt pocket. "This is a birthday card, which isn't unusual, however, inside is where it gets interesting. It's addressed to ' *Marianna, My dear friend. I wish I could be with you for your birthday this year but with the roads being such a mess there's no way I could drive there and of course, flying right now is out of the question. The trains are back up and running in a lot of places just not close to me. I doubt if we'll be able to travel at all for another year or so more. It's getting better but ,with all the strange things going on it's kind of scary to leave home. Luckily, food here hasn't been much of an issue. Our garden out did itself this year and I've been canning up a storm. Good thing I knew how to do that. How are things there in Colorado? Have you got your electric back yet? Ours here in Tennessee was*

restored in November but it's only on seven a.m. to ten p.m. Sure is strange isn't it how so many
people just disappeared. I heard that all the people in almost all of New Zealand, Australia and
most of South America as well as South Africa are just gone. And all these houses with no
basements? And no roads? What has happened? This wasn't the apocalypse that some folks were
expecting, but it sure is baffling. I was glad to get your letter saying you were okay. We've known
each other since we were young, hate to lose one of my best friends. Well, you have a wonderful
birthday next week. I'll be thinking of you! Love Esther."'

He stopped and looked around, "Here is the really strange thing. This was dated two
months ago. This Marianna apparently lived in one of those small towns the twister went
through. How did this card wind up here and now? What town? There's nothing above ground
for hundreds of miles! We can add this to the list of strange things we've encountered."

He shrugged and stepped back from the microphone, "Anyone with ideas is welcome to
speak. The mic is yours." No one got up. He nodded. "Well, report anything you find or see.
Eventually we'll get to the bottom of this."

People began to leave the room. Cora could see them being as bewildered as she was by
this new development to the plague of mysteries that they had experienced. At this point, no one
could explain any of it, besides the biggest question of all, what had happened?

For some reason, Eve, Sophie and BB seemed really agitated that night just before lights
out. Both of them paced and meowed until Cora finally gave in and let them go outside. They
headed straight to the garden tool shed that was on the far side of the tarmac. That wasn't
unusual, there were always mice and things to chase there, but most of the time they were
cautious, not at a full speed run like on this occasion. That puzzled her.

Then she suddenly heard a high pitched whine and felt a little dizzy. It made her seek out
something to lean on which turned out to be one of the trucks. She sat down on the running board
and waited as the whine seemed to disappear. As it faded, so did the dizziness. When she stood,
she felt a bit wobbly. It was chilling as she realized it was almost the way it was when she woke
up in the shelter, many months earlier. She gasped and looked around. The two guards on duty by
one of the other trucks were shaking their heads, they had heard and felt it too.

It was dark but there was enough of a cold moon to see that the cats were headed back to her. "Come on," she called. They came as fast as they had left. The three animals knew the dangers of being away from the shelter. Gray, the other cat from Eve's litter had already barely survived an attack by a coyote.

Once inside, it took a minute to find Virgil and tell him about the incident. He went out to talk to the guards and Cora took the cats back to their room. It was time for the lights to go out so she opted not to go back into the hallway. Whatever it was, it had evidently been nothing, so there didn't seem to be anything they could do in the dark anyway. It took awhile to calm down and fall asleep, but in the total darkness of her room she could. The cats made themselves comfortable, whatever had spooked them was gone and they were purring.

The next morning, several people at breakfast were talking about hearing the high pitched noise and either feeling dizzy or having a headache that went away in several minutes. All through the day everyone seemed to stay a bit nervous. By dinner, however, everyone felt a little more relaxed because the day had passed without incident.

The next three weeks came and went without anything unexplained. Nothing out of the ordinary had happened, much to Cora's liking. Everyone was busy helping stockpile what they could find for the winter. The days, while sunny for the most part, had been growing colder, to add to the urgency.

It felt like a time of wrapping things up. Sophie had her litter of kittens, who were definitely part Maine Coon, huge and beautiful. There had been four babies, two males and two female. Leo had already been neutered and Sophie was spayed shortly after the kittens were weaned. It was the consensus that they had more than enough cats and dogs at the shelter.

By late September, the last of the garden was, for the most part, harvested and either frozen or canned. The only thing left to bring in were several large pumpkins. Things had been calm around the shelter. No raids, they'd had better food during the summer and a good amount of food for the winter. People were cautiously optimistic that they were pretty well prepared to survive another winter.

Thanks to the tornado, they'd found another two wood stoves so each wing had its own wood stove and there would now even be heat in the work room. The storm also provided the fuel from the trees that had been uprooted or blown down. There were now two enormous stacks of cut up firewood just outside the doors of the shelter. It was fortuitous that they had wood because the gas to run the generator was getting more scarce. They'd had to forage much further all the time to find the fuel. It was the same with hunting and fishing. Still they had found a few game animals and caught dozens of fish, enough meat that the big walk-in freezer was nearly half full. They hoped that they would be able to use the freezer until the snow came and then that would be used to keep their food cold.

Two days before Halloween, winter sent a calling card that it was coming. They had awoken to ten inches of snow blowing drifts up against their doorways. It was a grim reminder of what was to come. The first snowfall didn't last more than three days, then a pleasant week of good weather returned. It seemed to ease the mood for a while. The days were bright and sunny even though the nights were definitely cool. Each morning before the sun had a chance to warm the ground they had to start their days of foraging in their heavy coats and trudge across the frost covered tarmac to the trucks.

It was a bone chilling morning when Lois and Cora headed for a rig that Mike was going to be driving out. They'd made the run with him several times in the last month, whenever the sun was out, so were they. As they crossed the pavement they could see Mike putting their equipment into the bed of the truck. He looked up and around. Cora started to wonder what he was seeing, then she heard it. Lois did too.

They both gasped and stood looking at the sky. It was the sound of that plane again. They hadn't heard it for months. But there it was back and it was getting closer. Cora could feel panic rising in her body. Her feet wanted to run from the noise, but her brain couldn't make a choice of direction or even if what she was hearing was real? She and Lois hurried over next to Mike and the three of them stood scanning the sky and listening intently.

Suddenly, Mike turned and looked to the west, "Oh my God!" he breathed, and he reached out and pushed Cora and Lois toward the ground. "Oh my God!"

CHAPTER NINETEEN

"What's going on?" Cora heard herself cry out.

"Stay down," Mike commanded. "There's a jet about to land, right on top of us."

Just at that moment Cora felt the heat of the jet's engine just a few yards above them. She felt Mike pulling her towards the shelter door. They were still in a crouching position, but both the women followed his lead to the doorway before standing up. Sure enough, when they stood and looked back at the tarmac a small jet had indeed just landed. It went to the end of the runway it was on and then it turned and taxied back over the rough, cracked pavement to where the three of them including Sergeant Marsh, stood. Several others, who'd come out to see what was going on, joined them.

The Sergeant walked out to the edge of the runway to greet the pilot. The jet came to a halt a few yards from him.

The pilot cut his engine and sat for a moment, then the he slid back the hatch and climbed out. Once on the ground, he stood looking around. Even from where Cora stood she could see the confused look on his face. His mouth was wide open as he took off his helmet. She moved a little closer to hear what was being said.

The pilot took the hand that Sergeant Marsh was extending, "Welcome to New Denver. You're the first plane that's landed here in a long time," he saw the name sewn on his flight suit, "Captain Havers."

"What is New Denver?" he asked, looking around. He looked down. "There's a runway here!"

Virgil looked around, "Yeah, there is. What were you expecting Captain?"

The Captain looked at him, "You're a marine aren't you soldier?"

"Yes sir, I am. There are some Air Force personnel here, but I am the ranking non-com. I am Sergeant Major Virgil Marsh." He snapped to attention and saluted. "Sorry sir, we've gotten a little informal over the last several months."

The Captain shook his head, "Don't worry Sergeant, a lot has changed everywhere. Just relax." He continued looking around. "Is this Colorado?"

Now it was Virgil's turn to look confused, "Yes, it is. Where did you think you were?"

The pilot shrugged, "I thought I was landing at the Denver airport. My plane was just about out of fuel and I was trying to set it down easy. Then I saw that hole appear in the haze. The next thing I know I'm seeing a runway, an honest to God paved runway." He walked a couple of feet out onto the tarmac and looked both ways. Then looked out over the barren countryside. He stood for a few minutes, then turned and walked back to Virgil. "Do you know what's going on?"

"Let's go inside and have a cup of coffee. I'll radio my commanding officer and see if they can send an escort for you to the base. I think there's a lot to talk about." As he passed Cora and Lois he stopped a moment. "Captain this is Cora and this is Sergeant Wilkerson, she is Air Force. If you would like I can assign her as your aide. She's a weapons expert."

It surprised Cora slightly to see Lois come to attention and offer a salute to the Captain. He returned the salute. "At ease Sergeant," he said with a wry smile, "I understand that things are less formal here and now." He continued into the building with Virgil.

Cora heard the Captain say to Virgil, "At least you have pretty girls here," as the two men disappeared into the building. "Well that was exciting," Cora said as she walked out to look at the plane. Mike was already out next to it giving it a once over.

He saw her come up beside him. "It's a T38 Talon training jet. Not a combat weapon, which is good. He wasn't expecting trouble, wherever he was headed. I can't wait to hear what he knows about what's going on."

Cora shook her head, "I'm not sure he knows any more than we do."

"What makes you think that?" Mike asked.

"I heard him talking to Virgil. He didn't know where he was. It sounded like he thought he was landing at an airport, not just a runway in a wide open deserted place."

Mike looked at the building, "Well that raises even more questions. Where was he coming from and where did he think he was going?"

It was all too much for Cora to worry about, "I think we were going out on a supply hunt. Shouldn't we go before it gets too late? If we don't leave by ten this morning we won't have but an hour or so to work."

160

Mike nodded. He motioned to Lois to head for the truck. She hesitated for only a moment, then grabbed her guns and got into the truck. They didn't get back to the shelter until after the escort from the base had come for the Captain. Cora kind of regretted that she didn't get to ask him some questions but it was enough that he was safe and they might be getting some new information soon.

Cora was about to walk back into the building after they had unloaded the few things they'd found in their salvaging run when she looked up at the sky. Mike was still cleaning out the truck. She walked over to him and pointed up, "I heard that Captain say he saw a hole in the haze just before he landed. Look up, doesn't the sky look a little lavender tonight?"

Mike scanned the sky, "I remember it looked a little that color when all this first started. It may have even been a shade darker. But I guess you could call it a haze. Been clear all summer, wonder why that color came back?"

A chill went down Cora's spine, "Now what? Are we going to have more of us disappear?"

"Maybe it has something to do with the Captain flying into our sky somehow. I wonder if it was this plane you heard before."

"Could have been, I guess," Cora muttered as she walked on into the building. More mysteries was not what they needed.

It was surprisingly warm inside the shelter. Cora had felt cold outside, but it might have been she had just grown numb to it. It was good to be able to take off her coat and go to her room and change into something much lighter for dinner. The supper that night turned out to be a very good, hearty bowl of vegetable stew with a decent amount of noodles in it. They'd all learned to be grateful to have anything to eat, let alone something that made you actually feel full. They'd found several cans of coffee in the tornado wreckage, but that was saved to be used for their breakfasts. At night the choices were always water or tea.

Lois had been disappointed that she didn't get to go back to the base with the Captain's escort. She had told Cora it had sounded like a good assignment to be his personal aide although he didn't seem to think it was necessary. She said that it felt like it would have been a promotion. Cora was sort of surprised that the formalness of the military and its hierarchy still held firm even though everything else was completely changed. They kept their ranks and everyone bowed to their presence. In a way, it was a relief to have something stay the same and orderly in the middle of a confusing collapse of things.

The next morning, Virgil was called to come to the base. Cora and Lois debated whether or not to go on their foraging run. In the end, they did go. Mike drove the large truck for this time out. They decided to go to some of the smaller towns to the east. For a change, Jake joined them because Clay wanted to look at what had been his home town of Bennett.

It didn't take long to find the townsite. Clay pointed out where his place had been and the cellar he'd been in smoking his cigar. Clay and Mike got out of the truck. Tears rimmed the boy's eyes as they walked across the ground where his house would had been. It hadn't had a cement foundation, just wood pillars. There was nothing to even show a building had sat there. Mike walked over and put his arms around Clay's shoulders and lead him back to the car. "Can't change things, son," he said quietly.

Clay climbed into the back seat next to Cora. She put her arm around him, "Kind of the way we all felt when we came out of our shelters that first day. It was hard for all of us, then we found each other and it's gotten better. Not the same, but better," she said as she smiled at him.

He nodded, took one last glance at the place then looked forward, "Let's go on to the next town." Mike started the car and they headed on into the day.

There were some paved secondary roads off of the highway they were on but it didn't look like there had been any major communities on them so they carried on into what had been Limon. Clay said he'd been there once or twice for school games, though it wasn't recognizable now at all. It was just flat treeless land. Here and there the suggestion of foundations was all that gave a hint that over a thousand people had lived there just a little more than a year ago.

Walking the fairly broad streets of the town wouldn't have taken much time on a warm day, but it was December and the days were short and cold. They all had their heavy coats, caps and gloves on, which made them sweat while their noses felt freezing.

Lois was the first to make a discovery. She had found a root cellar behind one of the houses. Of course whatever was in it would already be a year old and it probably was too much to hope for that anything edible remained, but Jake and Clay joined her immediately to help her move the heavy door that seemed stuck. Cora waited back a few feet and motioned for Mike to bring the truck closer. He had just arrived to help when the boys got the door open. There was a gust of stale air in their face as their reward. Inside the earthen room they were surprised to see dozens of jars of honey. "These folks must have been bee keepers," Cora said. There were some other home canned goods and several gallon jars of pickles and other vegetables in brine.

They decided to take everything back with them and let the cooks decide if they were still good or not. They carefully loaded everything in boxes and put them into the truck. There were some work gloves, some garden tools and a couple of bushel baskets so they took all of those things as well.

By the time they had finished walking the street they were on it was beginning to get dark. There was just one more building on the corner and it had a basement with a door to a room that probably went under the sidewalk to the side. It was locked, but they had a crowbar so it wasn't long before they had their flashlights and they were looking around inside the space.

"Oh my," Cora said when she saw the first item. "What shall we do with this lot?"

Mike laughed, "We could start a catering company, couldn't we?"

Clay and Jake were looking at the room lined with shelves full of serving dishes and platters. "Do we have to carry all this to the truck?" Jake moaned.

Mike shook his head. "We'll ask the cooks if we need it. We can always come back for this. In the spring we'll go out and see what's left of the tornado debris field, that's just a few more miles down this road. If they want it, we can pick it up then." He motioned and everyone left the room to wait. They secured the door and got back into the truck.

The ride back to the shelter seemed to take forever. It was well after dark when they arrived. The good news was that the honey was more than welcome, it seems that honey doesn't spoil. The dinner tea was much sweeter. That night for dinner the two jars of pickles that were deemed still good were offered as a treat for everyone. The spoiled foods were put on the compost pile and the jars kept for next year's harvest. It amused Cora that they had all become quite good at thinking ahead and recycling.

At breakfast the next morning the Sergeant Major, had come back and called everyone in to hear the latest news. Cora was curious but at the same time a little fearful. Things were confusing enough without more worries. She took her seat in the back of the dining hall, Lois stood by the door. If Lois knew anything more than Cora did she hadn't said anything.

Virgil got up to the podium and calmed everyone down. "I know you all are wondering about our friend, Captain Havers." He sighed. "He has an amazing story to share with us. I took the time to write it all down so I wouldn't forget anything because it is astounding." He looked out over the silent crowd. "So here goes. When I first met the Captain on the runway he asked where he was. To him, five minutes before he actually landed, he was coming in for a landing on the hard packed dirt runway at the Denver Airport. He said it was there and had been all along, although without a tarmac, no big planes could use any of the airports. They've been able to restore some airports in the east, but it's been slow going."

There was an even deeper silence as Virgil continued. "He told us that there had been three major sun flares, beginning with the one we all experienced just as we first found ourselves here. The next two were close behind the first and didn't do as much damage as the first one, but still caused some problems. The initial burst caused significant damage to the Earth's mesosphere. It was basically burnt, but we didn't lose all of it. It just turned a reddish purple, that caused a severe drop in the temperature for the rest of that year and into the next spring, but the planet recovered almost to normal within a year. The other two bursts were even faster than the first and did little changes, but for some reason, not to the atmosphere."

Someone at Cora's table whispered, "I saw that purple color when I woke up that day." Everyone sitting close by nodded. Cora, too, had witnessed that lavender colored sky.

Virgil went on, "He told us that the whole world is in chaos. There have been food riots, fuel shortages, droughts and all kinds of issues, however they've gotten the farming going and rudimentary distribution systems set up. Most places are still in a pretty dire situations, however, progress is slowly being made. Some of the already suffering countries found themselves in real peril. The whole infrastructure has to be rebuilt everywhere. Winter was extremely hard, many perished. Things had gotten much better by the next spring, they were growing crops, got some of the electricity back on thanks to all the solar plants and wind turbines." Virgil stopped and took a drink of water.

164

Someone raised their hand with a question. "I know you all have questions but please wait until I give you all my notes. Then we can spend the rest of the morning talking about all this. In fact, we'll probably spend the rest of the day trying to answer the questions all of this brings to us." He saw nods and then continued. "Okay, the Captain also confirmed what we learned from that letter we found not long ago. Australia and parts of South America look just like this, but that didn't happen until the second flare. A lot of cruise ships that were in the southern hemisphere at the time disappeared too.

The third flare didn't do anything they could find, but by that time, communication was in a pretty sketchy way so there might have been things that weren't noticed. The good news was that there haven't been any more flares for over a year now. Their scientists think that it probably means that the sun had just been releasing a small amount of it's hydrogen stores. It wasn't enough to cause major changes in the sun's mass, but it is a small foretaste of what is to come when, in a few million years, the sun begins it's dying cycle. When, and if, mankind recovers from this current situation, there is no doubt we have to devote ourselves to finding a way to move into space to find habitable planets."

Virgil took a deep breath. "One thing we have been able to establish is that the missing in Australia and South America are not here either. Which brings a huge question beyond just where are we? If they are not there or here, where then?"

He sighed and hesitated, as if he didn't want to talk about the next item of his notes. Virgil looked around the room. "There was one other thing, the Captain did say that there was one report they couldn't verify, but was something several people say they saw. There was a moment during the first flare and the others they saw a huge silver, shiny, looking disk in the sky that blocked out the sun for a split second." He shook his head, "I know that sounds a little hard to believe, but people did report it."

"There was one other thing. During the physical that they gave the Captain, the doctors found he had experienced much higher levels of radiation than we have here. While it wasn't a fatal level, it would seem, where he has been for the last couple of years has less protection from the sun's harmful rays because of the weakened atmosphere. He said that everyone has been asked to wear special clothing and stay indoors as much as possible. According to our best research here, our radiation has not increased to a significant level over what it had been. Of course, the worry is skin cancer." Virgil sighed, "I know this is a lot to process. I really don't have any answers for you. I think it would be best if you just think about it for a few minutes and talk at your tables while we have another cup of water or tea. I'll reconvene us in a half hour and let everyone express their thoughts." He saw people nod and look at who they were sitting with. He walked over and got his cup. Other's followed.

There was a tense silence in the room. Cora sat staring at her cup, debating whether she really wanted another cup of their weak tea. It did taste better now that they had honey to put in it, so in the end the sweet tea won. It only took a minute or two to get the drink and return to the table.

There were three other people at her table: Alex, an older man who had been a car salesman at one time; Gary, who was about Cora's age; Holly, who was an airman from the base. Lois came over and pulled up a chair to join them. "So what kind of questions do you have?" she asked looking at each of the others, and finally Cora.

Cora took a deep breath. "It's funny, my first thought when I stood alone in the middle of that road back in Nebraska was to ask myself if I was dead."

Alex looked at her in surprise, "I had the same thought. I'd been trying to find my dog. He'd ran into a culvert under the road in the park near my home. I went in to find him and the next thing I know I'm waking up totally alone. The dog is gone, the park playground is gone, the kids who were playing there are not there, my car, everything. I had to walk for about a mile, only to find that my house, my neighborhood and my town were also missing." Tears came to his eyes as he remembered that day.

Holly shook her head, "It could be that we are dead, just don't know it."

"We're not dead," Lois said firmly, "we just don't understand yet what has happened and how this world somehow got splintered into separate pieces."

"I wonder how many pieces?" Cora said absently, trying to imagine what that meant.

Virgil tapped on the podium, "Let's hear what everyone wants to say. Anyone come up with ideas?"

Lois raised her hand, then stood up. "It sounds like we've experienced a phenomenon that has somehow dumped us out like pieces from a jigsaw puzzle. When you go to put one together after putting things out on the table, some pieces are upside down, some have fallen off onto the floor and some might be missing if it's been worked before. I think what we all have to be figuring out is how to put it all back together." She sat down.

Someone on the other side of the room asked to be recognized then stood up. "Well that brings up several other issues. First, where are those missing pieces? Then which piece are we? Are we the missing ones or are they?"

Another person in a different part of the dining hall stood up. Cora couldn't see who it was but recognized Jay's voice. "I had a chilling thought. What if it all comes back, just as quickly as it went. We could be standing out there on the tarmac and a big jet land right on top of us, like the Captain's small jet almost did on Mike and Cora. We could be driving down the road on one of our foraging trips and a semi suddenly meet us head on. Think about that," Jay said as he sat back down.

Again the room was silent. Then someone else got up, "We might not like what we find if we get meshed back with the rest of the world. It sounds like things are even rougher there than here."

"We got family back there, lives and businesses," someone said without being recognized.

Jake stood up and looked around, "Has anyone realized that there aren't many kids here? I've only seen one girl my age so far this year." He sat down and everyone chuckled but they understood what he was saying. Out here on the prairie land there had not been many children with anyone at the time of the event. It might have been different in the cities on the subways or in other places, but not here. It would be a lonely life for the few children around.

Cora thought of her cats, even they were a precious commodity. Very few of them had been saved with them. It was all the more clear to her now since she only had Sophie and Eve. BB had gone off hunting early in the summer and had not returned. It broke Cora's heart to think he might have been taken by a coyote or bobcat. She had gone looking for him morning and night, calling at the edges of the runways for weeks.

167

Cora stood up to be recognized, "One thing that we can't be sure of is that we'll stay here forever. This may be temporary. There was a hole in the sky the Captain said that he came through. There was no hole there before, then suddenly he drops out of the sky almost on top of us. Those openings may occur at any time. How do we protect ourselves from something we can't predict or see?" She sat down.

There was a murmuring among the people for a few moments, then Virgil tapped on the podium. "We've got a lot to think about and I know that this conversation is spreading around the world, now that we know that we're not alone, just somewhere else. As information and new theories are shared, I will bring the latest findings to you. We're just an isolated pocket of people in this vast, whatever it is. Let's be patient, vigilant and supportive of each other. We have one big task ahead of us. We are going into another winter. We have limited supplies and will need to continue our foraging. The one big plus we have is, we have each other. You are not alone, remember that." Virgil switched off the mic and walked out of the room.

Cora sat sipping her remaining half cup of cold sweet tea. It was such a mind boggling situation, that it was really hard to even contemplate questions to ask. And who really knew any answers? Everyone seemed as dumbfounded as she was at the enormity of what had happened. As a child, she would have just gone to her bed and covered her head with her blanket so she didn't have to deal with a situation. All she had to do then was wait until it passed. Now, there was no blanket to hide under, this was not going to pass, or at least, it seemed that way. Still, dealing with the unknown was so hard.

Even the honey couldn't make the sour taste in Cora's mouth go away. She thought she might be going to be sick to her stomach. It was an accurate diagnosis, in just a couple of minutes her prediction came true.

CHAPTER TWENTY

Christmas came and went in an uneventful way. It had snowed several inches the day before and then, by New Year's Day there were twenty inches of snow on the ground. To boot the temperature dropped to some record breaking cold. The wind whipped the powdery flakes into a frenzy, causing whiteout conditions. Huge drifts had to be cleared away from the courtyard area at the bottom of the stairs leading into the shelter's two doors. The back door remained a little better protected and clear most of the time. Conditions stayed pretty much the same through all of January and most of February.

The wood supply for the stoves had dwindled to dangerous levels by the end of February. Had there been anyone keeping statistics, this would have gone on record as one of the harshest winters in history. The first week in March was still cold but the roads were almost bare, thanks to the wind blowing the snow to the sides. It was a necessity to visit the tornado debris field for more wood and resources.

All three of their trucks were uncovered and taken out on the hunt. Cora and Lois were among the ones who braved the cold to help. Mike drove the vehicle they were in. He had to go slow because of patches of black ice that nearly caused them to go into a snow bank a couple of times. Finally they did reach their destination.

Picking through the rubble this time was harder because of drifts of snow hiding the potential dangers. It was slow going and by the time they had to head back home, they only had one truck load of lumber and limbs from trees.

One unexpected thing they did find though were some tracks in the snow that Lois and two others followed. By the end of their time at the site, the hunters had brought back an antelope. Cora normally wouldn't have been anything but dismayed at the shooting of such a pretty animal; today it made her mouth water. The ingredients in the soups had been so scant lately that it was more like flavored water. The addition of meat to the broth would be a welcome treat for everyone.

The smell of the meat being cooked wafted through the shelter that night. Everyone was excited about dinner and no one was late when the bell rang. There wasn't much for each person, but it was more than they'd had in a very long time. Somehow, the cooks had managed to have enough rice to give everyone about half a cup of that with a nice slice of the meat with a few tablespoons of gravy over both. After what they'd become accustom to, it was a banquet!

Cora took her plate to the table. She didn't get her cup of sweet tea, she saved that for dessert. The aroma of the hot food swirled around her, making her feel almost euphoric. She looked around when she realized how silent the room was. Everyone was sitting looking at their plates. Tears came to her eyes, she realized just how really desperate their situation was for the first time. It hadn't really been obvious to her because the changes had been gradual and happening to her at the same time, but everyone had that gaunt look of a person approaching the edge of starvation. Cora looked down at herself, her shirt just hung on her shoulders and a belt now held up her slacks.

Slowly, she began to eat small bites of food, one at a time, savoring the taste of each morsel. It surprised her to feel full half way through her portion. She rested a moment and then willed herself to finish every last bit, right down to the last grain of rice. Looking around her own table, she saw everyone doing the same. She didn't lick the plate for the last taste of gravy, but she thought about it. When she was finally done, it was time for her sweet tea.

As others finished eating, there was a pleasant little murmur of people talking and commenting about the food. Cora relaxed with her drink and smiled. It had been a very good day. They'd made a successful trip and would have fuel for the fires for at least another week or two. She sighed and thought, "Maybe we'll have an early warm spring."

After she'd finished the last drop of tea, she went to check on Eve and Sophie. They had both been cooped up in the room all day. Cora loved the greetings they always shared when she came home from whatever project she was involved in.

After they'd had their petting and purring session, Cora took the cats to the storage area to forage for themselves. They, too, had grown fairly thin. There hadn't been a lot of prepared cat food around so letting them hunt for themselves had been a necessity. Luckily, there were lots of mice and vermin in and around the shelter. Just off the storage and maintenance rooms was the entrance to the utilities room that connected the airport with all kinds of services. The miles of utility pipes that ran under the former airport to the city were prime hunting grounds for the cats.

Even though that part of the facility had no lights, the cats were pretty adapt at finding their way around. They usually had themselves at least one rodent a day, they often brought the "best parts" like the heads back to Cora.

Shining her flashlight down the walkway, Cora watched as the two cats headed off down the pipes. They would come back on their own in an hour or so. Cora usually didn't wait for them, but came back for them before bedtime. She was just about to leave when she heard something. Looking down the corridor she saw Eve and Sophie running back to her. Then she heard voices and footsteps. Someone was coming towards the shelter. She opened the door to the maintenance room and the cats dashed in ahead of her. Once inside she locked the door and ran for Sergeant Marsh. Within minutes, several armed guards were at the door to the utility chamber.

Sergeant Marsh quietly opened the door and stepped into the next room, his gun was at the ready. Lois and two other armed soldiers were with him. There were no lights in the corridor so they shined their flashlights down the hall.

"Don't shoot," a small voice called out of the darkness. "Please don't shoot!"

"Who are you?" Sergeant Marsh demanded.

"I'm Kate Erwin, I'm with my mother Niva. She's really sick. I need help."

Sergeant Marsh nodded to two of the soldiers who cautiously moved ahead, weapons ready. They were back almost immediately, holding up an older woman who was having trouble even standing. They were followed by a teenage girl.

When they came into the other room where Cora was, she could see that both of them were thin and pale. She also recognized them as the two that she'd encountered on one of their earliest salvaging runs. "I know you," Cora said.

The girl looked surprised, "I don't remember you. I'm Kate and this is my mother."

"We weren't introduced then but I'm Cora. You and your mother were in a shelter in a basement. We accidentally opened your door when we were looking for supplies."

"I sort of remember that," she said looking back at her mother. "Can you help her? She's been running a fever for several days. We haven't had much to eat and we ran out of fuel for our stove. It's been pretty rough for the last month."

171

Cora watched as the older woman was whisked off to see their head medical person, an EMT. She followed along behind them. A quick exam was all it took to diagnose pneumonia and dehydration as the probable causes of her weak condition. Word was sent to the base to send a doctor as soon as one could get through.

The shelter, with the help of the EMT and a retired nurse, had set up a small emergency clinic in one of the unused rooms at the far side of the facility so Mrs. Erwin was given a bed there. Her daughter was to share a room with an elderly woman close to their clinic.

Once the girl's mother was settled and resting, Cora invited Kate to the dining room for some hot tea. "Hopefully there will be a little soup left we can heat up for you."

They walked quietly back to the other side of the shelter, to the dining room. There were still a few snow drifts in the courtyard that they had to maneuver around but they found enough wind swept dry spots to make it without falling down. They were in luck, there was enough soup left for the girl as well as a few crackers. Cora watched the girl eat her tiny meal like it was steak and potatoes. She thought to herself, "Hunger makes any of us grateful for anything we can put in our mouths."

Kate looked up after she finished her food, seeming a little embarrassed at how she had eaten so quickly. "That was really good, thank you."

"It isn't all that good, but it's hot and filling. That's the best we can hope for right now." Cora said, managing a small smile. "How did you get all the way out here?"

Kate shrugged, "Mom remembered you saying something about the tunnels. My uncle used to work for one of the utility companies and he worked on the pipes and stuff that ran out to the airport. Mom knew about them and figured that would be the safest way to get here." She looked at Cora, "I do remember you. You were there with a kid?"

"Yes, Jake."

Kate nodded, "Are there other kids my age here?"

"A few, Jake and a young man named Clay. There is one slightly older young man named Eddie. There is one of the soldiers, I think she can't be more than eighteen," Cora said.

Tears flowed down Kate's cheeks. "I wanted to find others last summer, but Mom insisted we could do it on our own. She thought it would all be over any minute. One time she scared me, she said she saw our house, sitting right where it always was." Kate looked at Cora, "It couldn't be, could it?"

Cora shrugged, "I'm not sure. Jake said he saw a house for just a second before a dog leaped out of nowhere and knocked him down. There have been reports of strange things happening." Cora thought it better not to tell her about the Captain and his jet that was parked out on the tarmac. It might be too much information for the fragile girl to cope with right at this moment. "Don't think too hard about it right now. You need some rest and we can talk again in the morning. Let me walk you back to your room."

As they started to get up, Jake came into the room and right over to them. He smiled as he saw Kate. "I heard you were here. I'm Jake."

"Yes, I remember you a little. It was such a shock to see you that day that I didn't think to introduce myself. I'm Kate. You seem a lot taller than I remember."

Jake laughed, "Yeah, I've outgrown most of the clothes I have." He pointed to the hem of his pants, "I've let them out as far as they'll go but they are still inches too short."

Kate managed a soft little giggle.

Cora saw an opportunity to step aside, "Jake, I was just about to walk Kate back to the other side of the shelter to her room. Would you mind doing that? I have to go get Eve and Sophie and take them out for their nightly hunt."

Jake smiled broadly, "Sure, I'll do that. Come on Kate," he said, offering her his arm.

Cora nodded, "Thanks Jake. See you tomorrow Kate."

The cats were a little hesitant to go back into the utility room, but their noses told them there was food available. In minutes, they were on the hunt and when Cora came back to get them, there was evidence that both of them had been successful. That night they purred contently, curled up beside Cora.

Cora mused on the idea that the cats sleeping so innocent and sweet beside her had, just a few minutes before, been stone cold killers, the terror of many of mice. At least to the cats, life seemed pretty normal.

Her world, though, was anything but that. Mrs. Erwin's vision of their house put more questions in Cora's mind. How could she see what wasn't there? Perhaps she had been just wishing she could see it. But then there was Jake, he'd never seen the house where he found Toby. How could he have imagined that?

She fell into a restless sleep and dreamt of houses, some she'd lived in and some that were grotesque and strange. Somewhere in her tossing and turning, both cats got down and went to sleep across the room with Lois.

Breakfast the next morning was just tea and not much else. Only the honey made it seem like something. Lois and Cora lingered over their cups as long as possible. Cora could feel her stomach cramping from being empty.

They looked up as Jake came into the room and headed for Lois. He whispered something in her ear. Lois looked a little surprised but didn't say anything, just got up and followed the boy out of the room. Cora sat wondering what was going on.

After finishing her tea, Cora went out into the hallway. A few yards away Jake and Lois were talking with Sergeant Marsh. Kate, the new girl, was there too, nodding as they talked. Lois looked around and motioned to Cora to join them.

"We've got a new place to look for food," Lois said quietly, "Kate knows of a stash but she was afraid to go there because of the people who built it."

Lois took Cora aside, "We're going out armed, but we'll have the trucks ready in case we are successful in finding the place and if anything is left. It may have already been cleaned out. Virgil thinks it's worth a shot. Go get Mike and one of the other drivers. We'll take two trucks. Tell them to stay back at least a mile from the troops." She started off, then turned back to Cora, "Tell him to come armed, just as a precaution."

Cora could feel the hairs on the back of her neck stand up. Were they expecting a fire fight? The pilot had said there were food riots where he'd been, would it come to that here? So far wherever they were, had been very civilized except for the raiders. Stoically she went off to find Mike and Jay. It wasn't going to be a good day if they ran into trouble. It was horrifying to think that it had come to this, having to fight someone for their supplies. So far they'd found things that were left behind or lost in a storm. Now, they might be having to take things by force? That was not what Cora wanted at all. She'd been proud of the fact that even though Kate and her mother, Niva had plenty of food and things in their shelter, no one had ever suggested trying to take anything away from them. They would have and did welcome them into their own shelter at New Denver.

Jake and Kate rode along in the truck with Mike and Cora. It took more than two hours to reach the site. It was in the mountains to the west of Denver. They pulled off the main road and traveled for thirty or so minutes on a dirt road before they got the call over the radio to stop and wait. Mike stopped and turned off the truck. It was very still, everyone was scanning the hillside and listening, but there was nothing but the bitter wind laden with ice crystals.

After a few tense minutes, they got the call to come ahead. Mike put his gun on the dashboard just in case he might need it quickly. That didn't help ease the situation at all. They continued to climb up the winding mountain trail. There was more lingering snow at this elevation so they had to stay in the tracks the heavier military vehicles had made. Finally, they crested a hill and were surprised to find themselves in a forested valley.

Cora laughed, "This is another one that looks a whole lot like that one we found in Nebraska."

Mike nodded, "Sure is good to see trees and you know there will be some wildlife here. This might even have been where that antelope we got came from."

Mike kept plowing through the snow until he reached the soldiers at the end of the valley. They motioned for him to stop and park. "This is the spot," Lois said as she came to the truck. "Kate, where exactly is the entrance? It doesn't look like anyone has been out here since it snowed, which was months ago."

Kate got out and sighed, "I only heard about it. My dad had come out here once with one of the guys who helped build it. He was trying to get my dad to join up with them. Dad thought they were a little too radical for him, even though he thought they might be right. They were doomsday preppers. He had already built the shelter in our basement in case of a tornado. It wasn't very big, so he enlarged it to the two rooms it is now. He started really stocking it up about a year before all this happened. Mom and I just happened to be down there organizing some of the shelves when things changed." Tears came to her eyes as she looked around. "Dad said there was a really pointed rock on the ridge right above where the entrance to this place was."

175

Everyone turned around looking up at the rimrock. Mike pointed to a place about twenty yards further into the canyon. "Think that's pointed enough?" He was indicating a spot in the stone face of the surrounding rock. It did stick up a bit higher than anything else. Two of the troops trudged through the snow drifts to the spot directly below the outcropping. They disappeared into a crevasse and then came out and waved.

Sergeant Marsh and Lois went to investigate. In a minute, Cora heard what sounded like a bullet being fired. She braced herself for someone to come out shooting, but it was just Lois motioning for the rest of them to make their way to them.

It was hard walking on top of the icy snow drifts, with every other step they'd break through up to the top of their legs in snow, then would have to crawl out and try again. Finally they reached the spot where they could see behind the ledge of rock to where a wooden door lay open, it's lock shot off. Cora laughed, "Well, who needs a key?"

"This is unbelievable," Lois said shaking her head. "These people must have really thought it was going to be awful."

As Cora stepped through the door, she recognized the sound of a generator being started. Suddenly there were lights in an enormous cavern. It was filled, floor to ceiling with all kinds of food and supplies. Kate walked over next to Cora, "Dad said that the plan was to have at least three to five years worth of things. They thought that there might be a nuclear war and people wouldn't be able to go outside for a long time. My dad didn't think that would happen. He thought it would probably be something like a pandemic or an asteroid hitting the Earth."

Mike looked at the dust on the floor and the foot prints their group had made, "No one has been in here since the event. They must have been outside when it happened. They never got to use any of this stuff."

"We have to thank them though," Cora said as she walked over to one of the shelves and looked at cases of chicken noodle soup. "They may have saved our lives."

Jake was looking at one of the boxes. He opened it quickly and got a smaller box out. He quickly opened it and came around to everyone, "If you're as hungry as I am this will help." The box contained peanut butter protein bars. There was enough for two each of the people in the room.

Cora eagerly took her bars and ate one without stopping, her stomach had shrunk so much that a single portion was all it took to make her feel full. The other one went into her pocket for later. "So what do we do first?" Cora asked Sergeant Marsh.

"Let's load up the trucks as full as we can get them. And put as much in the back of the military rigs as we can. Then we'll secure the door again. We'll have to obscure our tracks into this place so the raiders won't find it. We'll come back tomorrow or the next day for another load." He looked around, "My guess is that it will take at least three trips out here to get it all."

They didn't hesitate, Mike brought his truck as close as he could to the entrance and they started loading. Having to walk back and forth on the hard crusty snow made it hard work. There were many big, heavy bins of things that weren't labeled, but had numbers on top. The crew didn't open any, they just left that to the cooks at the shelter. It looked like enough that they would be able to give some to the base, which had began to run out of supplies too.

In two hours, the trucks were loaded to capacity and ready to go. They moved them to the edge of the the valley and went back to do the best they could to erase any sign of their being there, but it was still pretty clear that there had been activity in that area. "We will have to come back tomorrow for sure," Mike commented as he took one more look back.

Cora sighed, she was really tired and hungry again. She took out her second protein bar and ate it more slowly than the first. She relaxed. Without meaning to, she feel asleep.

CHAPTER TWENTY-ONE

The second trip to the cache was uneventful. The two trucks came back as full as they had on the first run. Everyone was quite excited and happy that for the first time in several months they were able to have real meals. That evening the cooks had made biscuits with creamed tuna over them.

Cora would normally not like anything creamed, especially made with powdered milk, but this was not a normal time. Without hesitation she ate her two ample biscuits smothered in the mixture with gusto. There was even enough to save a little of her portion to share with Eve and Sophie. The cats were ecstatic and didn't even beg to go hunting that night. It felt so good to go to bed that night with a full stomach.

The next day, the shelter awoke to a surprise. A late snow storm had moved in over night and there was at least five inches of snow on the ground and it was still coming down. Everyone was certain that it would be much worse in the mountains so no trip out was planned for that day. That seemed okay with everyone. They'd had pancakes for breakfast with jam and peanut butter, and coffee with powdered creamer in it. It seemed almost the way it used to be. But of course, it wasn't. Nevertheless, most people were in a good mood.

Several board games were brought out and mini-tournaments were set up. Cora wasn't a game fancier so she opted to go to the storage room where they were sorting what they'd brought back and arranging it for the cooks. When she saw everything, it surprised her to see there was a lot more than just food. There were rakes, hoes, shovels, a small plow, a couple of generators, blankets, canning equipment, inflatable mattresses and boxes of all kinds of seeds, as well as things she wouldn't have thought of. There were personal items like toothpaste, deodorant, shampoo, lots of hand soap and a goodly amount of first aid supplies. Cora shuddered and thought to herself, "They really did think they'd be starting over from scratch."

Mike was working at one of the tables, looking through a stack of books as Cora walked over to him. "What are you reading?"

He turned and smiled at her, "This is really interesting. They had books on how to do everything, from canning to building shelters. The people who put this away were creating sort of a Noah's Ark of information and things they'd need for their 'forty days and forty nights.' I'm surprised we didn't find any animals in there. Probably just hadn't brought them there yet."

"Well, there's a lot here. I guess we better start labeling shelves in the storage room. We might even have to use part of the maintenance area. How much more was left to bring back?"

Mike thought a moment, "Probably another two or more full trips worth, maybe have to go back with an extra truck."

Cora nodded and began sorting the canned goods, putting the ones with the longest shelf life in the back, she was amazed at how many cans there were. Then there were the multiple big seventy five gallon fiberglass airtight shipping barrels, full of rice, dehydrated potatoes, dried milk, powdered eggs, whole wheat flour, oatmeal, and beans. Mike and another guy moved the bigger stuff to the back of the storage room. "How lucky we have such talented cooks in our group, they're going to have to be very creative to make something out of all this," Cora mused to herself.

It was three days before it stopped snowing, then the sun came out and the temperature rose to above freezing. The beautiful white powder became slop. It was too slippery and wet to even walk out on the tarmac, let alone drive. It was two more days, before they were able to take the trucks back into the mountains. Cora and Lois were with the trucks this time to help out.

When they pulled to the top of the valley the lead truck stopped and motioned for the others to back up. Two soldiers got out of the lead truck, their AR47's drawn and ready. They crept into the valley. Mike got out his pistol and Lois quickly got out of the truck with her weapon in hand. Cora stayed in the truck, looking around and staying low in the seat. Her heart was racing and she began to shake.

Lois motioned for Mike to stay with the truck. Carefully, she made her way to the first truck. She watched from behind a bush what was going on ahead of them. Then she motioned to the driver of the first rig to drive on, then to Mike to come forward. Mike got in and drove to Lois, stopping long enough for her to jump on the running board and hang on as they slowly went into the valley.

Once they crested the hill, Cora could see the reason for their concern. Their secret had been found out. There was a rusty old pickup that looked like it was stuck in a snow bank just outside the entrance of the stash. The snow had been plowed through and there were deep ruts in the road leading out of the valley. Cora hesitated getting out of the truck when Mike stopped the truck. Lois motioned for Mike and her to stay in the vehicle. Mike turned the truck around in case they needed to make a hasty retreat. It was a very tense moment. Lois stood guard at the entrance to the storage area while the other soldiers went inside. They were back in a minute, talking quietly to Lois. Then the soldiers got back in the first truck and Lois came back to Mike and Cora. She got in and motioned to Mike to get going. He didn't hesitate.

No one said anything as they drove out of the valley, all scanning around to see anyone. Lois kept her rifle on her lap and used her binoculars to look beyond what could be seen with the naked eye. She seemed to relax when they got to more open ground. The tracks from whoever had been there seemed to lead off to the north, not the way they were going. "They didn't take much, but no telling if they were planning to come back. Didn't look like a big party of raiders, it seemed like just a couple this time." She radioed the base and asked for backup.

By that afternoon, three trucks and several more soldiers from the base arrived and headed for the stash site. Much to Cora's relief, no civilians were invited on this run. Lois went with them and so did Sergeant Marsh driving one of their trucks.

When they came back, all the trucks they had taken out were full. Three of the truckloads of goods went back to the base. Five of the additional soldiers stayed at the shelter in case someone came looking for what they'd taken.

Cora finished her work in the storage room and went to get the cats for their daily hunt. They were excited as they headed off down the corridor along the pipes. There had been a bumper crop of mice without many predators, so her two cats, Gray and the already grown kittens Sophie had were having success once or twice a day. The seven felines who were good at being cats, stayed fairly healthy and well-bodied. Leo it turned out wasn't a hunter at all. He preferred to be served his meals, so he had grown thin like his human family.

The dogs, Toby, the Jack Russell and Speedy, the border collie, had lucked out. There had been four big fifty pound bags of dog food among the stored items. They'd been living on meager scraps for months so a full stomach for them too, was a great treat.

The next three or four weeks went well. It was spring and the snow was gone. Wildflowers popped up everywhere, including in the middle of the tarmac. Without constant maintenance, the forces of nature were restoring what mankind had stolen away.

The gardening crew used the golf carts to more or less plow up the land just beyond the tarmac, enlarging what they had for a planting area the year before. Several people with building skills revamped the makeshift greenhouse from the year before. It was made out of PVC pipes with plastic for some of the less hearty crops. Little seedlings had already been started inside so they were ready by the end of April to start putting things in the ground again.

There had been no sign of the others who had taken some of the items from the storage site in the mountains. Cora wondered about them. It could be that there was another shelter out there with people like them, just trying to survive what ever had happened. She wished them well and, perhaps someday, they would come to their shelter and become part of their community. It surprised her when she thought about "her community." It had become so normal, everyone so much a part of everything, it was like having a big family. But unlike most families, she hadn't really seen anyone at odds with each other. There had been people a little out of sorts but nothing earth shaking.

One sunny morning in early May, Cora took the cats outside to chase whatever they could find in the fields near the garden. While they explored and enjoyed the sunshine she began her old job of sweeping dirt and things that the wind had blown up around the back entrance to the shelter. Jake and Clay were having a game of basketball five or six yards down the tarmac. They'd rigged up a hoop out of PVC pipe and had what looked like a large kid's rubber ball. Cora enjoyed the sound of their laughing and joking around.

She hummed as she work, then she stopped. The boys were quiet. Turning around, she saw them walking towards the edge of the tarmac, looking at something. She saw it too. There was a ten foot circle, something like a smoke ring, that was a slightly purple color. It was just undulating in the air about three feet off the ground. Cora remembered the pilot saying that he'd come through such a circle. Dropping her broom, Cora ran towards the boys, "Don't go near that thing!" she yelled. "Stay away from it."

181

But it was too late, Clay laughed then ran and jumped into the the middle of the ring. Almost as soon as he did, he jumped back out and rolled on the ground. His eyes were wide open and he looked frightened. Within a minute the smoke ring disappeared. Cora reached him and threw her arms around him. "Oh, are you all right?"

Clay sat up and looked around, "I think so," he got to his feet. By this time, the people who were working in the garden had come to him.

"What happened?" one of them asked. "You disappeared when you went into that."

"I just thought it was a cloud," Clay said shaking his head. He was shaking. "I thought I could just go through it." He looked at Cora. "It was strange, I could see the circle from that side but wherever I was it was like the sun was already setting and the sky was very purplish red. I saw things moving around and I knew I had to get out of there so I jumped back through the circle." He looked back to where the anomaly had been, "Where did it come from?"

Jake put his arm around his friend, "Did you see what it was that was moving?"

Clay sighed, "I'm not sure, I was in a hurry to get out of there, but I think it might have been something like a deer or an antelope."

Jake laughed, "I think that you were right." He pointed at the end of the tarmac. Four deer and a couple of fawns were heading away as fast as they could. "You didn't come back alone."

In the distance the frightened animals swerved away from the runway and headed in the direction of Barr Lake.

Clay shook his head, "I wonder what they were running from. It could have been me. I may have scared them."

Cora shrugged, "Well, the important thing is that you're not harmed."

"There was one other thing," Clay bit his lip. "Off in the distance. just for a moment, I thought I saw headlights and just caught the sound of a truck or something like that."

Cora and the rest of them looked out across the open fields.There was nothing they could see, but it was evident that Clay had seen something. It would be the subject of discussion for the next several days.

As the group walked back into the shelter, the cats came running and joined the group going inside. Cora was surprised how common strange events were becoming. Soon someone would have to find an answer. She looked back once more to make sure there were no more odd cloud formations to menace them. No one went outside for the rest of the day, not even the gardeners.

It took several weeks before everyone stopped watching the skies every time they went outside. Sergeant Marsh had taken Clay to the base to tell them of his experiences. The boy became quite a celebrity for a few days, which he seemed to enjoy.

It was mid-summer before they visited the tornado debris site again. They were hoping to salvage whatever wood remained for their winter needs. All three of their trucks went out as well as most of the teams that had gone before, including Cora and Lois.

Cora, Lois and three soldiers were dropped off at one end of the rubble and an equal amount of people were placed at the other end with the idea that they'd meet at the middle in a few hours. A truck was to follow each group. The other truck was starting in the middle, which was where the field was widest and had the most debris. It seemed a good plan.

Cora had her "picking cotton" bag, as she called it, around her shoulders and set off with her walking stick and gloves. She found several things that might be of use, like a pack of safety pins and several hair brushes.

Turning over a large piece of plastic that looked like it was part of a sign of some kind, she was surprised to see a pair of spiked high heels. She picked them up and cleaned them off with the edge of her bag. The name embossed on the sole said "Jimmy Choo." They obviously were an expensive pair.It struck her odd that they seemed so alien now. No one dressed in anything except found clothing, shoes were usually tennis shoes if they could be had or boots. No one even thought of things like these she'd just come upon. For some reason, those went into her bag, even though they'd probably never be used.

The morning passed for their group, with nothing major being found. There were several armloads of wood, mainly from fences, small limbs, and buildings, but not enough to sustain the shelter during another winter. Some fixable pieces of furniture had been loaded on the truck by the time Cora reached it with her bag of new things to sort. The truck took them back to the agreed upon meeting spot for their lunch break.

The group at the opposite end of the tornado's path had more luck. They'd found a tree on the other edge of the area. The guess was that it would yield about a cord and a half of fuel. That was a good start, but much more would be needed. So it was back to the hunt after everyone had their cup of water and biscuit.

Cora was probing along with her walking stick when she heard a sound that sent her running. "Snake," she yelled as she moved away from the area as quickly as possible without falling. Not only did you have to worry about stepping on a nail or falling into an unseen void covered by debris, but being in an area that provided so much cover for the reptiles made the work twice as dangerous. One of the earlier scavenger team members had been bitten.

Here and there, among the broken pieces of walls and shattered glass were little personal items, a photo of a child that might have hung on a fridge, a piece of mail, mail order catalogs, a bit of a toy, some part of something unrecognizable. After a while, Cora had taught herself to ignore most of it and only look for the stuff that still had some possibilities.

Her bag was nearly full again when she heard the truck driver's whistle signaling it was time to come in. It wasn't as late as she thought they would be staying, but she didn't hesitate. It was back to the truck.

Lois was already there when Cora made it. "Hey," she said to her friend, "find anything interesting?"

Lois laughed, "Wasn't looking for anything, but wood. Too hot to pack anything but my rifle." She helped Cora put her heavy bag in the back of the truck. "Seems like you found plenty to sort later."

"Just little stuff," Cora said. "We've pretty well picked it clean."

The other soldiers came back with a good sized log over their shoulders that they'd found. When they had tossed the potential fuel in the back of the truck and everyone was accounted for they went to find the others.

"Wonder why we're leaving so early?" Cora said as she leaned back in her seat.

Lois tapped her on the leg and pointed out the window. "I can guess," she said.

Cora was sitting in the middle of the seat between Lois and one of the other soldiers so she had to lean around her friend. "Oh, yeah," she said. Off in the distance the horizon was black.

The thick clouds were swirling. Shafts of rain could be seen even though it was miles away. Cora knew it would be a race to make it back to the shelter before the storm crossed their path. It was a storm like this coming one that had brought the debris field to them. You couldn't help but wonder if another one would bring more? In this uncertain time, one couldn't know for sure what would happen.

The old truck they were in seemed slower than ever as it lumbered back towards New Denver. The other two trucks were miles ahead when the rain began to beat down on them. The tension rose in the vehicle as the driver tried to keep going slow enough not to hydroplane. He was doing pretty well until they started across a small but deep ravine.

The soldier sitting next to her was the first to see it. He yelled and pointed up the gorge, but it was too late for the driver to react. The impact of the flash flood hit the passenger side of the rig first and the truck was spun around, the force of the water catching the driver's of the vehicle and tipping it. The soldier next to her was swept out as the door next to him gave way. Cora tried to hang on but she, too, slipped out. Lois was calling her name, but it was all she had time to hear. In seconds, she was swimming for her life in rushing, cold, muddy water.

A large piece of wood hit her in the back, she rolled over and grabbed onto to it. She never felt the other one that was to give her a black eye. All she could remember thinking, was that she had to hang on.

CHAPTER TWENTY-TWO

Cora didn't open her eyes, her head hurt too much. It was also too hot, and she felt wet all over. It felt better just to sleep and hope it was cooler later. So she did. At least, she thought she was sleeping.

When it was finally light, she opened her eyes. Then she closed them again and tried to remember where she was. Cora tried to sit up, but her head was reeling.

"Hey, let me help you," a soft voice said. "Let's do this easy okay?"

Cora accepted the offer of help in coming up to a sitting position on her bed. "Her bed?" she thought. It just didn't seem right, as she opened her eyes. It took a minute to focus, but what she saw was a bit unnerving. This was a place that was new to her. Looking around she found herself face to face with a woman she'd never seen before either. "Who are you?" Cora was surprised at how hoarse she was.

The woman smiled, "I'm Hayley Norman. I imagine you wonder where you are. Well, my husband would say I shouldn't tell you because you're from the airport place." She moved to the end of the bed Cora was in and sat down. "We've been watching you for the last year or so. We see that you go out looking for supplies like we do." She handed Cora a cup, "You might want to sip on this first before you try eating anything too solid."

Cora recognized the smell of canned chicken noodle soup, they'd had enough of it from the cache they'd found. She gazed over the cup at the woman. She appeared to be about the same age as Cora. She was thin, but muscular, probably from the hard work of trying to survive, Cora thought to herself. "Thank you, this is good."

Hayley nodded, "We got it the same place you did, I reckon."

Cora shrugged, "We wondered who'd been there."

"We were lucky to find it before the one's with guns did. I think they used to call themselves a militia of some sort. They would have stayed and shot most of you. We just took enough to get us through the winter."

Cora looked around, "Is it just the two of you?"

Hayley shook her head, and looked down. "No, there are three of us. Me and my two kids, Hayden and Janice." She took a deep breath, "My husband died of fever about the middle of winter during that big snow storm we had."

Cora was moved to reach out her arms, "I'm so sorry. You and your kids are out here all alone?"

Hayley took the offer and the two women wept onto each other's shoulders. Strangers, but the only comfort available was eagerly accepted. When they sat back Cora looked up and saw the children standing in the doorway. The boy looked to be about twelve or so, tall and thin like his mother. The little girl was much smaller, probably not more than eight years old. Both of them rushed to their mother and the three of them embraced.

Hayley sat back and smiled at Cora, "These are my precious kids, Hayden and Janice. Hayden is the one that found you. They both helped me get you down to our shelter."

Cora nodded, "Thank you so much. I thought I was going to drown out in that flash flood. I don't know how far I travelled and I don't know where I'm at now, but I am grateful that you helped me. My name is Cora Mason and if there is anything I can do to help you, let me know."

The two youngsters acted shy and left the room quickly. Hayley chuckled. "They haven't seen another person outside the four of us for a long time. At least anyone they trusted."

Cora felt much stronger after she finished the soup. After handing the cup back to her rescuer, she began to wonder about some things. "How long have I been here?"

"About three days. You've got a nasty bump on your head. My guess is you had a concussion." She smiled, "I don't have a mirror so I'll just tell you, you've got a real dilly of a black eye. It was so swollen the first couple days I thought you might lose your eye, but the swelling is way down and I can see you have vision. You have a couple of scrapes and bruises but those are healing."

Cora looked at the bandages on her legs and arms, "Thank you for taking care of me." It was humbling to know how close she came to dying and how three people in need themselves came to her rescue. "Thank you again."

Hayley nodded, "So where were you when all this craziness began?"

"I was in the basement of a medical facility where I worked in Nebraska. They had an old shelter, kind of second basement, that we kept our old dead files in. I was down there when I passed out. Where were you?"

"Believe it or not my husband had a feeling of something bad about to happen. He'd had moments before where he'd had premonitions, and about twenty percent of the time he'd been at least partly right so we humored him and came down to our root cellar for lunch. I made a picnic meal and brought it down here. We'd had it stocked up for a disaster for a long time, just in case but never expected to have to use it. My husband, Avery, built it himself. He made the two rooms large enough to stay in for awhile. He was friends with the people who built the storage place you folks found. But they got kind of radical so he backed off having much to do with them. He didn't know the actual location of their place until you people found it. He never told them about this shelter he built."

"You'd been watching us?"

"My husband was a computer geek. He worked at the airport and put in all the surveillance cameras. He had them wired so he could keep tabs on the systems on his phones in case they needed maintenance. He could correct a lot of things from home in bad weather. The little surprising thing was that he could hear and see what was going on in many places including the downstairs there. So yes, he watched you anytime the generators were on. He also had made a trip to the airport once or twice to put trackers on your trucks. He wasn't sure if this had all been something the military had done when he saw their presence everywhere. That's why he wanted us to stay hidden. He was always afraid of a military takeover."

Cora thought a moment, "There was a pickup stuck out at the storage place, how did you come to have a vehicle? How did you get back without it?"

"That first year we went foraging in the opposite direction you did. Avery knew where you were looking so we went another way. We were walking towards the west and we came to a gorge and when we looked down from the ridge, we saw a little farm with several outbuildings. We went down and knocked on the door. Nobody answered and the garage door was open with no town car in it so we figured that the people who lived there had either been at work or out shopping when all this began. We found one really old pickup in the barn. Another was sitting out next to it. So Avery got the old one running and he drove it back close to our place and I drove the newer one. Who knew Avery could hot wire cars? Later, we found the keys in the house," she chuckled. "Anyway we left the pickup when it got stuck. My son had brought our four wheeler and it's trailer so we loaded what we could on that and came home."

She sighed, "I hated stealing from those people, but I guess that's what all of us here have had to do, right?"

Cora nodded, she hated the idea of taking from people she'd never met but she always told herself it was survival mode. "I know what you mean."

"So tell me about life in the airport?"

"Not much to tell. The soldiers are there to help us in case the raiders try to break in again."

"Do you know who they are?" Haley asked.

"No, I think they weren't doomsday preppers though. One of the young men that was with them, actually kidnapped and forced to join them, was wounded and left behind. He's turned out to be a great kid. He said they were just a group of anti-social, government haters who'd basically withdrawn from society."

Hayley shuddered, "So the crazies showed up there."

Cora nodded, "Yeah." She put her feet on the floor, "Could I go outside? I really think some fresh air would help me." She stood up and realized she was in a large flannel nightgown.

"Sorry, that's all that I had extra," Hayley said.

"I think I was lucky to have something that you could put on me. I think I was pretty wet."

Hayley nodded, "Wet and ripped to shreds."

Cora felt wobbly as she walked towards the door. Hayley got up and put Cora's arm around her shoulders. "I'll help you. It might be a little chilly out there. It's about midnight."

In the brightly lit room there was no way of knowing day from night. Hayley had been right, when the door opened to the out of doors a cold breeze greeted them. Cora felt pain in every part of her body as she was guided up a rather steep set of stairs. Once at the top, the sky seemed to be right on top of them, the stars brighter than she'd ever seen them before.

189

"Really pretty isn't it with no city lights making it hard to see them," Hayley said as she stood next to Cora. "There's no moon tonight so that makes the night even more intense."

They stood there for several minutes, then the breeze gently reminded them that it had cooled down significantly from the daytime. Cora shivered, "I guess it's time to go back in but it is breathtaking. Thank you for letting me come out to see this. It's fantastic." She turned and waited for Hayley to lead the way down the steps.

Once they were back inside Hayley turned on one dim light in the main room. The children were sleeping in bunks on the far side of the room. "I've been sleeping out here on the couch so you could have the bed. Tomorrow I'll take you back to where you can walk to the airport." She motioned for Cora to go on into the bedroom, "We'll talk tomorrow. Good night."

Cora turned and hugged her, "Thanks again for rescuing me."

Hayley smiled, but didn't say anything as Cora went to the small room Hayley called a bedroom. In normal times, they would had probably classified it as a closet, but you could get a double bed in it so it worked for this period in history. She didn't care, her body ached and her head was throbbing. Sleep was a welcome relief from the pain and the unanswered questions floating around her mind.

Without the lights on, it was hard to tell if it was morning or night in the Norman shelter. Hours later, Cora got up quietly and tiptoed into the other room, feeling her way along towards the door. She was almost to it when a small light came on. She turned and saw the children in the bunks starting to wake up. "Good morning," she said quietly, "I hope I didn't wake you."

The boy, Hayden, sat up and rubbed his eyes, "No, you didn't wake us. The light comes on every morning at eight to let us know it's daylight outside." He got down from the top bunk and helped his sister out of her bed. "Mom is usually already outside in the garden."

Cora looked at the door, the bar was off so she guessed Hayley must be outside. "I'll go see if I can find your mom."

It was an overcast morning although it was already feeling like it might be a hot day later. The garden area was a little way from the shelter, down in a small swale. It wasn't visible from the entrance to the living space. As she walked away from where the Normans were living she noticed it too was down in a small gully, not easily seen from the main part of the valley or any

190

of the roads that crisscrossed the prairie in the area. Nor could they be seen from the airport, which was just at the horizon from where she was now. "They did well," Cora thought as she walked. "No wonder they could watch us without being seen themselves."

When she reached Hayley, the woman was dripping with sweat. She smiled when she saw Cora and wiped her brow. "This dirt doesn't give without a lot of work."

Cora nodded, "The gardeners at New Denver have complained of the same but they've managed to grow a pretty good bit. Really helped get us all through."

Hayley went back to hoeing, "I'll take you back when I'm done here."

"Won't you come with me?"

Hayley looked at her, then away. "I don't know. My husband was firm about wanting to stay separate, even before the change. He worried about so many things happening. He told me on his deathbed to stay here." She looked up for a moment. "But if something happened to me my kids would be alone and I don't think they'd be strong enough to survive. I wanted to come over and at least see for myself what it was like there. At the same time, I didn't want to go against his wishes, especially since I saw soldiers."

"I can only say we've been a pretty good community. We eat together, forage together, work for the benefit of one another and watch out for each other. It's just been me and my cats at our shelter and I've felt perfectly fine having the soldiers there. They are only soldiers when they need to be, the rest of the time you can't tell them from anyone else. And to be honest everyone is confused and a little scared of what's happened and all the mysterious things that keep happening."

"Mysterious things?"

Cora nodded and began to pull weeds as she told Hayley about all the things that no one had been able to explain, right up to Clay's experience. "So it's kind of comforting to know you're not alone when these things happen."

"Where would we stay?" Hayley said as she moved some seeds into the rut she'd just dug out. "I mean we're pretty comfortable here."

Cora thought about her first place of safety in Nebraska, it had been hard to leave the 'known' for what might be the alternative. "Why don't you come visit us for a few days and if you don't feel safe there you can come back. I won't tell anyone where you are out here so your secret with be kept. We can wait until dark and then go. No one will know."

Hayley worked a little more as she thought of the offer, "All right. That sounds like a plan. I think we could stay a day or two."

Cora heard something moving towards her. She wasn't prepared for the child jumping on her back and giggling. "Honey, you're heavier than you look," Cora said as she face planted into the dirt.

Hayley grabbed her daughter, "Jannie, baby, you could hurt Cora!"

Tears started running down the girl's cheeks, "I'm sorry Miss Cora."

Cora sat up and opened her arms to the child, "I wasn't hurt honey, just surprised. Come here, let's be friends. I have a surprise for you. Your mom and you are coming to visit where I live. And I'm going to introduce you to my cats Eve and Sophie."

"We have a cat. He's a good mouser," Janice said with a smile.

"Where is your cat? I didn't see one around the shelter?"

Hayley laughed, "He slept on the bed with you for the first couple days you were here. He wouldn't leave your side. But being a cat he went hunting yesterday. He usually stays gone a day or two. He'll be back later I'm sure by dinner time."

Cora and Hayley went back to work. Soon the two children were helping with the weeding and planting. It turned warm by mid-afternoon and everyone went in for a nap. Hayley left the door open to let in a little fresh air and a possible home coming cat. If it hadn't been so isolated it would have been an idyllic place to be.

Cora wasn't aware of how long she slept, but when she awoke she found herself staring into a familiar face. "Oh," she said, tears welling up in her eyes, "Oh, BB! So this is where you've been." She buried her face in his fur as he purred and she wept with joy.

Hayley came to the doorway of the bedroom and witnessed the reunion. "You know this cat? We call him Chester."

Cora held him close to her chest, he continued to purr. "Yes, he was one of my cats, Eve's kittens. He left us some time ago. We thought he'd probably gotten taken by a snake or coyote. I'm so happy he's been with you!"

Janice came up beside her mother, "Are you going to take him?"

"No, honey," Cora put the cat down and he ran into the waiting arms of the child, "I think he's as glad to see me as I am him, but you can tell who he really wants to belong to. He's claimed you as his person."

Hayley smiled. "The sun will be going down in about an hour. Let's eat before we go. I'm just going to take a suitcase for now so I'll get busy and pack that."

It was just a little after the airport shelter's dinner time had started when they arrived. Cora lead Hayley and the children into the dining hall. Everyone cheered when they saw her, but then grew quiet when the others came in.

Cora went to the front and introduced the new comers. "Thanks for the welcome," she smiled at Hayley. "These are our new friends, Hayley, and her two kids, Janice and Hayden. They are my rescuers. I was knocked unconscious during that flash flood that swept me away. Somehow they found me and took care of me until they could bring me here. They're going to be our guests for a few days. I know you have questions about how they've been getting along on their own, but let's be gracious and not too nosey. We're a big group and pretty intimidating. They need to get used to us. I think there are still one or two rooms on the far side that are open for our guests so I'm going to get them settled in."

Jake got up from his table and came to help, "I know where a room is, it's got two sets of bunk beds so it should do." He picked up the Normans' suitcase and led the way. Hayden tried to keep in step with Jake. Clay met them in the hall and the three boys sped down the hall ahead of Cora, Hayley and Janice.

The room lacked the charm of the Norman's shelter, but at least it was good sized room with a couch besides the bunks. It was also right across the hall from the bathrooms. Hayley was delighted to hear there were showers and that they were available in the morning for the women and the evening for the men.

As Cora said good night to her new friends, BB opted to come with her. It was a joyous reunion when he saw his mother and sister. Cora could hardly find a spot to lay that night in the bed, being surrounded by so many cats, but the purring made it worthwhile. In the morning, though, BB left to seek out his new family.

CHAPTER TWENTY-THREE

The two day visit by the Normans stretched into almost a week because of a series of rain storms that went on for several days. Hayley thought her crops would be fine since they were getting more water than she normally would have had to haul all the way from the river. The New Denver gardeners were equally as happy to see the gift of rain on their crops, although they were a little worried that too much rain wouldn't be good either.

It turned out that Hayley had some sewing skills and began mending clothing for people. It didn't take long for her to feel needed and one of the community. The kids joined the few other youngsters in going to a couple of hours of school everyday, led by two former teachers.

Hayley decided to stay on at New Denver and went to get some of their personal things from their shelter. Cora and Lois went with her. The children stayed behind, which turned out to be a good thing.

When they arrived at the Norman place they found it had been raided. Two of the culprits were just finishing off the last of the carrots that Hayley had planted. She ran at the deer yelling "Shoo, shoo!" And they did with amazing speed.

There was evidence that the inside of their place had also been vandalized. The door was standing open. Lois went first with her gun ready. She carefully stepped inside and switched on the lights. She motioned for the other two to stay back, just before she fired several shots. Finally she motioned that it was all right to come in.

Cora was dreading what they might find. She prayed it wasn't several people that Lois had killed. When she rounded the corner to where Lois was standing she gasped. Laying there in a pool of blood was a pretty large black bear, even bigger than the one that had tried to break in at her shelter earlier. Cora sighed and laughed to herself, "Well we ate that one, if the cooks think there's nothing wrong with this one, we'll probably eat this one too."

Lois went outside to call for some help in rendering the bear. Within minutes, the truck and some able bodied men were there to assist with the job. Cora helped Hayley get her things gathered up and in the pickup. Lois assured Hayley when they left they would clean up the mess inside and really secure the door this time.

Hayley stood outside for a moment and looked around at what had been her home for the last few years. Before leaving, she and Cora picked what was left in the garden and then loaded it into her rig. The drive back to the airport was bitter sweet for both of them. Cora understood that feeling of loss. She'd experienced that several times during this trial.

Word had gotten around that there might be fresh meat for dinner and everyone was excited at the shelter. Almost everyone, not so much Cora or Hayley, they'd seen the creature lying on the rough floor, bleeding out and watched it take one last rasping breath. It had been enough to turn a person's stomach. Cora would have preferred vegetable soup that night.

The bear turned out to be tough as shoe leather. It must have been an older animal, because it was missing most of its teeth. The chefs were concerned about its health so they really cooked it, so as to kill any potential germs. In the end, most of it went to making some baked dog and cat food. Cora was very glad they did indeed have the veggie stew as an option. Only the really adventurous took the meat.

Life seemed to fall back into a more normal pattern over the rest of the summer. The foraging crews had been to all the small towns surrounding the area that were within driving distance. So very few went out any more. Instead more work was done on harvesting.

Hayden had led the way to the valley where the farm had been discovered. The real treasures they found there were several pieces of farm equipment including a tractor and seed planter. By the end of the summer there was enough ground plowed for a crop of spring wheat for the next year.

The also had found bags of seed. Seeds of watermelon were also found and were now doing quite nicely in the greenhouse. Everyone made a trip out to the garden to see how they were doing, even Cora. It would be such a treat if they could get them to maturity before it got too cold. The pumpkin and squash were doing better than the melons, but still it was the fruit that was the rare item.

The farm also had several apple and pear trees, that would be ready for harvest in the fall. It had been the talk of the shelter for weeks, and the anticipation was growing.

Everyone fell into the kinds of work they wanted to do and life at the shelter seemed to be going well. Thanks to finding the cache and the creativeness of their chefs, the food had been adequate and tasty, most of the time.

There had only been one small scrimmage with the raiders. One of the foraging teams had run into them in a small town near the foothills of the Rocky's near one of the national parks. There had been an exchange of gun fire, but no one was hurt, the combatants were at least a mile apart. The New Denver people had turned around and left the area to the others. The report was that it seemed there were only a handful of people doing the firing. The truck and troops returning were sure no one had followed them.

In late August, Sergeant Marsh was called to the base. When he came back, he had someone with him. A man in civilian clothes got out of the truck at the back door of the shelter. He was walking with a cane.

Cora was doing her usual job of sweeping the tarmac of debris. She was about half a block from the back door, but she recognized the man with Marsh. The tears came immediately as she dropped the broom and ran towards the new arrival, "Eldon," she screamed, "Eldon!"

He dropped the cane and held out his arms, Cora accepted the invitation, hugging him so tight that they both nearly fell over. She steadied herself and him when she felt how thin he was. There was no longer a robust, strong man in her arms. She looked at him, she could see the lines in his face and a scar that was partially hidden by the hair above his ear. "I'm so glad to see you. I've thought about you everyday, wishing you well." She stood back at arm's length.

Eldon sighed, "For months I didn't remember anything. But I had this nagging feeling that there was someone I had to find. Then last winter there was a snowy day and I went outside to enjoy the cold for a bit. As I stood, there a face drifted into my mind." He looked at her, "It was your face. I didn't have a name or place, but I knew I had to find you. I worked with a nurse at the hospital and eventually we were able to piece together where I'd been. I thought if I could get back here and find you my memory would come back."

Cora looked into Eldon's eyes. He still didn't know her, it was clear to see. "I'm really happy you've come back, Eldon. I'm Cora Mason. I was with you the day you were shot. I may have been the last one you saw before you went unconscious." It was all she could do to keep from bursting out into wild sobbing. The man who'd asked her to go away with him, whom she had loved, was standing in front of her, but he hadn't really come back to her. The pain would be hers to bear. She felt as alone as she had on that day on the road in Nebraska.

At that moment Mike came out of the shelter and came quickly to greet Eldon's return. "Eldon, it's good to see you fella," he said throwing his arm around him. Eldon responded hesitantly. Mike looked at Cora with a questioning look on his face.

Cora sighed and stepped up next to Mike. "Eldon, this is Mike. He was with you too, that day we came under fire and you were wounded. There were a couple of others that you might want to meet. You were stationed here as our military contact before Sergeant Marsh." She looked at Mike who nodded. He could now see that the Eldon they both knew had not really returned.

"Well, Lieutenant you will have to tell us all about where you've been. Would you like to go in and have some coffee or tea?"

Eldon nodded, "I'm not in the military anymore. They mustered me out because of my memory and my balance. I need the cane to help steady myself." He walked ahead of Mike slightly as they headed for the door. Mike looked at Cora and silently mouthed, "I'm so sorry."

Cora stood and watched them as they disappeared into the building. Then she turned and went back to her broom. Her hands shook as she left pools of tears while trying to finish her sweeping. It was all too much. She went into a small gully so she was out of sight of the shelter and lay on the ground and sobbed until she was almost too sore to stand. When the crying finally stopped she sat for a few hours just pulling the weeds within her reach. Her life seemed like the parched ground she was sitting on, hard and full of wild grasses that looked pretty for a while, but would finally reveal what they truly were, dry and useless.

That evening Sergeant Marsh took Eldon back to the base so he could return to Arizona where he'd been living. Cora had seen him at dinner, he was sitting at a table with some of the soldiers he'd known at one time. When he got up to leave, he waved at her and smiled. She managed to return his wave and smile, but her heart was not in it. It felt like she'd lost him twice, and this time was for good.

Cora spent the next few days back in the sorting room, making an inventory of what they had left. It was a big job, but being busy kept her from thinking too much. It was a form of therapy for her.

One afternoon, Hayley came and joined her, looking for material or clothing she could repurpose. "Hi my friend," she said cheerfully. She stood watching Cora for a minute. "Hey, what's the matter? I didn't see you at breakfast this morning or dinner last night. What's going on?"

Cora looked around, at the moment they were the only ones in the storage room that they used for sorting things. She motioned for Hayley to follow her to the bench. While they were sitting there, Cora explained her involvement with Eldon and what had just happened when he visited. After she finished she put her face in her hands and cried quietly again.

Hayley put her arm around Cora's shoulder. "Oh, I'm so sorry. I'm not sure why life is so hard, but I think sometimes we're just not meant to understand, just endure it. At least he's alive and mostly well. One thing that I found helpful after my husband died, was to find one thing every day that I'm grateful for. Some days that wasn't easy but I felt better if I did. I'm not sure that will work for you, but it wouldn't hurt to try." She patted Cora's back, then got up and went to the table of unclaimed clothes. "I was looking for some jeans that I could use for patching material. Have you seen any?"

Cora took a deep breath and dried her eyes, "I think I saw some in the stack of things in the far right bin, that's where I've been putting men's clothing." She got up to help with the search. Hayley found what she was looking for and nodded. Soon Cora was alone in the room again. She decided to go outside.

It was another warm day, just a few wispy clouds here and there. Cora thought about what Hayley had said. Looking around she thought to herself, "I guess I'm grateful for a pretty day."

Not to far from her the guard of the back door was helping one of the other men who was working on a truck. They had the hood up and were doing something to the engine. That didn't interest her so she walked over to their large garden. Three or four people were picking vegetables and doing various things like weeding and watering in other areas.

"Cora," one of the called to her, "don't be late for dinner tonight. One of the melons is ripe enough to eat. We'll be bringing it in soon."

Cora laughed, nodded, and clapped. "That will be really nice!" she called back, then walked on to where she could see the mountains to the west.

She was standing there, admiring the view, when she heard a scream from behind her. Whirling around, she saw a huge aperture within a familiar looking smoke ring. For a few seconds she could see through it. And what she saw caused her to scream also. Heading straight for them was a huge jet, coming in at an odd angle. It appeared that it would land right on top of the gardeners and then her. She was frozen in terror.

Then all of a sudden the ring began to close and just before the plane reached it, the whole apparition was gone. Cora was still shaking like a leaf when Lois came running out the door and to her. "What was that? I thought I heard a big plane." She looked around wildly. "What happened?" She looked at Cora, "Honey you're as white as a sheet!"

Cora shuddered, "I don't know how much longer I can take this. There was a plane coming in for a landing, right here!" She indicated the flight path to Lois. "It was just about to hit the gardeners over there and as fast as it was going there would have been no chance I could get out of it's way in time." Tears were running down her face, "It was coming through another one of those rings like Clay went through, but this one was huge!" She wiped her eyes on the edge of her shirt. "Then just like you see now, it was gone. The ring closed up and it's just as it was."

Lois steadied Cora as everyone on the tarmac and in the garden went inside. Lois went to get Sergeant Marsh. A hasty meeting in the dining hall was called and everyone flocked in to hear what had happened.

A woman, who was known as Stella, got up to relate the incident to the group. "I was in the garden with at least four others," she pointed out the others, "and Cora over there was on the runway looking out over the prairie. We heard something, and, when we looked up we were staring at the front of a big passenger plane, could have been one of those Jumbo Jets. It was still miles off, but it had begun its descent. I was so horrified that I just started running but Jennie over there stood for a few minutes after I took off. Jennie would you come and tell them what you saw?"

An older woman got up and walked to the microphone. "I couldn't take my eyes off the plane for a couple of seconds, but something else caught my eye." She looked out over the group, "I may have been hallucinating, but I saw the Airport. You know this place had a pretty unique look to it before we all wound up here. And I saw part of the airport! It was a quick look, but it was there. And I saw another plane sitting outside of it." She shook her head, "How can that be? We're here, and all that is too, but we can't see each other?" Jennie continued to shake her head in disbelief as she walked back to her seat.

Stella went back to the podium, "Cora you want to tell people what you saw from your angle?" She stepped aside.

Cora swallowed hard and went up front, she was embarrassed and didn't want to sound like a fool. "I saw basically what you did," she said quietly, more to Stella than the audience. Cora thought a moment, "I did see one thing, now that I'm remembering more. I saw distant hills beyond the airport and I think I saw houses on that hill. It was only a flash because the ring closed so quickly, which is the only thing I think saved our lives. That plane was headed straight for us." She shrugged and moved away from the front quickly.

Sergeant Marsh stepped forward and Stella went to find a seat. "Well folks, this is just another in the growing list of things that are unexplainable. But we do now recognize there is a danger to us to be on the runways around the airport. The base commander and I've been discussing these issues since the Captain arrived through one of those rings or openings, whatever you want to call them. We've been discussing the possibility of moving our shelter to a safer place. Somewhere that there were no buildings that might come crashing down on us or airplanes might land on someone. When Mrs. Norman and her children arrived, they told us of a little valley not far from here that had not been taken. It's an established farm and where we got the equipment we've been using to grow grain and other items. The family that lived there must have been away at the time. Anyway, she showed it to me and the base Commander and he thought we could possibly move our shelter there. There are several out buildings that could be converted to living quarters. They might not be quite as private or well established as this one but we don't know what's going to happen in areas that used to be busy like this one."

The room was silent for a minute, then Mike raised his hand, Sergeant Marsh nodded go ahead, "I've been thinking this wasn't as safe a place myself. I didn't know about the farm but if it's big enough for all of us I'd certainly be willing to move."

Small murmurs could be heard all around. Stella got up and moved back to the mic. "I think if we are going to move we need to do it now before winter hits us. Remember this is Colorado and it can snow early. We're about ready to harvest the rest of vegetables and we've got the spring wheat planted. So we could take down our greenhouse and move it to the farm."

Sergeant Marsh nodded as Stella went back to her seat. "I would like as many as we can get into the trucks to go to the farm and start planning where we'd house everyone and what needs to be done. The rest of you can start figuring out what the important things to take are. Make a list, those going to the farm and those staying behind. We need to do this quickly and in an efficient way if we're going to do it." He motioned to Mike, "We can take five in each truck so I need fifteen volunteers to go to the farm." Several men stood up and in seconds more than the needed number were headed out the door.

Cora opted to stay behind. Lois got up in front and asked for team leaders, "Cora will you be the head of the storage area team?" She saw Cora nod and then she went on to name several other areas and appoint people to do the chores. "Remember we're just making lists of what would be important to take from each of these areas. Don't start packing yet." She turned off the mic and went to the door. "Let's meet back here at dinner and go over our lists." Then she went to advise the guards of what was going on.

Cora asked several people who had been taking turns working in the storage room to go with her to make the lists they needed. In the end, it turned out that she, Jake, and three others were the ones who would make their list. When they were in the storage room, Cora asked them to gather around a sorting table. "We've pretty well cataloged this area, but now we are being asked, what are our priority items that should move with us. So if we look around we've got things on shelves, in bins, in drawers, in closets and on the sorting tables. I'll take the drawers." She motioned to two other women, "Nancy and Beth, would you take the closets? And Jake and Maryann would you start on the shelves?" Everyone nodded and headed for their area.

By the time the people who went to the farm returned, the lists Cora and her team had made were ready. Dinner was about an hour late so rather than have a meeting then, they decided they'd meet right after breakfast with their recommendations.

The next morning, everyone was in the dining room early. Breakfast served rather quickly because it seemed everyone was a little anxious about the possible move. The table talk was all about the pros and cons of such an undertaking. Some people were fearful, others all in favor of getting out of the cramped conditions they had at New Denver. Cora wasn't sure about anything, especially for her cats.

Mike was the first to get to the front. "Hey everyone," he said and waited until people stopped talking around the room. "I was one of those who went to the farm. Sweet little place, I imagine the people who lived there would have welcomed us. We found three large sheds that had really big farm equipment, like harvesters, various kinds of big harrows and plows as well as tractors. My guess is they lived in the valley, but farmed up on the plateau above them. The big problem is that there wouldn't be enough room for all of us to be there. We have more than eighty people here and that's more than we could put in the house. There are a couple of bathrooms on the property besides the two in the main house, but even with that it's just not enough space. My suggestion is that we just stay here and be very vigilant until spring and then decide how we're going to proceed. It may turn out that half of us go to that farm and the other half goes either back to the main base or on to some other area." He nodded to Sergeant Marsh, who came right up as Mike stepped away.

"Okay, thanks Mike," Sergeant Marsh said. He looked around the room, "Who has another thought?"

Another man came forward and was given the podium. "I think we should go back to the main base. It was there in the beginning and so nothing's going to change for it. Here we might find ourselves buried. If people are there, just without what was underground, like this place, they may have filled the holes that were left with all kinds of stuff that we'd be under if it all comes back together again."

For once Lois went up to say something, "We heard the Captain telling what life was like on the other side of that ring. It was really rough for awhile because they had to build their infrastructure all over again. With that many people with no power, limited resources, and panic around the world, it was a nightmare. At least here we've had time and space to figure out how we could survive and since there weren't many of us we've had time to adapt. The fact that plane was landing means they had rebuilt their runway so what happens when it comes down on top of the one out there? What happens if we're driving one of our trucks out on the highway and a full section of a major freeway drops in on us? Moving to some open space may be a great idea but how do we know it's still an empty spot? I for one would feel safer being back at the base." She walked to the back of the room and leaned against the wall.

Clay was the next to go to the mic. He took a deep breath and began, "I wasn't too smart I guess but when I saw the circle, smoke ring, whatever you want to call it, I thought I'd be cool and jump through it. I didn't realize until I was on the other side that it was somewhere else. It was a scary place. The sun was up there, but it was a hazy, reddish, smoky looking sky. You couldn't see very far. It was warm, but not as warm as it had been before I went through the opening. I saw something move so I jumped right back. It was just seconds, I don't know. But it was time enough for those deer to come through the ring after me. They were as scared as I was." He looked around the room, "I know we all have someone we miss, but I think it would be a rough place to go back to right now." He sighed and walked back to his seat.

Murmuring went on around the room again, Sergeant Marsh stepped up to the mic once more. "I know everyone has opinions on what we should do and questions about what's going on. The facts are, as I see them, that we can't control what happened to us or what's happening on the other side of those rings. The only control we have is over what we do and how we protect ourselves from harm. So far, Jake has been the only one hurt that we know of; last year when that little dog came out of nowhere that caused him to fall into the open basement of a former house and he got a concussion. There have been some other incidents in other places though. At the last briefing at the base, a report came in of a truck driving into a ring that appeared right in front of it and was never seen again. Our debris field from that tornado last year was not the only one reported. They found one in Mississippi. So there have been unexplainable things in several places. No one this far has been able to explain what's happening. The ones who usually have the most credible ideas are leaning towards the multi-dimensional theories, but even that seems pretty far out there. I still think the most important issue for us today is to not panic, but plan for what is the safest thing for us to do. Is that 'stay put' or is that 'move'? Is it 'stay together' or 'disband into smaller groups?'" He shrugged, "I do not know. I will yield to majority consensus."

Mike stood up, "Give us at least two days to think this over."

Sergeant Marsh nodded, "Is that okay with everyone?" He saw no disagreement so he went on, "We'll do that. There will be two issues to decide and based on those results we'll probably have another set of things to decide, but our two items to vote on will be: Do we want to move from this shelter and secondly, do we want to stay together? Do we want to stay together or break into smaller groups? We'll assemble here again day after tomorrow at the same time." He turned off the mic and walked out of the room.

Cora got up and went to her room. Eve and Sophie hadn't been out yet so it was time to let them go hunting or playing, which looked pretty much the like same thing. Within minutes Cora was at the back door with her little companions. She reached for the door, but hesitated a few seconds before opening it. It was a nice day outside although she wondered if she'd ever feel safe out there again. With a shrug she opened the door enough for the cats to go out, then peeked around the edge. Everything looked normal so she stepped out. The cats seemed to sense no danger so she followed them as far as the edge of the field.

A small flock of birds flew by and headed towards one of the lakes in the area. It dawned on Cora that she'd seen several birds lately. In the beginning the only place there had been any kind of bird were those green spaces in gulches and valleys they'd seen. The hair on the back of her neck started to rise, why were there more birds now? What else could be suddenly appearing? She looked around, trying to see if anything else seemed out of place. It was a small relief that nothing seemed new or different.

That was until she looked up. There was a definite lavender tinge to the sky, just as it was the day she found herself alone. "Oh no!" she cried. Looking around, there didn't seem to be any of the other shelter folks out. The cats were not too far from her so she called to them but they were too involved in what they were doing to pay any attention.

With a sigh, she thought, "Maybe it doesn't mean a thing." Then, as she felt a bit dizzy, she remembered that first day, the dizziness, fainting and then.....before she could finish that thought she was laying in the tall grass and weeds. Then, for her, the world went dark.

CHAPTER TWENTY-FOUR

Cora was afraid to open her eyes. Laying on the warm ground seemed as safe as anywhere. Her mind seemed reluctant to take the chance on waking up, only to find herself alone again. Her thoughts raced as she tried to lay still and wait, thinking if she didn't see what was around her, everything might be all right.Could it had all been a bad dream? Finally, she took a deep breath and looked up at the bright blue, clear sky. Taking that as a good sign, she sat up and risked a look around. Everything looked as it had when she had fainted or whatever. The garden was still growing on the other side of the runway from where she was sitting. Their foraging trucks were in the makeshift garages just beyond the end of the shelter. She stood up and shook the dirt off of herself. "Silly me," she said, chiding herself.

Eve and Sophie were back at the shelter door waiting to go back in. Cora had no idea how long she'd been laying down, but it was at least long enough for the cats to get tired of being outside. She felt a little stiff as she walked back. Once they were inside, she realized how quiet it was. The usual din of people talking, making jokes and laughing couldn't be heard. She walked on into the main hallway. There was no one there. For a moment she started to panic but then she heard a voice that was coming from the dining hall. It was music to her ears as she hurried on.

Inside the room she quickly found a seat next to Lois, the cats followed her and Eve jumped into her lap, Sophie into Lois's. Cora looked around and saw that there were some new people standing with Sergeant Marsh in front of the group.

"Where have you been?" Lois asked quietly, "We went looking for you this morning."

Cora shrugged and looked back at the people in front of them. "Who are they?"

Lois shook her head, "Newcomers."

Sergeant Marsh began to introduce the three people standing next to him, "This is Jude Williams, Elliot and Marge Garcia. They will be joining us." He looked at Jude Williams, "These folks were driving to Kansas to an Air Force Base there when a ring appeared right in front of them, and long story short, they drove into it and wound up here. They tell us people are as confused there as we are here, but there are so many problems to solve, that the disappearance of a few people seems like a minor thing." He scoffed, "It doesn't feel like a minor thing to our new friends here, or us, but there's not much we can do about it. Remember tomorrow's vote." He switched off the mic and escorted the new people out into the hall.

Cora got up and headed to her room. Lois caught up with her, "Is it my imagination or are these unexplained things happening more often?"

"I wish it was your imagination, but it isn't." Cora walked quickly down the hall to their room and put Eve inside. Lois put Sophie into the room too, then walked on to talk to the Sergeant. Cora didn't want to think much more about the choices that lay ahead. She decided to go into the courtyard and up the steps to the front of the shelter. It was windier up there, but the breeze on a warm day was pleasant, not like in the winter when that same wind would chill you to the bone.

Outside, Cora walked past the two guards at the top of the stairs and then on across the parking lot area. The boys, Jake and Clay, had Toby and Speedy out in the open area playing frisbee. The dogs were happy and the boys were enjoying a few worry free minutes. It seemed so normal, yet nothing was.

Cora just kept going and soon found herself what would have been several blocks from the shelter. It was so unreal to her, the whole situation. How could this have happened? Was there a way to restore the world? The enormity of their issues seemed overwhelming. She was just staring into the sky until she heard a dried weed or something snap behind her. Whirling around she was surprised to see one of the new people standing there.

"I didn't mean to scare you," the woman introduced as Marge Garcia said.

Cora sighed and smiled, "Nowadays, almost everything seems to scare me. I'm just a little jumpy."

Marge rubbed her arms, "Me too." She walked over next to Cora and looked up. "I saw you walking out here and thought it would be safe if I was with you." She looked around. "This is so strange. This should be one of the busiest places in the country and it's empty."

"I've actually gotten used to it," Cora said. The truth of that statement surprising herself. " By the way, my name is Cora."

"Hi, Cora." She smiled then looked around. "Everything is so quiet, I haven't heard one coyote or many birds. Are there wild animals?"

Cora nodded, "There are a few animals, but not many. We have three dogs and a bunch of cats, but they're all in at night. But yes, there are things still here. We've had to kill a bear or two. There's lots of snakes and small animals, a few deer, but not much else we've found so far."

"How long have you been here?"

Cora had to think about that, "A little over two years, I guess. Hard to keep track of time now. It's more the seasons. Its been two winters at least."

"So you were among the first to wind up here?"

"Yes, I think so," Cora answered.

"Was it hard at first?"

Cora nodded, "The hard part was knowing you were alone. That is a gut-wrenching feeling. I remember standing in the middle of what should have been a pretty busy highway, looking left and right and feeling that terrifying moment when I realized I was totally on my own."

"How long was it before you were found?"

Cora thought a moment, "It wasn't so much found as it was that I joined forces with a couple of guys, Mike, Jay and Jake, Jay's grandson. The four of us didn't see another person at all until we got here."

"Our family had a farm in Southern Oregon so I stayed there until Jude came up from San Francisco on his way to his new assignment. We decided it would be safer if we came with him. We were just across the Idaho border when we drove through the opening. We only saw a small group of men after that. They had guns and took a few shots at us so we just kept going."

"Ah yes, there are some around here like that. We call them raiders, others call them survivalists, but they're just folks who want to live separately, so we leave them alone and so far they've only tried to steal from us once here."

"Well, it was much worse on the other side. People in the beginning were scared and trying to get and save resources for their families before the systems got up and running to deal with the situation. It was odd to say the least, not to have running water, sewer systems, all that you take for granted. Everything had to be hastily installed and made to work. The lucky things were the solar farms and wind farms were already in place. That eased some of the need for

208

lights and electricity. Although that was limited, it helped. Lucky for us we lived on a pretty rustic farm in the first place. We had a well and a wood stove."

"What was the worst thing?"

Marge thought a moment, "Driving on dirt roads. We always thought potholes were bad, driving on a dirt road after a rainstorm meant up to your hubcaps in mud!"

Cora laughed, "Well, we had the highways, but very few vehicles to drive on them."

The two women continued their walk, arcing in a big circle until they were headed back to the shelter after an hour or so. They laughed often as they compared their lives over the last couple of years and beyond. Finally when the shelter was in sight, Cora asked one last question, "Where did you say you were going when you went through the ring?"

"My brother, Jude, was going to a base in Kansas and we were driving him there. We have a small car that gets really impressive mileage with each charge. We were following a convoy of military trucks, so we felt pretty safe in making such a long trip. We'd never been there so it was a bit of a vacation for us and reporting for duty for him. I guess he's considered AWOL now."

"Probably not, we have lots of military from all branches of service here. They all report to the commander of the base in Colorado Springs," Cora said. "As a matter of fact, just recently a Captain, a pilot, flew his plane through a ring and landed here. He was an Air Force guy."

"I'll tell Jude. He might be able to report in to him. I hope he doesn't lose his position. He's just been promoted to First Lieutenant. He's been a part of a flight crew before, so hopefully they'll have something for him to do here."

There it was again, people clinging to the way things were. Cora thought it was remarkable that even though it seemed the whole world had changed, some things like the chain of command among the military, continued to stay pretty well in tact. She didn't say anything, but it was one thing that seemed to remain consistent.

When they reached the courtyard, they parted company until breakfast the next morning. Marge's family had been assigned quarters in the other side of the shelter. Cora was pleased to seem to have a new friend.

Just as she opened the door to go inside to her part of the building someone she hadn't seen for awhile was coming out. It was Boyd Harms, one of the fire fighters she'd met when they first arrived in the area. "Boyd," she said, "how have you been?"

"Hi Cora," he responded with a smile. "I've been good. It's not quite as nice at the main base as it was here."

Cora nodded, "I knew I hadn't seen you around for a while. I had forgotten some of us went back just before the summer started. What have they had you doing?"

He shook his head, then looked around and then moved closer to her to talk more privately. "Let's go outside, I want to tell you something I heard."

"Okay," Cora said and turned and went back up the stairs to the parking lot.

They walked quickly by the guards and over to the edge of the field and sat down on a curb. It was beginning to be twilight so their time would be short to make it back inside before dark so they huddled together and talked quietly.

"There is something going on," Boyd looked around, "it's more than just a little odd. We heard that the people in South America and Australia aren't in either this part of the world or the other, remember? Now there are more areas where the people aren't in either place. It would seem China and a good deal of Russia have disappeared too. Our satellites, of course, were lost immediately so we couldn't see what was going on, but we do have planes flying now and one reported seeing a huge silver disk looking thing on the horizon just before they lost ground communications with China."

Cora felt sick, she remembered seeing the glimpse of something like the silver thing in Nebraska. "I may have seen the same thing. in Nebraska."

Boyd shook his head, "The scuttlebutt is that they're leaning more towards something that isn't the Russians or Chinese for sure," he pointed up to the sky.

"You mean E.T.s?"

He nodded his head. "What else could make millions of people just disappear? Or for that matter, send a lot of people to here and the other place, and be in the same place at the same time? Man, just saying that makes it sound so crazy, doesn't it?"

Cora scoffed, "Crazy isn't the word for it? The roads are here, the cars are there. and never the twain shall meet?"

"They're working on how to keep the gateways or "smoke rings" as some people call them, open. They come and go so quickly that maybe a few birds come through or something that just happens to be there, but not enough to communicate or pass any supplies. Both sides it seems, know about the 'rings. Some people are trying to find them to get here. The few people we've met who've wound up here say conditions are really rough on their side of the rings. Bad air, radiation, food riots, vandalism, you name it. Everyone is armed just to protect themselves. Aliens aren't doing that, that's just people who are scared and have turned violent against their neighbors. Not a place to be. So I'm not sure that keeping the openings open is a good thing."

"Sort of sounds like we've had the better of the two halves. At least we've mostly all worked together to get through."

Boyd nodded. They sat for a moment watching a little last bit of sunlight over the Rockies begin to fade. "We'd better go in before we can't see where to step." He stood up and offered a hand to Cora.

"Thanks," she said as they walked back to the building. "You going back to the main base?"

"Yes, tomorrow, I've got to help with setting up another camp in the downtown area."

Cora nodded, "Always something more to do, isn't there?"

"Yeah, but to what end?" He reached for the door for her when they were back at the bottom of the steps. "I don't know what lies ahead for us, but I'm glad you're doing well." He smiled at her and then stepped over and kissed her on the cheek. "Take care of yourself. I'll look you up when I came back out here." He smiled and watched her walk inside before he closed the door.

Cora nodded and shrugged, she did remember liking him. It was nearly lights out but she took the cats to the tunnels for awhile. She took her flashlight so they could find their way back. This night, they didn't have to go any further than the storage rooms before the cats went into full hunting mode. They were successful almost immediately. While they did what they could do best, Cora sat on a bench and thought about what Boyd had said. "Could it be aliens? Did they cause all this to happen? Were they here to to kill the whole human race?" She felt a chill as she continued on with that thought, "Were they succeeding?"

The cats came back to her and wanted to go back into the hall. Eve brought a portion of her kill along; Cora discouraged her from taking it any further. Reluctantly the cat dropped her prize and went back to the room. Cora kicked the remains aside until the morning, when she'd have to come back and clean up after her "children." She sighed and headed down the dark hallway to bed. After her conversation with Boyd, she doubted if she would be able to sleep very well. If it were aliens, what could they be trying to do?

CHAPTER TWENTY-FIVE

It has been a quiet two months since her conversation with Boyd, but Cora thought often about what he'd said. He'd gone back to the main base shortly after their discussion so she hadn't seen him again. Could there be aliens? If they were so powerful that they could wipe out huge parts of the population, why not all? Hollywood couldn't have made a scarier movie! Usually when she started to think about all the possibilities she just felt overwhelmed so she just tried to concentrate on something else.

Cora stepped outside into a pretty, bright clear, late September morning. It was going to be a nice day, she could tell. There wasn't a cloud to be seen anywhere. The air was fragrant with the smell of warm earth and a soft breeze stirred the dust on the tarmac. Everywhere more weeds than ever were poking up through cracks in the pavement. It wouldn't be a scorching hot day like the last of August had been, but it would be pleasant.

With broom in hand, she pulled a heavy trash can to the middle of the runway and began her job of the day. Across the way, the gardeners were already out tending the remaining crops. Most everything except a few things like the squash and pumpkins had already been harvested, canned, dried and whatever they could do to prepare for the reality of winter they all knew was coming.

Beyond the vegetable patch, the men and women driving the farm equipment were getting ready to plow the stubble under from the summer crops to plant the winter wheat. They'd planted corn and potatoes that had already been harvested. They didn't have enough seed or equipment during the first year to plant a huge piece of land, but this year they had more because of the farm they'd found, thanks to the Norman family. The place had been a gold mine. Now they had twenty to forty acres under cultivation.

Marge Garcia was among those in the garden. When she saw Cora she waved and walked over to see her. "Hey, beautiful day isn't it?"

Cora nodded. "You're up bright and early this morning. I didn't see you at breakfast."

Marge laughed, "I can't take too much heat so I try to get my work done in the mornings." She smiled, "Did you know I am going to have a baby?"

213

With a laugh, Cora reached out and hugged her friend, "That's wonderful. When?"

Marge shrugged, "I think by March. I am not sure. They tell me that I'll probably have to go to the main base this winter just to be close to the doctors and hospital. I haven't been to the base, have you?"

"Yeah, that's where we were to begin with, before New Denver was established. It's okay, just a little strange to be inside a mountain with no natural light. But it's huge, bigger than I expected."

"My brother, Jude is already there. They've got him working as a co-pilot on a helicopter they brought in from Arizona. I think he's happy with that assignment."

Cora looked across the fields as a fairly large bird flew up in front of an oncoming plow. "Look," she pointed. Just as the bird started to lift above the machine a small shimmering ring appeared and the bird disappeared. "Oh not again," she sighed. "We haven't seen any of those things in a while. I was hoping they were gone for good."

Marge wrapped her arms around herself and sighed, "It happened so fast that day we wound up here. We were just driving along on the rough dirt road. It all happened too fast to stop; one of those circles appeared right in front of us. It was a big one, lots bigger than that one. We were in it and through it in just seconds. It was so strange. One minute there was dust all around us, the next the air was clean and we were skidding on a paved highway in the middle of what looked like a pretty barren land."

"That must have been a shock," Cora said as she reached out and patted her friend's arm.

Marge shook her head, "I get so scared some days. I have no idea what will happen in the future but now with the baby coming...I worry I'll be taken or Elliot. I think one of us here and one back in the other part of the world would be awful."

"What was it like for you before you wound up here?"

Marge sighed, "It was pretty rough in the beginning. The day of the first big sun flare there was no time to do much, just an hour or so before there was a bulletin flashed around the world that something was about to happen. Wasn't the news stations though, it was some scientist on the internet. So only a few heard it. Then it happened. In a flash of blinding light, our sky became purple, with tinges of orange. Houses shifted, trees toppled, roots in the air! There

214

was no running water, no sewers, no pavement. It was really hard for a few months. No one had answers, just big questions. It was like mass camping out. Everyone was homeless until they secured their house or building. Temporary shelters were set up and resources were amassed. It was much like what you did here only on a global scale."

"Where were you when it all changed?"

"I was in town. I had just finished up the last of my morning duties as a hostess for a restaurant. The place opened at five in the morning, my shift was until noon. My job was not only to seat people; I had to keep things like napkin holders full and supplies the waitresses needed available all the time. I can't remember what I had gone for, but I was in the basement storage when everything changed. I imagine it must have been something like that for you?"

"It was a little different for us here, almost everyone got dizzy and passed out. When we woke up we were here." Cora thought, but didn't say aloud, "Could it have been the aliens trying to kill us?"

"Doesn't seem to have done any permanent damage."

Cora laughed, "Well, not too much at least. I seem to keep forgetting what the date is. Somehow that used to seem important when you had a job to go to and weekends. It kind of reminds me of the time of the big pandemic, when we all basically lost those years."

"Yeah, I remember that. I was in the second or third grade I think. I met Elliot in high school. We got married a few years later at a quiet little family gathering. Was fine, just not what my mother had wanted for us. You know how mothers are."

Cora sighed, she felt a little guilty having not thought about her mother and sister in a couple of months. "I hope that my mother did all right through the chaos where you were. She's a strong woman and very level headed, I'm sure she found a way."

Marge shrugged, "Most of us did." She looked around towards the garden area. "Well I suspect I'll get fired if I don't get back to work." With a laugh, Marge headed back across the runway.

Cora started sweeping absentmindedly, humming some little melody she couldn't remember the words to. It was almost noon when she heard a caravan of trucks approaching. She was surprised when a number of soldiers jumped out and ran into the shelter. It was a little unnerving to see anyone in such a hurry. She started to walk towards one of the trucks when the driver hopped out and began running towards her.

When the driver was about thirty feet from her, Cora recognized that it was Boyd, the fireman who'd gone back to the main base earlier. "Hey, what's up?" she called out.

He was almost breathless by the time he reached her. Taking a deep breath, he took her arm and urged her back towards the shelter. "We've got orders to bring everyone from the shelters back to the main base. The scientists that we have think there's going to be some more solar flares. These could be as bad as he first ones. We don't have much time. They've seen the same kind of small ones that proceeded the big one before."

"Okay," Cora said as they picked up the pace and basically ran to the shelter.

"Can't take much with you, the trucks are for people," Boyd told her.

"I can take the cats can't I?"

"Yeah, the cats will be fine." They reached the door to the shelter, "I'll help you get what you need."

"Thanks, Boyd."

The two of them quickly headed for Cora's room. The cats, Sophie and Eve, seemed on edge as Cora put them, along with some food and water, in the crate she'd found in the storage. The crate had been used for transporting medium sized dogs on airplanes, but it worked well for the two cats. However, before they were done, Gray and Leo as well as BB were in the carrier too. The other cats and Sophie were just put in boxes. It looked a tad bit crowded for the animals, but under the circumstances, it was the best anyone could do. The dogs, Toby and Speedy, were just loaded into the back of a truck. All their little companions seemed to sense the urgency and didn't bark or howl, just settled in and sank down in fear.

It only took about a half-hour for the trucks to be loaded and, one by one, they headed south to the main base. It was odd how quiet everyone was. All that could be heard was the drone of the truck engines and sound of wind rushing by those in the open beds of the trucks. It was an uncomfortable ride. The rough benches on the sides were hard as a rock and sitting on the floor of the truck was jarring. Ten or more people were in the back of each truck and six more inside so it was crowded.

216

They did stop once for a stretch, but were back on the road in ten minutes. The caravan was made up of several heavy trucks, and civilian rigs like the fancy cars they'd found and Mike's old pickup brought up the rear with personal belongings people were able to grab quickly. That included Cora's one old suitcase.

They were more than half way to the base before Cora's stomach began to settle down. She aways got a sick feeling if she had to hurry or was under any stress. These seemed to be one of those times when she was just about to the "all she could take" moment. Closing her eyes sometimes helped, but not this time. The movement of the old swaying truck didn't help anything either.

Cora was sitting right behind the cab of the truck. She could see Boyd driving and waved to him when he glanced around at her. Immediately he pulled the truck to the side of the road and got out and came back to her. "You okay?"

"Just feel a little nauseated. I think if I can just walk a bit I'll be okay." She hopped out of the truck and stood there for a moment. Then, even though her legs were feeling like rubber she managed to walk around the truck.

Boyd was waiting for her. He gently lifted her into the back of the rig and then climbed up and sat down beside her next to the crate of cats. "I'm letting one of the other guys drive the rest of the way. I'm just going to keep you company in case you get sick again."

Cora chuckled, "Thanks my friend." She leaned over and checked on the cats. "They turn out to be better travelers than me." She managed to smile at Boyd as the truck started off again.

"Just another hour and we'll be safe," Boyd said reassuringly.

Cora nodded, there was nothing she could say that would be heard over the sound of the engine so she just huddled down against Boyd and repeated to herself, "You will not throw up, you will not throw up."

They'd only gone another mile when the world seemed to go white, a blinding white, for just a second. The truck careened to the side of the road and stopped. Then it went dark, the kind of darkness Cora had only experienced once during a total solar eclipse of the sun when she'd been a child. When she and Boyd looked up, there was a huge round disk in the sky, effectively blocking the sunlight from the Earth. It was too big and too near to be the moon. Everyone in the back of the truck was staring up, open mouthed and almost breathless. Then in the distance, in one of the other trucks, someone screamed and everyone began to panic.

Instinct said run and all the people with Cora except Boyd jumped off the sides or out the back and ran towards the sides of the road. Cora stayed with the cats and Boyd stayed with her, looking around, trying to figure the best course of action. "What is going on?" she asked more of herself than Boyd.

"I don't know Cora. I think that might have been a sun flare, but I haven't got any idea what this big black thing is." He sat looking up.

Suddenly a huge, shimmering wave started out from the object above them. This time it was Cora who screamed, "Oh God, look at the size of that ring it's forming!"

Sure enough, there was a ring forming that looked the size of the planet. "Come here," Boyd said as he reached out and pulled her behind him in a protective move. "Stay down." He threw a blanket over her and him, covering the cats as well. "Be quiet." He crouched down as far as he could. Cora was almost laying down, curled up tight against the cat carrier.

For a few moments, no sounds were heard, just the labored breathing of themselves and the cats. Then it began, the high pitched noise that both of them had heard before, just before they'd passed out the day it all began. Cora looked at Boyd, she saw the panic in his eyes that he must have seen in hers. She reached out and drew him to her and kissed him on the cheek. "Thank you," she said as the world began to sway and she slipped into the darkness again. The last thing she remembered was feeling the tears running down her face. Her last thought was, "At least this time I'm not alone."

CHAPTER TWENTY-SIX

It felt a little like swimming in a hot tub. Cora stretched a little, moving slightly side to side. Her back ached, so she tried to get more comfortable. The movement helped a little and she was able to drift back into sleep. There was only time for one thought, and that was that she must be dreaming.

Something touched her arm. Cora wanted to open her eyes, but the effort to do so hurt. Wherever she was seemed to be spinning. There was an odd noise, sounded like some sort of high pitched whine of an engine. It was a sound that was all too familiar. Cora fought to come upright and see what was going on, but her body just wouldn't respond.

"Cora," a gentle voice called into her hazy mind, "it's okay. You're going to be just fine. You are safe."

It was a voice she sort of recognized, but yet not quite. She took a deep breath and managed to open her eyes just enough to see a blurry image staring down at her. Concentrating was hard, but she managed to stare long enough for the face to come into focus. It was a man, just a few years older than her; somehow he looked like someone she should know. He reached down and helped her sit up.

"What," she tried to speak, but her throat was dry and it hurt to even swallow.

"Don't try to do much right now," the man said. "It takes a little time to come out of the deep sleep they put us all in. You and your companions are safe though."

Cora looked around the small, half empty room. She was surprised to see Boyd laying on a bed close to her and the cat's crate lay the between the beds. "Oh, my babies?" she managed to whisper.

"Yes, Eve and her kittens are fine. Even the other cat, the Maine Coon is alive and well."

It surprised her that the man knew the name of her cat. "Who are you?"

He looked down and then at her, "It's been awhile, but it's me Cora, Eldon."

Her mouth fell open! "What happened? The last time I saw you, you didn't remember me at all." Looking around, she had other more pressing questions. "Where are we?"

He smiled, "That's the million dollar question. We are in space, headed for a new planet."

Cora shook her head, "Am I going to wake up and this has all been a nightmare?"

"No, you're not dreaming. There's a lot to tell you about what's going on, but it would be best to wait until you're fully awake. It takes a day or two to get all the deep sleep out of your system." He looked over at Boyd. "You came in with him. Are you two married or a couple?"

Cora glanced at the sleeping figure on the other bed. "No, he came to help get us all back to the main base because of another solar flare coming. He was one of the fire fighters who came to the main base early on." She looked at Eldon, he was older looking than she remembered. Of course it had been some time since she'd seen him. "What happened to you?"

He chuckled, "Well, the folks who rescued us were able to fix me. And the first thing that I remembered was that I had someone very special to find." He took her hand and kissed it. Tears were streaming down his cheeks. "The hard part has been the wait. Honey, it's been nineteen years."

"Nineteen years?" she stammered.

"Yes, you were in deep sleep for nineteen years. I was only in deep sleep for twelve. We didn't age while we were under, but the minute we come out things go right back to normal. They woke some of us up so we could help the others when we got close to where we're going."

Cora swung her legs over the side of the bed and sat up. "Where are we going?"

Eldon shook his head, "It's quite a story and I'll tell you all I know, but first you need to take it easy. Don't try to stand. Your body will take a while to adjust to the gravity here on this ship."

"Ship?" Cora looked around as Boyd moaned and started to stir. Eldon went to him and reassured him as he had for her, then he came back to her.

"Yeah, you're on a space ship so big that most of the population that was left on Earth is here. They've kept us in different sections, but pretty much in the groups we were picked up with. Even with that, it took me over two years to find you."

"I need to see Eve," Cora said trying to edge off of her bed.

Eldon stopped her, "No, not yet. She's not in the kennel. They've got all the livestock and animals in deep sleep in another part of the vessel. You'll see her when we get there. It's amazing how they keep track of every breath, health condition, you name it, of all of us, human or animal."

Boyd managed to sit up, "What's going on? Cora are you all right?"

"Yes," she answered hoarsely, "just a little shaky. Boyd, we've been here nineteen years!"

"Nineteen years?" he looked around, "how did we...."

Eldon put his hand up, "Listen, both of you take it easy for awhile. Just sit here until you get used to the gravity and the pure air we're breathing. You'll find you're stronger and healthier than you've ever been. These creatures who saved us have amazing abilities and they've cured most of us of whatever ailments we might have had." He put his arms around Cora, "I've waited a long time to say this, I love you Cora. I hope we can pick up where we left off before I was shot." He kissed her tenderly, then stepped back. "There will be a group dinner for this section in about two hours, not that time really matters out here, so rest a bit and try not to do anything strenuous. Take it real easy, okay? I have a few more people to help wake up. Tomorrow you'll probably be doing the same. I'll join you for the meal and tell you everything." He walked over to a wall and a door appeared and he walked out of the room.

Boyd looked around. "I wonder if there's a privy here?" He slid off his bed and wobbled to a wall. He felt his way along until a doorway appeared. He looked out into a long empty corridor. He pulled his head and shoulders back into the room and the opening disappeared. "Bloody hell!" He continued feeling his way along the wall. In a moment, he found another doorway. "Success," he said happily as he stepped through into the next area. He dropped a handkerchief from his pocket just outside the door before it closed, "Just in case you need to come looking for me."

Cora sat staring at the cloth laying on the floor. She hadn't even thought of trying to stand yet, but Boyd finding a bathroom made the thought seem suddenly more urgent. Easing herself off the bed, she did indeed find the feel of gravity alien. It was hard to walk, even holding on to the edge of the bed. She shuffled along around to where the bed touched the wall and then leaned against that, scooting along until she reached the spot where the cloth lay on the floor. It was hard to wait for Boyd to come out. When he finally did, she rushed by him.

It was comforting to find an almost normal looking bathroom. It had a common toilet and pedestal washbasin. There were two or three green towels that seemed out of place in all the stark white of the place. Behind a small swinging door was a shower stall.

The thought of a bath seemed to right thing to help her fully recover. She stripped off quickly and turned on the faucets. Nothing seemed to happen so she stepped into the shower to see what was wrong. Instantly things began to whirl around her, she could feel moist warm air blowing at a tremendous speed around her. Her hair was whipped up and her arms were drawn out from her body. There wasn't a part of her that didn't feel the sensation of tiny beads of liquid being flung at her. Then that stopped and a warm massaging surge of air flowed over her several times. When that stopped, she was dry and felt exceptionally clean.

There were no mirrors or glass to see her reflection in, but if she had to guess, even the pores on her face must have been clean. Her skin felt as soft as if she'd been rolled in lotion. Whoever their benefactors were did have some amazing technology for sure. She picked up her clothes and realized they were the ones that she'd been wearing on the day they'd left the shelter. "That was nineteen years ago?" she whispered aloud. "Boy, I need some new clothes."

There was a ding, the sound of small motors and then an opening appeared in the wall. Cora was a little afraid to look, but there hadn't been anything that seemed threatening so far so she risked it. There was a small package in the cabinet in the wall. She picked it up and sat it on the edge of the sink. It wasn't sealed so it was easy to open. Inside was a green jumpsuit, a pair of underwear, a pair of green socks, a pair of tennis shoes and a bra. "What?" she said to herself, "I said I needed new clothes and all this appears? In my size too boot?"

It took a moment, but it was worth trying. Cora looked around then said, "I would like a glass of water."

Again the unseen cabinet door opened and there sat a glass of water. "Holy cow!" Cora took the water and sipped from it. The liquid felt so good going down her parched throat. She stood there, naked and drank the whole glass of water. She put the glass back into the cabinet and the door closed.

She immediately donned the new outfit and went back to the other room. Boyd was sitting on the bed. "What took you so long?" he asked. "Where did you get that outfit?"

Cora went over and sat down next to him, she leaned over and whispered, "Try something. Just say 'I need new clothes.'"

Boyd gave her a funny look, then shrugged. "Okay, I need new clothes."

There was the sound of a motor running and suddenly a small cabinet opened in the wall near the bathroom door. Boyd got up and went over. He laughed when he took a pair of green coverall's out, along with underwear, socks and a pair of tennis shoes. "Well, I'll be darned." He brought the clothing items to the bed. "I guess we wear one piece suits from now on. I'll go change." He headed back to the bathroom.

"Take a shower while you're in there. It's pretty unusual."

Boyd laughed, "Isn't everything now?"

"Just stand in the middle of the stall and then turn the handles." Cora laughed as the door closed behind him.

In a few minutes he came back out in the green suit. "Okay, that was great! Who knew you could feel so clean without water?"

"Wonder how they did that?" Cora said.

They didn't have time to continue their talk at that moment because a soft bell began to chime and the door that Eldon had left through opened. Boyd held out his hand to Cora, who eagerly took it. It was great not to be alone in this place. Cautiously they walked out into the hallway. Several other people, including Lois were also coming out of rooms.

"Cora!" Lois called as she made her way around several others. The two women embraced as they met. "I wasn't sure I'd ever see you again." She looked at her with astonishment, "You look just like you did the last time I saw you."

"You haven't changed either!" Cora said with a laugh.

"And we wound up together?"

"Eldon said they tried to keep us together with whoever we were picked up with,"Cora said.

"Your Eldon is here?"

Cora nodded, "Yes, and he's well and he still loves me." Cora couldn't help the tears in her eyes.

There was a slight unsteady minute for everyone as the hallway became an elevator and everyone was moved to the next floor up. When Cora and Lois looked around, they saw long picnic type tables set up with plates, glasses and silverware. Everyone seemed to understand they were to sit down, so Boyd, Cora and Lois found seats together. There turned out to be the eighty plus people from New Denver group and about three hundred from the main base in Cora's section.

As soon as everyone was seated the center of the table began to move and trays of various foods began to be paraded by them. There wasn't anything fancy, just corn on the cob, hot dogs in buns, carrot and celery sticks, jello cups and slices of oranges. The food was followed by school type cartons of milk, bottles of coffee flavored drinks and glasses of water.

Cora was surprised how hungry she turned out to be. She ate two of the hot dogs and a serving of everything else. It wasn't fancy food, but it really hit the spot. She felt really much better after she'd eaten.

Towards the end of the meal, Eldon and two others came in and walked to the front of the room. A stage seemed to appear out of nowhere and a podium with a mic came next. He walked up to the microphone and tapped it. It sounded just like they always did.

"Hi everyone," he began, "today was a big day for all of you and for me too. I know you have more questions than I can probably answer right now, but I will do my best. Before your questions though I want to give you an update on what has happened, why we're on this ship, where we're going, that kind of thing." He took a sip of water from a glass that hadn't been there a moment before.

"So let's start with the day you left Earth." There was a murmur in the room and he waited for it to die down. "There was a massive solar flare, even bigger than the first one that separated our peoples into two dimensions. The Iridans, that's what they call themselves, knew it was coming so they placed a protective shield between the Earth and sun to give them time to get us off the planet before our atmosphere was burned up, which it did this time. They tried to shield us from the first series of flares, but the shield wasn't big enough, so some of the flare hit the Earth and the people who were in the other dimension experienced the burning of part of the sky and exposure to the radiation of outer space. Unfortunately, they tell me that the people in a great part of Europe where the radiation was the worst did not make it." Eldon paused for another sip of water. "It may not seem like it to you, but all of that was nineteen years ago."

"On a more positive note, you and I are here. We have to look forward, not backward. The Iridans are taking us to a new planet for us to call home. None of us have seen it, but they have shown photos, actually images, to those they woke up early. It's beautiful, much like Earth because they've been aware of what our sun would do for centuries. They have been trying to make the new planet over in Earth's image for all that time. They live a long time and are sort of fascinated by us, especially our development as a species. They have been taking key people from Earth to help them develop the planet for us so it would be ready when we needed it." He looked around the room, "Thousands of people used to disappear every year around the world. It was just a fact of life, people explained it away often as a mystery, only to be remembered by a few, but these people and their families have been living on this new planet for hundreds of years, waiting for us. The Iridans have brought trees, made forests, brought various other things that will make a new life for us. Right now there are some pretty happy Australians and folks from South America who have been there for about five years. From what I hear they're happy to be there, koala bears and all."

"I know it will be a big adjustment for us all, but it truly is a new beginning. We are truly blessed that a benevolent race came along just at the right time." Eldon paused, "Now what are your questions?"

"Why did they wake you up and not one of us?"

Eldon nodded, "I was in their hospital being fixed, if you will, and they had to wake me up to make sure I was okay. Some of you will remember that I was shot in the head and side before I left Colorado. I lost my memory and had to walk with a cane. When I wound up on the ship, after repairing me, they left me awake, telling me they wanted me, as well as several dozen others, to be ready to help the people who woke to be ready before we got to our destination. They began to educate us on the planet and them."

Another hand went up, "Tell us about these Iridans; What do they look like? Why did they do all this?"

Eldon thought a moment, "They are tall, probably well over seven feet. Sturdy, but quite thin, have huge chameleon eyes that move independently. Kind of small sweet faces, look like they're about to laugh, although I've never heard them laugh, or make a sound for that matter.

They don't actually have hair, but they do have something like short bristles on their head that look a little like a crew cut. They come in all kinds of splotchy colors. They walk upright like us, have a thick tail that reaches the ground that they use for balance, kind of like a kangaroo does. They have hands with four opposable fingers on the end of their super flexible arms." He chuckled, "They also have really big feet."

He sighed, "As for why they did this to save us." He shook his head, "I think we may be more of a novelty to them. I got the impression that they were kind of fascinated with building a planet home for us the way people got into building Legos things back on Earth. Remember that craze? People were building amazing things with those little plastic blocks," he shook his head. "They don't strike me as so much saving us, but as preserving us because they want to know more about us. They tell me they will leave us as soon as we are safely established on the planet. My guess is though, that they'll continue to watch us like they have for the last several hundred years. According to them, there isn't as much sentient life out here as one would think considering how big the universe is. A species like ours turns out to be quite unique."

Another hand shot up, "Where are we going? What is this planet called?"

"The Iridans don't have a name for the planet, but the people they've already taken there have been calling it Magna Terra, the latin term for big Earth, or just Terra. According to what we've been told, it is a huge planet, probably more than eight times the size of Earth, nearly the size of our Neptune, almost ninety-six thousand miles in circumference, compared to Earth's not quite twenty-five. It's in a galaxy just beyond what we call the Needle Galaxy known to the Iridans as 76321.12. The twelve means there are twelve solar systems in that galaxy that they've explored. It has a lot of lakes and rivers. There are two oceans, one at the top and one at the bottom of the planet. It's the eighth planet around a slightly larger star than our sun was. It's a relatively young star so it's probably going to be okay for a few billion years or so. Our sun was about four to five billion years, in the middle of its life, but was just beginning to change into being less stable. The climate seems to be very Earth like. It has north and south poles, all the normal seasons, however it wobbles less on it's axis so the seasons are due more by it's slightly elliptical orbit. It has over a five hundred day year and a thirty hour day, which will take a little getting used to."

There was a slight pause before the next question was asked, "Will we get to meet the Iridans?"

"Yes, they like observing us. They don't have a spoken language, but they do understand us and can communicate directly with us by thought transfer. If you ask them a question, they will answer it and you'll know what they're saying. They're very curious about us. We have sort of abstract minds in their opinion. They have art and culture, but everything is more or less uniform, not much individuality, which, of course, is what we're all about."

A young man put up a hand, "Do they have kids?"

Eldon chuckled, "Yes they have children, but they are neither male or female. They don't have to mate to have a child. Each Iridan in its long lifetime will give birth to one offspring. There are children here on this ship. They usually stay with their parent for a hundred or so years I've been told. They grow very slowly. They're all pleasant, if a little stoic. They have few enemies I understand, but they can defend themselves if necessary. They've been a little perplexed by humans always fighting one another. They just don't have a class system or any need for competition for resources."

Eldon looked over his shoulder, "I've been told that Zitau, one of the Iridans, is ready to meet you. They can't breathe our air nor can they be in our presence because of the bacteria we carry on our skins and in our lungs. The way we meet is here, with them on the other side of a glass wall." He turned to the wall and it dissolved into glass. On the other side was a tall being looking back at all of them, its eyes shifting to see everyone in the room.

The stunned group immediately heard and felt a "Good to see you" in their minds. A collective gasp went out from the crowd.

CHAPTER TWENTY-SEVEN

Over the next three weeks the sight of an Iridan became less and less strange. They appeared friendly and, as Eldon had said, curious. They asked a lot of questions. It seemed that even though they could speak into a person's mind, they never knew what the person would say in answer to their inquiries. Human ability to think in the moment fascinated them somehow.

Cora and her group were introduced to several people who had been with the Iridan crew all of their lives. Their ancestors had been brought to the new planet to help get it ready over several hundred years. The Iridans had been teaching humans about space travel and planetary development for centuries. It was amazing how much they'd been taught. In some ways the people looked primitive, yet their knowledge base was astounding.

It also explained a lot of the "disappearances" that went unsolved every year on Earth. Everyone either assumed that their person had been kidnapped to some foreign country or ran away from their lives on purpose, lost in a war or worse, were murdered and buried, never to be found again. It was awful and good, at the same time, to find many of the missing really had been involved in saving the human race.

One of the people assigned to their section was a young doctor named Benjamin Lowe. His parents were of Chinese and Canadian decent. He looked to be about thirty something, but he astonished everyone by telling them his true age was seventy-two. One of the things that the Iridans had thought was important was improving the health care system humans had. An advanced school of medicine had been one of the first things they'd built on Terra. Doctors trained there now could treat not only humans, but the Iridans themselves. Dr. Lowe told them that there were now hundreds of Doctors waiting to be spread out among the people coming to help the doctors from Earth catch up.

Others came as technicians and began the process of introducing some of the advanced technologies they would have in their new society. Solar power was the main source of energy although some of the rivers could be used for hydroelectric plants; creating dams for power wasn't as efficient as solar had become at the hands of the Iridans. There were no fossil fuels because it had been a barren planet before the Iridans found it. An overhead tram system would keep the land from being scarred by roadways and would allow more land for cultivation. Only local cities and communities had paved streets developed so far. Many large farms had been established. To travel the vast distances from place to place, a suborbital shuttle system was already in place.

Finally, the day came when they were told that they would be arriving at Terra within the week and to be prepared to be transported off the ship. Everyone was to take whatever they had with them. People with pet animals could request them be brought to them. Cora could hardly wait to see Eve and the other cats. Jake and Clay were anxious to see Gray, Toby and Speedy.

No one was disappointed. The cats and dogs had come through their nineteen year ordeal in good health and without seeming to age a day. The reunion was a joyous one! Cora spent the day in her small chamber holding Eve. Brenda had come for Sophie and the Hayden children had come for BB so it was just Eve and Cora now. Eldon had a lot of work to do helping get people organized and so he didn't spend as much time with her as Cora would have liked, but there was no doubt that they would be together when they were finally off the ship. Boyd had moved to quarters with his friends from the central base so Eldon had claimed the other narrow bed in the small room with Cora. It was a little like being in a goldfish bowl while on the ship; the aliens were watching all the time and everyone knew it. It wasn't a mean thing, it just gave everyone the willies at times because of the lack of privacy.

That evening, Cora opted to have dinner in her room. She had gotten used to just asking for things and have it appear in the cupboard. It had surprised her when even kitty litter and cat food were also available, even if it was a little different than the cat was used to. Eve loved whatever the cat chow was, so it seemed just fine. The cat was in the middle of Cora's single bed, purring away when Eldon came in.

"Hey, honey," he said as he crossed the room to embrace her. "I think we're just about ready to depart. I can't wait to put my feet on solid ground again."

After a kiss or two, Eldon sat on the side of the bed next to Cora and petted the cat. "She seems happy enough."

"It must seem as strange to them as it is to us though," Cora answered. "What do you think our new home will be like?"

Eldon sighed, "I'm not sure. What I've been told is that they are going to be putting us in as close to the type of climate as we were found in. So I would imagine they're trying to figure out what North America was like for us. One thing I do know is that we'll be a long way from other groups. I tried to ask several times for them to convert things to miles as we know it. The closest I got was the United States had a little over three million square miles to its land mass, making it the third largest area on Earth. The Earth had about 500 million or so total square miles of area on the surface. On Terra, we should have about twelve to fifteen million of its nearly two billion square miles and it still have enough for every other part of our world to have double or more of what they had before plus wide open spaces between the settled areas."

He shrugged, "There will be some problems to overcome. Some people have trouble with the gravity. Because it is a huge planet and the days are longer because the rotation isn't as fast, the gravity isn't quite the same as it was on Earth. People feel heavier and a little sluggish at first. It takes a lot to adapt to, some never do. The soil has been and will need to be worked on constantly to keep it healthy. It was not worth anything before the Iridans brought people from Earth to start working it. They've got most of the areas good for farming in usable condition, but there are climate issues that make it challenging. Since they developed our kind of an atmosphere for the planet it has become quite stormy at times. Nothing like hurricanes, but monsoons and flash floods especially close to the mountains that kind of divide the planet into several different sections. Some of those mountains make Mt. Everest look like a mole hill, they say."

"Wow," Cora said as she tried to imagine how high that mountain range must be. "Wonder if people will want to climb those."

Eldon laughed, "Probably. We humans tend to think we can do anything. And we love a challenge." He looked at her, then scooted the cat over on the narrow bed. He held out his arms to her, "Come here. I want to talk about getting married the minute we're off this ship. I'd have the captain do it here, but I'm not sure which one that would be. They don't seem to have a hierarchy. Anyone who is close by does whatever is needed."

Cora didn't hesitate. She lay down on the bed next to Eldon with the cat at his back. They couldn't move, but it didn't matter, they were together as a family. It was the way she hoped it would always be.

It was hard getting up the next morning. Her back was cramped from laying on one side all night. She stretched and laughed to see Eve doing the same thing. She'd slept the whole time next to Eldon. He got out of bed the last, but showered first since he had to get to work. He had breakfast while Cora showered and was gone before she came back into the bedroom. She sighed, "Another day of wondering what lies in store for us."

There was no telling really if it were morning or still night. All that was different about the times of days was that the lights dimmed a minimum to indicate night for so many hours, then were fully on for what everyone supposed was fourteen hours. Cora was surprised to learn the Iridans had been systematically increasing the times of both for fifteen to twenty minutes each day since they were awoken to help them get a little more used to what their days on the new planet would be like. Without a clock or the sun cycles they were used to, there was no telling time. For a human, that was an oddly unsettling thing.

All during the day Cora found herself drawn into a conversation with one or another of the Iridans. They were most curious this time about Eve. Several came and went on the other side of her bedroom wall. There would be a soft bell sound, then the wall would be glass and an Iridan there to visit with. Today was no different.

The cat didn't seem afraid of the huge beings, so Cora just sat on the bed while she was asked questions. It kind of gave her a headache if they stayed too long, but she tried to be patient. "Why did you name the animals, your pets?"

"We always name our pets, we kind of think of them as our children, like part of the family," Cora tried to make it simple to understand.

"We understand the concept of family, but you did not birth these creatures?"

Cora laughed, "No, we adopted them. We got them and made them part of our household, like another family member who we could love and take care of. In return, they love us and give us pleasure."

The Iridan shook its head, "We are trying to understand the concept of love and pleasure. It is something that we have tried to emulate, but we have not perfected that yet."

Cora couldn't imagine life without love or pleasure. "So do you have families?"

"Not that live together, past being with our parent until we are mature."

"Do you not love your parent?"

There was a silence for a moment, "The parent is responsible for protecting, feeding, educating, and making sure we grow well. We appreciate those things, but they are expected and what we are obligated to do. There is no long term attachment. We live independently."

"That sounds lonely," Cora said softly. "Not to have anyone that you can reach out and hold in your arms or really get to know and cares about you is hard. Believe me, when I found myself alone on a highway that should have been crowded with people I nearly lost my mind! Humans need each other. Sure we fight and countries fight, but everyone of us needs someone to love or to love us. People get strange if they don't have that."

"We have seen humans do very unloving things, like kill each other."

"Most of us really hate those kind of things. It is a crime to us, heavily punishable, to kill someone, yet there are gray areas where it does legally happen."

"What is the difference?"

"Well, we do go to war over a variety of things, we don't like it when people hurt innocent people. In World War II for instance, a very bad man came to power and through his words of hate convinced a lot of people in his country that they were better than others. He got those followers to kill the ones he didn't think were worthy. Someone had to stop him so many countries, England, America and many others went to war with him and his country. Sometimes in our country at least, if someone kills another person, the courts and a jury can decide that person doesn't deserve to live either, so they can have him put to death. So you can see that the human race has come to a strange place in its development."

The other being just remained silent for a moment. "Perhaps it is time to change all that? You are such unique individuals, to lose even one of you would be a terrible loss."

Cora smiled sadly, "I think so too." She picked Eve up and cuddled her for a moment.

"I wish I could experience what you do when you are with your pet. But, we can't touch you or them. Just too many unknown bacterias and it's just too big of a risk, but I see and sense the joy you feel and they feel too."

"Can you read their thoughts?" Cora asked.

"They have more images than thoughts like you do. You think in sentences, they think in pictures. When it thinks hungry, it sees its food bowl or a rodent of some kind, when it thinks sleep, in its mind it's an image of you or the bed."

Cora was excited by what she was learning, "Do they feel our love toward them?"

The being made a sound, a bit like a chuckle. "It feels warm and safe when it thinks of or sees you. It has a lot of feelings, it can be cold, hot, tired or even worried, which looks like nervousness to you."

Eve purred loudly as Cora kissed her on the face. "I like knowing she feels safe with me. I always feel better around her too."

Cora looked up to say something else to her guest, but the glass was gone and she had a wall back in her room. She kissed Eve again, "I'm going to go find Jake and tell him about my conversation. I think he'd be interested in finding out what dogs think."

It took a few minutes to find Jake and relate the conversation she'd had with the Iridan. He couldn't wait to get back to his room and see if he could talk to someone himself. If he could find a way to talk to Toby, he'd be thrilled.

People were milling about since it wasn't meal time. There were several long corridors to walk in so that was the main activity they had to keep fit and fight boredom. Cora walked to the end of the hall and was just walking back to her room when an announcement was made that everyone heard. "Please return to your rooms. We will be descending into the planet's orbit soon."

It was nearly a stampede as people tried to hurry and get back to the perceived safety of their own spaces. Eldon met her about half way down the hall. "What is going to happen?"

He shook his head, "I know just about what you do. I wasn't told we were this close. I thought it would be at least two or three more days." He took her arm and led the way through the crowd. By the time they reached their door, they were nearly the only ones left in the hall.

"I wonder why we had to come back to our rooms?" Cora said.

"My guess is that it's safer to transport us when we're asleep. Every time they've moved us, they put us out first. So don't be surprised if you suddenly find yourself passing out again.

233

You'd better lay on your bed with the cat." He walked over to his bed and lay back, looking around and waiting.

Cora felt a little apprehensive as she called the cat to her and stretched out on her bed. The animal didn't seem nervous or anything, but soon Cora heard the high pitched noise she had heard before and looked down at her baby. Eve was already asleep, "Eldon, I think...." she called as she looked across the room. He didn't answer before she, too, was out like a light.

There was nothing, just that dream of swimming in a warm hot tub again. It wasn't scary or awful, just a feeling of lightness. She sighed and went back to sleep. The bed was soft and the cat was purring. Everything was just fine. There was a gentle sound she recognized as rain on the roof. Again it felt like she had been dreaming. She opened her eyes and looked up at the ceiling. She didn't remember her room having a plaster ceiling.

Eve stretched and yawned, then jumped down off the bed and ran over and hopped up on the window sill to watch the rain.

Cora rolled over on her side to watch Eve try to catch the little drops of water running down the glass. She smiled, then it dawned on her, her room in the shelter didn't have a window and there certainly hadn't been a window on the ship. She swung her legs over the edge of the bed. Across the room, she could see Eldon still sleeping. "Hey, Eldon, honey," she called softly. Then a little louder, she tried again, "Eldon, wake up. Honey, please wake up." She was relieved to see him stir a bit and then stretch his arms out.

Eldon took a deep breath and sat up. He had to hold his head for a few moments before he could focus enough to look across the room at her. "You okay honey?"

Cora smiled and nodded, "Feel like I think being hung over would feel, but yes I'm okay. Look," she pointed to the window. "Rain?"

Eldon laughed and staggered to look at what the cat was watching. He gasped when he realized what was outside the window. Cora managed to wobble over beside him. Before them was a vast area of small dwellings, looking like a huge housing project. Every few blocks, they could see large buildings. There were also parks and tree lined streets. There were small cars in front of each of the houses. Outside their building were a hundred or so people standing under

234

umbrellas. It looked from where they were, that the building they were in was at least three or four stories high.

As people came out of their building, the ones waiting in the rain would hand them a paper and give them some instructions. "Guess that's what we need to do, check out what comes next," Eldon said. "You ready?"

Cora smiled, "You wanted to get your feet on solid ground as soon as you could. I guess this is your chance."

Eldon kissed her and then looked around at what had been brought with them. "Look at that," he pointed to a suitcase, two umbrellas, and the cat crate. They thought of everything."

Cora leaned against him for a moment. "You also said that you wanted to get married as soon as we got here. Still think that?"

He kissed her again, "More than ever." He walked over and put Eve into the crate. "Grab an umbrella."

Cora grabbed her umbrella. The two of them, with their precious little family member, headed out the door. Much to their dismay there wasn't an elevator on their floor so they had to walk down three flights of stairs to reach the line of people filing out into the rain. It took a few minutes of standing in line for it to be their turn.

Just as they turned the corner so that they could see the front door ahead, the rain stopped and the sun came out. It was beautiful. "That must be a good omen for us," Eldon whispered as he stepped one pace closer.

Finally they reached the doors and were greeted by a young woman, who introduced herself as Alani. "Welcome, we're glad you're here and part of our family. There are about one hundred of us assigned to this section. We can help you get settled, find your way around, figure out what jobs you want, get you involved with the local governments, many things. We ask that you first find your homes, then rest for a few days and when you're ready we'll start having our community meetings in the large halls that are in each neighborhood. There are providing machines in your quarters just like you had on the ship. You just have to ask. They will be in place for about five to ten more years. We will talk about that later." She handed a piece of paper to Eldon, "Are you two a couple?"

Eldon smiled, "Yes, we are."

Cora felt a blush, but she was happy with his answer. She was more than happy.

Alani nodded, "You will find your house marked on the map. There will be a community center near there. One of us will be on duty at all day there to answer questions or help. Please follow the map to your house and check it out. Best of luck and again, welcome." She looked over their shoulders, "Next!"

Cora folded up her umbrella and took Eldon's arm. "So we're a couple now?"

"Yes, now and forever." He smiled as they walked away and looked back at what was a simple looking apartment building. "I hope our house is a little more appealing than that is," he said as he began looking at the street signs.

"Amazing, they have street signs and look." Cora pointed at the houses that they passed, "There are six alternating styles of houses and about as many different colors on each block. Looks like some neighborhoods in the old suburbs of the sixties and seventies."

"Let's hope they're not that on the inside."

They continued to walk for what seemed like forever. Eldon had been right about the gravity. Cora found even the umbrella felt heavy. Poor Eldon strained under the weight of the cat in the carrier and the suitcase. Their house was about a mile from where they started. Cora was glad when they finally reached it and were pleased that their place was on a corner. The next block was a big city park with a playground and various kinds of courts for basketball and tennis as well as other activities. What looked like a school and large community center were just beyond that.

When they double checked the house number against what was circled on their map, they stood for a moment gazing at the modest looking little place. It had a small front yard with roses planted on either side of a nice sized front window. There was a pretty dark blue door with a window in it as the front door. The house itself was a pale blue color. It had a one car garage and a small solar car was parked just in front of the garage.

Slowly, they walked up to the door. Eldon tested the handle and the door swung open easily. "Wasn't locked," he stated as he sat the cat carrier down. In one swift motion, he picked Cora up and carried her inside, sitting her down just beyond the threshold. "I wanted to make it official, you're mine. Piece of paper yet or not." He kissed her and then brought in the cat and the suitcase.

Cora laughed and walked to the center of the first room, "Well, the living room is small, but enough for our little family...now." She smiled as Eldon came and put his arm around her with a look of surprise.

"Now? Are we talking children already?"

"Hmmm," Cora said softly, "could be more cats."

They both laughed as they turned to look at the dining area with a nice wooden deck just outside a set of patio doors. The kitchen beyond that. It wasn't a terribly large room but, again it was adequate for the two of them. Cora was pleased when she opened the cupboards and drawers to find them fully stocked with silverware, pots, pans and dinnerware. "Wow, they did think of everything." She found a bowl to use as a water dish for the cat. "We better let her out soon. They said there's a cupboard supply place here somewhere?"

Eldon looked around, then said loudly, "Okay, we need a litter box and twenty pounds of litter." They weren't disappointed. A cupboard next to the small refrigerator swung open. There was a large pan and a large bag of litter, just as ordered. Then as soon as he'd removed the stuff he had ordered, he closed the door and called out his next wishes, "We need ten cans of cat food and one bag of dry cat food. And a bottle of champagne."

"Champagne? The cat doesn't need that!" Cora said laughing.

Eldon reached over and grabbed her for a quick kiss, "No she doesn't, but we do. It's a night to celebrate."

Cora heard the familiar whirring sound, "First let's find a place to put the cat's stuff." She walked through a doorway off the kitchen into an eight by ten foot sized utility room. Just inside the utility room, there was the door to a small half bath, before the laundry area. There was plenty of room for the washer and dryer and for the litter box along the far wall.

Within minutes, everything was ready and the cat brought to the laundry room. Cora designated a space right next to the kitchen door for the food and water area, a few feet away from the litter box. Eve seemed to be happy with the arrangement, eating first, then taking a turn on the other side of the room.

Eldon and Cora continued exploring. There was one large bathroom between the two equally nice sized bedrooms. Each bedroom had a walk in closet. They were surprised to see a collection of jumpsuits in sort of one-size fits all style and several long kaftan robes, in colors and fabrics for men and women. "Guess that's work clothes and at home wear," Cora said with a smirk.

Eldon just scoffed and walked over to one of the two small dressers. It was filled with socks, women's underwear and various other things. "I think this one is yours."

He looked in the other. It was empty. He quickly walked to the other bedroom and came back with an armload of men's items. "This goes in the other dresser in here." He made quick work of bringing his things into the same room as Cora's. She sat on the bed and watched him in secret delight. When he was done, he turned to her and smiled brightly. "I don't actually know what to do now?"

Cora looked around, "I think this is a queen sized bed isn't it?"

Eldon walked over and looked at it. "Yes, I think it is, looks bigger than a double, but not as big as a king."

"Wonder if that cupboard could produce a king sized bed set at some point?"

Eldon laughed, "Okay, it might. Or we might break it trying."

Cora shook her head, "Well, we better not try then, I certainly wouldn't want to break it. I think this might be enough room, don't you?" She scooted up until she could lay down. Then patting the space next to her, she called to him, "Lay down over here and see if it's going to be big enough for two."

He practically ran and jumped onto the bed next to her. "Oh yeah, honey! I think it will do just fine."

They both laughed as they embraced in the center of the bed. The champagne waiting on the kitchen counter was completely forgotten.

CHAPTER TWENTY-EIGHT

The first three years on Terra had been harder than expected for the newly arrived people. The remaining population of their former home, Earth, was now on the huge planet and they were spread out all over the globe. The first people brought to Terra had been mostly living in one area, in the most temperate climate.

Terra's orbit was slightly elliptical and, unlike Earth, it didn't wobble on it's axis. That meant that it's Northern Hemisphere and Southern Hemisphere were experiencing the same seasons throughout the long year.

The humans had to count on the Iridans quite a bit for help in the beginning, as they fought to save themselves and the animals during the worst of it. The winters were so brutal that even the wild animals had to be brought into shelters during the coldest months. Luckily there were only three of the months, December and two of the three newly added calendar months, when they were at the furthest point away from their new star. During those months, it felt so cold that Antartica on their former world would have been considered a vacation spot. By the fourth winter, however, the Iridans had figured out how to use the shields that protected the earth from radiation, to reflect the limited sunlight during the coldest months onto Terra. That made the winters more bearable. They were able to warm up the entire atmosphere to more Earth-like conditions.

The best parts of the year were the long spring and fall, when crops could be grown and harvested. The summers were a little hot, but livable. There was now a new month added after July which was the warmest month, and August was the beginning of the move to fall.

Of course there were rainy times too. Many rivers raged to flood stage often, causing some damage to towns that had been developed too close to waters. The Iridans were able to change the courses of some of the rivers. If the town was small, they would move the town.

While surviving the winters was paramount, there were other issues. During their first year, they discovered that the solar storage plants weren't enough to support the needs of so many humans. With the help of the Iridans they did manage to get several hydroelectric plants up and running before the next winter cycle. It saved a lot of lives in the New United States. Now as their fifth winter lay ahead, everyone felt more confident. There was a power plant next to almost every community on the planet.

It had been a busy time for everyone on Terra. Cora worked four days a week, of their nine day week, at the Administration Center, helping compile directories of who was in their large city of about two million people, that they called New Denver. They were at least eight hundred miles from the next big community to the west, New Salt Lake and to the east, about nine hundred miles from New Kansas City. Five hundred to a thousand miles was about the average distance the large communities were from each other. The smaller settlements were usually at least a hundred miles from any large one. There didn't seem to be any communities smaller than twenty thousand residents though. The bigger cities of Houston, New York, Los Angeles, and Chicago found that their boroughs had been placed in communities of their own, at least fifty to a hundred miles apart. The Iridans considered the land for farming more important than covering it over with cities.

Cora enjoyed her job as she helped families that had been separated on Earth find family members. No one was paid for their work, but everyone pitched in as though they were. Through her research she'd even been able to find her mother and sister who were living in New Houston, a huge community near the southern ocean. Her mother had been ill with slight radiation poisoning, but was recovering nicely at one of their new and improved hospitals. It would take a while to be able to go see them because the suborbital shuttles were already booked a year in advance. But Cora was happy just knowing that they were okay and on the planet, even if they were thousands of miles away.

The military was still a presence on Terra. It was still unknown if any of the old factions that had dominated the various countries would resurface or not. However, they were not a funded entity, like anything else. Nevertheless, the military personnel remained a committed group, functioning much like the National Guard in the communities. Facilities for them to train and be prepared were established on the perimeters of the communities of the United States, which all of the them still identified themselves as. One huge difference, however, was that no weapons of war, tanks, bombs, or the like had been brought to Terra by the Iridans, nor had anyone found anything with which to make such weapons.

240

Now that Eldon was fully recovered, he resumed his rank of Lieutenant and was a part of the new military, attending trainings a few times a week. He was also on the neighborhood council that met once a month for progress reports on how things were going in their sector and what problems had come up. Beyond those jobs, he helped with the maintenance of the food processing plants. The Iridans had set up some very sophisticated canneries. They had developed methods of recycling that took their efforts to the cutting edge. Hardly even a leaf was lost. What couldn't be eaten by the human population became nutrition for the pets and livestock around the world.

For the most part, things had gone well for Cora since they landed on Terra. Eldon had been adamant about them getting married, even if some thought that an old fashioned idea. He found a minister within a week and a few days later, in front of what felt like half their neighborhood, they were married. They found a good use for the champagne he'd ordered on the first day in their new home. It and a few more bottles made a fine addition to the party they had with several of their friends from the shelter, who also lived in the New Denver.

One bright and sunny morning, Cora slept in. Eldon was already at his job at the cannery. She wasn't due at her job for another two days so it was pleasant not to have to hurry to do anything. After a leisurely shower, dressing, then a light breakfast of toast and an egg, she went out on her back porch. It was warm enough to just wear a sweater over her long kaftan.

In the beginning they'd made a rough guess at the time of year and the months, even the time of day. They still called their new star The Sun. Somehow, people who do those kind of things, had come up with a calendar roughly based on what they were used to, by adding three months to the year and three days to the week. According to the latest edition of that, it was the fourth week in May, a Wednesday. Cora laughed at that. She could see the kitchen clock from where she sat on the porch. According to her now thirty hour clock, it was ten-thirty.

Cora didn't think too much about the bigger picture at the moment, sitting there on the back porch of her little cottage. Her garden was up, weeded and a few precious fruits and vegetables were already starting to grow on their stems. Looking to the trees in the yard she could also see pippins on their two apple trees. The pear tree had blossoms as did the cherry. Just outside her yard, the roses were already as high as the fence.

She sighed. There would be a lot of work ahead when all the things in the garden were ripe. The neighborhood center had given classes on all the ways to preserve food. The last growing season she'd canned tomatoes, frozen green beans, learned how to dry certain things, and how to preserve more things than she realized she could. She'd become quite good at bartering what she had extra, for foods her neighbors had. It was very good to find neighbors she liked too.

As it turned out, Brenda and Grady lived just a few blocks from them. Lois had married Boyd after Cora introduced them. They had both been living in the single peoples dorm, where Cora and Eldon had been when they woke up on Terra. The new couple were given a house in their neighborhood, too.

Sitting there letting the sun warm her, Cora couldn't help but think of her incredible journey to this day. When she had found herself standing alone in the middle of that road so long ago, it never entered her mind that, years later, she would be on a completely new planet with a wonderful home and a beautiful husband. It made her smile.

There had been that first day when she had actually thought she might die, if not of loneliness, then of some unseen menace. It had been scary at times, and really hard at other moments, but it had been all leading the way here. She'd had nothing, but the clothes on her back, no one to love or to love her. Then she found the cats, that was the first spark of hope. Then Mike, Jay, and Jake came along. The thought of that day and the joy of knowing there were others alive, still brought tears to her eyes. It hurt a little that Jay and Jake had opted go to New San Diego. Mike had gone with them. But they stayed loosely in touch.

Then there were the years of trying to survive, being hungry, worrying about where the next meal would come from, yet somehow they made it. Then the mysteries of things appearing and disappearing, that perplexed them all. And the best thing, meeting Eldon, that made her smile and feel warm.

Eve came out of the house, having learned that she could open the screen door herself. The cat jumped up onto Cora's lap and settled in, demanding to be petted. That was pleasing to Cora; Eve had been right there to comfort and love her. They had been through so much together over the years. Eve's purring became loud and regular as Cora gave her what she wanted. It made Cora laugh softly, "Silly old girl," she said to her sweet companion.

The two of them sat enjoying the moment, then in an instant something changed. Cora sat up and Eve awoke from her half sleep and looked up at her master. "Was that you?" Cora said.

Then it happened again, a slight flutter in her lower stomach. Cora held her breath and looked down. The third time there was no doubt. "Oh honey," she whispered to the cat. "I think you're going to have a new playmate." She couldn't wait until Eldon got home. She hadn't said anything to him, waiting until she was sure, but the movement she felt confirmed what she had been hoping for.

Eve bent down and seemed to sense what Cora was feeling, she lay down again, but this time she wrapped herself around Cora's stomach rather than having her back against her master's belly. She purred loudly, cuddling as closely as she could. Cora felt such joy that she couldn't help the tears.

* * *

The weeks flew by, winter came and lingered to the last of January, Cora was getting pretty close to time. Finally just before her due date the weather improved a little. By the end of February, they were a family of three humans and one cat. The new, tiny human that had joined the Elroy family was named Jennette Ellen after both of their grandmothers.

Eldon could hardly contain himself when he held his daughter for the first time. When he was able to bring Jennie and Cora home, he went around the neighborhood passing out cupcakes he'd had made and frosted with pink icing. Cora laughed at him being so silly, but thought it wonderful.

The baby was officially christened at the local non-denominational church where they had been married years before. A few days later, some neighbors, Evan Terrence and his wife Trisha, came to call. They had seen Cora and Eldon out walking with the baby in her stroller and wanted to congratulate the family and see if they could help in any way. They were a little older, their three children were all grown and living in the Los Angeles suburbs.

Somehow, as it usually did on Earth, conversations on Terra always swung around to those two subjects no one was supposed to talk about, either politics or religion. Evan served on

243

the City Board of Commissioners, that the neighborhood council that Eldon served on reported to.

Cora wasn't one to hold back when questions crossed her mind. She didn't hesitate. "So Evan, what's going on in the city government?"

He looked surprised for a moment, then smiled. "Well, as far as serving as a commissioner, I don't think it means much. The country is still trying to figure out if we should be one or many different governments. We're so spread out. It used to be just three thousand miles from LA to New York, now it's more than twelve. And so much land in between cities. We don't have the continents dividing the world either. Just several thousand miles past LA is China, although they lost some of their people to the radiation." He took another sip of his lemonade.

"There is a congress of sorts trying to form up again, with representatives from each of the areas," Evan said thoughtfully. "Lots of people would like to remain independent of the bigger areas. I don't exactly know what to think. On Earth we used to say 'God works in mysterious ways,' when we weren't able to come up with an answer. I think that applies now more than ever. I've wrestled with that question since the day of the first big flare, that took so many of us into the other dimension, or wherever we were. I was in Seattle at the time, on a tour of the underground city with about twenty-five other people that day. I questioned 'why' many times. My children were not with me. I'd already been a widower for five years. I felt really lost." He looked at Trisha, "I met this fine lady about two years later. We were married by a Priest, who had been in the basement of his church when it happened." He shook his head, "So many stories!"

After a moment, he continued. "I was talking to one of the Iridans on the ship and relating my story to him, or it, whatever they are. Anyway I asked him why they rescued us? And how, since their home world was so far from us, did they find us? The Iridan, who called himself Zevi, said that one of their oldest Iridan members had a dream or a vision. He'd seen a star in a far off galaxy about to go nova. It was emitting large bursts of radiation that fried everything in its path to a crisp. Being a curious species, he said that they sent out scout ships to locate the galaxy and the star. They went looking for many of our centuries, ship after ship going to the corners of the known universe examining the galaxies one by one. Finally they came to the one we called The

244

Milky Way. They then looked through the millions of stars until they found the one emitting the solar flares. They didn't find anything special about it so they watched where the flares went, watching what it destroyed and what was touched."

Eldon shook his head, "I can't imagine the enormity of their efforts. It just boggles my mind."

Evan nodded and continued, "Finally, they were passing by our solar system and saw that the light from one of the flares probably was visible from it. They studied the planets in this system and found us, a species capable of learning what they could teach. They were fascinated by the fact that we were such a complex species, more so than any other they'd encountered. We accumulated knowledge from one generation to the next as they did. What was more interesting than all that, were our feelings as well as our caring for each other in our short lifespans. They live a long time, but it is just being alive and doing their duty. We had something they wanted to understand, but had never known, love and joy. They had seen hate and war in other species but still, our ability to forgive and make amends was new to them. They saw our star was going to be entering the same phase as the one they'd come to find so they decided to save us."

Cora shrugged, "Wow. I guess you were right Eldon, they were interested in us." She looked at Eldon, he had a very serious look on his face. "What are you thinking honey?"

Eldon sighed, "Well, that is just another mystery that will probably never be answered."

It was Cora's turn to look puzzled. "What do you mean?"

Eldon shrugged and looked at Evan, "Why did they spend so much time looking for that star that the Elder Iridan saw in his, dream or vision in the first place?"

"You said they were a curious people, isn't that what they always do? Go searching out new things and people?" Cora said.

Evan got up and shook Eldon's hand and motioned to his wife that they were leaving. He smiled at Eldon and glanced at Cora, "They are a curious people, but the Iridans don't sleep as we know it and no Iridan had ever had a dream or visions, until then or since then." He bowed slightly to Eldon and Cora. Then he and his wife left quietly.

Cora looked at Eldon, who was still heavily in thought, "Is that true?"

Eldon looked at her and nodded, "Early on, right after they'd healed me, I heard that myself from one of the Iridans on the ship when I asked almost the same questions. I just passed it off as so much talk. But as I got to know the Iridans, I found they don't lie, don't make up stories, don't have much of an imagination, but would go to great lengths to help others they deem worthy of learning about. I often wondered why they would do all that for us."

Cora took a deep breath. Suddenly, she remembered what her friend Hayley had told her so long ago, "Find something to be grateful for everyday." She smiled, today that was easy. "Somehow they knew of our need, or what we would need," Cora said softly as she began to feed the baby. "Whatever the reason, I'm so grateful to be here with you and Jennie."

Eldon, sat down next to her and watched the baby eagerly accept the breast that was offered. "Yes, I really am grateful too."

# # #